DEATH BEFORE LIFE

DEATH BEFORE LIFE

JOHN F. GORMAN

GMS Publishing

To my lovely wife and steadfast partner of 40+ years, Janice

Part I:

The Kill

CHAPTER 1

"Beat 1814?"

"Yeah, this is 1814," Patrolman Ed Jackson barked into the radio velcroed to his shoulder.

"Woman calling for help behind 1844 N. Lincoln," came the dispatcher.

"10-4," Jackson said.

Jackson's partner, Beth Opanski, took a U in the middle of North Avenue, in front of the Old Town Ale House. It was just letting out at 3:55 a.m., and the hard-core drinkers were oozing out of the tavern.

"The back end of that address is Lincoln Park West, isn't it, Ed?" Opanski asked.

"Yeah. Take Wells here."

She swung a hard left.

As they approached the back of the address in this fashionable neighborhood of townhouses and three-flats, a white-haired woman ran up to the squad, pointing to a silver Jaguar XJ-8 with the passenger side door ajar.

"You'd better look in there. It looks bad," the woman said. Opanski swung to the rear of the Jag and threw the squad into park.

The street was deserted at this hour as Opanski approached the driver's-side door. As Opanski peered inside the Jag, she saw a young blonde sprawled across the driver's seat, an ice pick protruding from her neck. The light tan leather seat was bathed in blood. Her eyes were open, as if surprised, the pupils dilated and fixed.

"Don't touch a thing," said Opanski, five years older and a decade wiser than Jackson. Careful not to touch any part of the car, she reached in to put her index finger just above the ice pick on the girl's neck; there was no pulse.

"Oh, shit," Jackson said, bending down to look inside the Jag from the passenger side. "I'll call it."

Fifteen minutes after Jackson notified Zone 1 Radio, the neighborhood was alive with blue and whites, Mars lights flashing. A murder in Old Town was rare. Million-dollar homes tend to keep the riffraff away.

Sgt. Tom Sheehan, the supervising sergeant in the Near North District, was the first supervisor to arrive and quickly took over.

"Did you run the plates?" Sheehan asked Opanski and Jackson as he approached the Jag.

"We've done nothing since we called it in and secured the scene," Jackson advised. "You want us to?"

"It's gotta be done, yeah?"

Sheehan looked inside the car. He slipped on his latex gloves and then turned the body to see if she was lying on her purse. Good guess. He pulled the small purse out from under the body. He looked at the blue eyes and thought how they still looked somewhat disbelieving, the emotion she had taken into eternity.

"Still looks shocked, eh, Sarge?" Jackson quipped, having not moved yet on the plates.

"This funny to you, son? Go run the plates."

Jackson hustled back to the squad car to check the plates' registration. By this time, Opanski had asked a few perfunctory questions of the gathering throng of yuppies who were coming out in the predawn to gawk. She was getting nowhere fast. This was not a neighborhood where everyone knew each other. Residents in the same three-flat often were strangers. It was bars, restaurants, and clubs, just a stone's throw from Second City.

After Jackson notified Zone 1 of the body, detectives were launched from Area 3 Homicide. The zone would also reach out to the Medical Examiner. Any homicide also drew the Deputy Superintendent on the overnight shift. Sheehan snapped open the purse and saw the driver's license and smiling face of Jennifer Cavaretta. No money, no credit cards. No cell phone. But pepper spray. A whistle on the car key chain lay next to the body. Besides the driver's license, he found a student ID from Northwestern Law School

"Jesus F. Christ. I hope it ain't *that* Cavaretta," Sheehan mumbled to himself. But Opanski heard him.

"Whattya mean?" Opanski asked.

"As in—State's Attorney Thomas A. Cavaretta."

Sheehan knew the State's Attorney had a daughter, and he recalled that he'd heard she was in law school.

Sheehan would take no chances on this one. Young, white, pretty, law school student-- and she may be the State's Attorney's daughter. He pushed down on his two-way.

"Dispatch, get me the Deputy Supe on call, pronto." Sheehan wanted to personally let the top-ranking cop on duty know who the victim was.

Just then Jackson ran up to the sergeant.

"Plates come back to a Thomas A. Cavaretta, 109 Pine, River Forest, Sarge."

Sheehan retreated to his Crown Vic and quickly dialed his old classmate from the academy, Dan Delaney, the sergeant on overnights who was dispatching the dicks this morning from Area 3.

"Danny, it's Tom. Got a bad one here. You'll hear from the zone and then the shit is going to start hitting the proverbial propeller. You're gonna need your best guys on this one—the victim is the State's Attorney's daughter."

For once, Sheehan thought, Delaney was speechless.

CHAPTER 2

A peregrine falcon stopped Mike Halloran dead in his tracks. It was perched on the sidewalk adjacent to the tennis courts at Sheridan Park just north of Taylor Street.

Its eyes fixed on the human threat, its feathers around his neck taut. In its talons was some unfortunate creature. Breakfast.

Halloran was on his way to swim at the Sheridan Park pool on Aberdeen Street. He was hot-stepping his way for a quick 20-minute swim in the ever so slightly beat-up but free park district pool.

But the veteran homicide dick's fascination with predator birds froze him. At first, he couldn't make out what the falcon clutched in its talons, and so Halloran just eyeballed the strange sight for a full minute. A few years ago, he had seen one of these magnificent predators sitting on the 13th floor ledge at the grimy tower at the Criminal Courts complex at 26th & California while he was in the midst of a heated argument with a veteran prosecutor over the credibility of a witness.

That argument flashed through his mind in the seconds that he and the falcon stood silently appraising each other. After a minute, Halloran decided he had better swim now before he got called in to work on this beautiful Saturday morning. He took another step. That was enough to spook the falcon. It took off, clutching what turned out not to be the rat that Halloran, with his 1984 Orwellian phobia, thought the falcon was grasping. No, it was the flying rat--a pigeon--quick enough to dodge kids and creeps on the plaza at the Daley Center, but a step, or flap, too slow for the falcon's dive. But as the bird took off, Halloran's beeper bleated out a summons. Sgt. Delaney's desk number appeared on the beeper screen.

After 20 years of being on his own on the streets, Halloran got stuck with this electronic leash a few years ago. He knew it was for the good, but it was still a huge pain in the ass to have to answer these—especially just a good stretch of the legs short of the pool locker room.

Swimming was boring, but it gave him time to think. The exercise was the best he could do since his knee operation. He had been a tight end, a good one, almost All Big Ten as a sophomore. At 6'5" and 250, he was big enough to go pro, or so he thought up to the point that a Purdue safety made a perfectly legal and career-ending hit on him in the first quarter of the first game of his junior season.

For a second Halloran considered not answering, telling Delaney later that he had been in the pool, unreachable. *But this early on a Saturday,* Halloran thought, *it must be pretty hot.*

So, he did a pirouette, and headed back to his stick-shift Jeep Cherokee and his cell phone—his other leash. He dialed the number for the desk at Area 3. Delaney was the first-shift guy, crossing off the days from the calendar until his retirement.

"Yeah, Sarge. Halloran here."

"Halloran-where?" Delaney asked abruptly.

"In my car," Halloran deadpanned, yanking the sergeant's chain a bit.

"No shit, asshole. Where in your car?" Delaney demanded.

"Front seat." Halloran was now certain that this would send Delaney into early morning orbit.

"Okay, wise guy. Wherever you are, get your ass—forthwith--to 1844 Lincoln. Get there. Now. And talk to Sheehan. He's got the scene. And, Halloran, save the jokes today—your humor may not be appreciated." Delaney slammed the phone down.

And you have a nice day, too, Halloran thought.

Delaney, Sheehan, Halloran.

"Jesus Christ," Halloran mumbled to himself. "An Irish conspiracy. Are there no Jews on the Chicago Police Department? Yeah, Larry Schine and some other guy, maybe."

As he pulled onto Taylor Street, Halloran spotted the falcon perched atop a streetlight, pulling at the remains of the pigeon. The peregrine falcon. An urban predator, ridding the city of the pigeons on the streets and the rats in the alley—the city's vermin.

As a cop, he reflected, I guess I'm an urban predator, too.

CHAPTER 3

"Heater" cases were nothing new to Halloran. If you solve them in a hurry, they didn't get a chance to heat up. But the press was relentless and intrusive when it was a heater.

He parked a block from the scene, across the street from Ranalli's Pizza joint on Lincoln. The television trucks with the antenna towers extended were there already, their reporters hoping to get something for the early broadcast.

"Halloran, whattya got? What can you give me?" implored Becky Thompson from Channel 7 when she spotted the detective moving hastily toward the wooden barricades blocking the street.

"I got nada." Halloran edged past the camera and mike, slipping under the yellow plastic crime scene lines at Lincoln and Lincoln Park West. "You probably know more than I do."

"Yeah, right. Don't stiff me on the way out when you *do* know something," Thompson yelled to Halloran's back.

Halloran waved her off, but as he did, he noticed the Sun-Times guy, Frank Marone, taking notes at the first-floor landing of a nearby three-flat from a woman with a housecoat pulled tightly against her.

Marone probably does know more than I do at this point, Halloran mused. *But not for long.*

"Whattya got, Sarge?" Halloran asked as he approached Sheehan.

"This is huge, a shitstorm in the making, Mike. Brace yourself. It's the State's Attorney's kid--his daughter." Sheehan nodded to all the brass hovering by the car. Lots of silver stars on the shoulders and crisp navy-blue uniforms. Standing in the middle was Supt. John Johnson, his black, bald head gleaming in the early morning light.

Christ on a crutch, no wonder the press is salivating, Halloran thought.

"You seen my partner, Sarge? She's hard to miss. Hispanic, drop-dead beautiful, carries a .45 the size of a cannon." Sheehan tilted his head toward the far side of the Jag.

Detective Sylvia Ortiz was crouched down by the rear tire, engaged in a gesture-laden conversation with one of the forensic technicians.

"Everything in the car, everything outside in a 25-foot radius," Ortiz insisted through clenched teeth as she stood up.

"Gimme a break. I know my job," the tech complained. The scene was messy. Blood all over the front seat, murder weapon still protruding from the neck. And the victim's clothes were a bit messed.

"Take a look at her clothes," Ortiz told Halloran as he walked up.

Before Halloran could even fake a move toward the car, Chief of Detectives Matthew Mallory planted himself in front of Halloran. Mallory had 15 pounds and 15 years on Halloran, but they saw eye to eye, physically at least. Mallory had played center at St. Rita's when 6'4" and white could still dominate at basketball.

"By the book, Halloran, no shortcuts, no cute ploys, no hunches. I want to be apprised of any development, no matter how small. I'll be watching you, and so will he." Mallory tilted his massive head to Johnson, standing near his car and talking on the phone in hushed tones. "You need help, you call me."

"Always by the book, boss. Now can I take a look—please?"

After pulling on his latex gloves, Halloran stuck his head and shoulders into the open passenger door of the luxury car. He immediately spotted what Ortiz was talking about. The three top blouse buttons were open.

Whoever killed her may have been trying to molest her. It was a chill October morning; she would not have had those buttons down. As he studied the inside of the car, he bent down further and spotted a crushed cigarette on the floor of the Jag. Camel unfiltered, he noted. Not very lady-like, Halloran thought.

"What we got so far, Syl?" Halloran asked over his shoulder. Halloran exited the car and squired his partner by the elbow a few car lengths away from the brass.

"Tough to say. Woman's heard screaming for help. Lady calls it in from the pay phone half a block away. The beat guys are here in 90 seconds, two minutes tops, after the call comes in. And she's dead. Top buttons on her blouse are open. She's been smoking apparently, and there's money and credit cards missing. But she's on top of the purse. What's he do? Stab her, take the money out of the purse and then lift her up and drop her back on the purse? Doesn't add up. Too many cross indicators."

Cross indicators, Halloran thought, *Police Academy jargon. Ortiz was new school, her partner old school. How about--it doesn't quite make sense?* He held his tongue, though.

"Yeah, could be robbery, a carjacking. Maybe he robs her first, then comes on for a little sex. She resists. He whacks her. Could be attempt rape. But what's she doing here at 4 a.m.? Where's she live?" Halloran asked.

"At home with her parents. The supe is going to inform the family himself. She's the only child. Jesus."

A second after Ortiz was finished, Johnson broke from a conclave of deputy supes and walked slowly toward the Jag. A squat African American, Johnson bent down to peer at length at the victim. He leaned in and peered into the back seat, spying a nearly empty water bottle among some old newspapers on the rear floor.

He emerged, wiping something from his right eye. He had known this young woman in life. The State's Attorney and his wife were friends.

"Don't forget to bag that bottle," Johnson said to the tech hovering nearby.

"Absolutely, boss."

"And don't miss that butt," Halloran added.

Johnson walked away and spoke briefly to Mallory, then walked slowly over to where Halloran stood with Ortiz.

"Once you guys are through with the scene, you call my cell," Johnson said, handing Halloran a card with the number on it. "We're all going to go to the State's Attorney's home to make notification. And I'll do the talking, Halloran."

Ortiz and Halloran nodded.

No shit and no problem, Halloran thought, but his mouth stayed shut.

CHAPTER 4

Once he was finished at the scene, Halloran slipped under the yellow crime scene tape. He hoped to get past pesky Becky Thompson. But she spotted him, head down, trying to tunnel-vision his way to his car.

"C'mon, Mike, don't try to sneak away. You said you'd talk on the way out," said Thompson, her camera crew scrambling 15 paces behind her.

"I didn't say shit, Becky, and you know that. And I don't know shit. You know what I know for sure. We got a dead body. We don't even have a positive ID yet. You can try to call me later."

Don't abuse the press; use the press.

Those were the wise words of Halloran's first homicide sergeant. And don't lie to them. That will really screw you. He hadn't really lied; they wouldn't have an official ID until a family member identified the body. And the reporters knew this was big--why else were they there at 7 a.m. on a Saturday?

"And I'm gonna call, Mike," Thompson yelled to his back.

He raised both hands up over his head, waved, and kept walking.

He started the Jeep, slipped it into first gear and pulled away from the curb, glancing in his rearview mirror to see Thompson retreating to the television truck. Halloran headed over to the Outer Drive via Clark Street. The streets were empty this crisp autumn day as he passed Lincoln Park Zoo.

***

The supe was being driven to the State's Attorney home in River Forest while Halloran and Ortiz made their way there on their own, Syl driving her family van. The media didn't know who was dead yet, but it would only be a matter of hours before this leaked.

As he approached Oak Street, Halloran marveled at the beauty of the city in the early morning. Chicago's skyline was striking on this cloudless day, the Hancock building looming over the squat greystone splendor of the stately Drake Hotel.

Heading south on Lake Shore Drive, heading into town, Halloran sang softly. *Alliota, Haynes Jeremiah—did they ever make another song?* LSD was a great song, reminded him of his youth, heading down to Rush Street to bartend. Standing behind the bar, it was easy to search for the future Mrs. Halloran, as he liked to call her, whoever she might be.

His reminiscence was broken as a Cadillac cut him off and brought him back to the present. He got over to the right to turn off the Drive to get onto Lower Wacker at Grand to head to the Eisenhower Expressway, focusing now on the grim prospect of telling the family. It was a thankless task every cop hated, but at least this time, it was the supe who would be doing the talking. *He'd made that clear enough.*

What do we got so far? An ice pick, possible sexual assault--know more after the autopsy--missing credit card or cards, no money. Upscale neighborhood, though, so not likely a street crime.

Halloran picked up his cell and called Syl.

"Yeah, Mike. Whattya think?" Ortiz said, spotting Halloran's number on caller ID.

"I think that we'd better hope somebody saw something."

"At 4 a.m.? Fat chance."

"The canvass may pick something up. Sheehan was a dick for five years before he made sarge, so he knows what to do." Halloran switched lanes on the Ike.

"I called dispatch and the original call came from a woman at 3:57 a.m. from a pay phone in front of Ranalli's," Ortiz said. "Left no name."

"Jesus Christ, must've been the only woman left on the North Side without a cell phone."

"Yeah, and calling on the last pay phone in Chicago. Ranalli's closes at 2 a.m. on Saturday. Wonder who was passing by who heard the scream."

"Could be a passerby, but don't discount the pizza joint's help coming out at 4 after cleaning up and having a few pops or maybe smoking a jay. Let's get back there this afternoon after they open up. Can't be anyone there for Sheehan or his guys now."

"I don't think she was raped," Ortiz volunteered. "But we'll know soon enough. No signs of a struggle. I'm wondering if she could've screamed once she was stabbed."

"We need to make sure Doc Powers does the post," he said before disconnecting.

Halloran had seen Dr. Jane Powers testify numerous times. She was unflappable and professionally condescending when she lectured even the shrewdest defense attorneys during cross-examination. Juries loved her; so did prosecutors. Halloran dialed Mallory as he drove, looking up at traffic and down at his cell.

"Chief, need a favor, not a big one. Can you put in the call to the morgue and make sure Powers does the post? This looks simple, but we don't want this fucked up, right?"

"That-- is a good idea, Halloran. And it will remain a good idea to keep me posted, right?"

"Right." Halloran pulled off the Eisenhower at Harlem and started heading toward Cavaretta's home. He sighed. *This is gonna be a real fucking bitch.*

CHAPTER 5

After a meteoric career as a prosecutor, first in the State's Attorney's office and then in the U.S. Attorney's office, Tom Cavaretta joined one of Chicago's top law firms. It was all walnut paneling and leather chairs and sofas, handmade oriental rugs, and magnificent views of the lakefront and the riverfront from the 38th floor corner office at Keenan Levin and Prentice.

In between prosecutor jobs, Tom married Joyce Dennehy, the daughter of longtime North Shore Congressman Bill Dennehy, who was a confidant of mayors, senators, governors and several Democratic presidents. Joyce was to the manor born, but no snob.

A Northwestern Law School grad, Tom flowed easily in the high echelons of the Chicago legal literati. No one seemed to remember Tom had gone undergraduate to Creighton in Nebraska, or Moo U, as some disparaged his alma mater. Joyce met Tom when he clerked in the Corporation Counsel's office one summer in law school.

In 1996, the Cook County Democratic Party turned to Tom after the Republican State's Attorney got caught in a messy divorce and looked vulnerable. As expected, Cavaretta had no opponent in the primary election.

In the general election in November, the divorce flap, Tom's sterling resume and the mobilization of the Democratic machine's ground troops all combined to give him a 2-1 margin over the incumbent. The papers hailed it as an upset. But the smart money always went with Democrats in Cook County.

Before rejoining the public sector, however, Cavaretta had 20 years of private practice as a white-collar criminal defense attorney, charging $500 an hour for court time. He was not ostentatious about his wealth, but he was financially comfortable. The Cavarettas lived in a classy Tudor on a cul de sac in tony River Forest. Five bedrooms, three and half baths, and a three-car garage.

As State's Attorney and the guy who put bad guys in prison, Cavaretta had a driver/bodyguard to take him wherever he went. When the driver arrived each morning, he would park the black Crown Victoria Police Interceptor far enough forward in the circular driveway so the boss could see the car from the family room post, where he devoured the Tribune and Sun-Times over coffee.

On this Saturday, Cavaretta had not expected the head of his security, retired Chicago police detective Frank Moran, to arrive until 10 a.m. *Strange,* he thought, *when he saw a Black Crown Vic turn into the driveway and park in front of the house. It was only 8:40.*

Then just as he stirred himself to go outside to speak to Moran, a Jeep Cherokee pulled up behind the Crown Vic, and then a van behind the other two vehicles.

"What the hell is this, so early and on a Saturday?" Cavaretta said to himself as he walked to the front door.

When he swung open the front door, he was shocked to find Supt. Johnson standing before him, looking grim. Johnson was a serious man, and they were always dealing with heavy issues, but this unexpected visit was immediately unsettling.

"John, how are you? What brings you out on this bright October day?"

Just then, a tall, muscular detective filed in behind the superintendent, and a pretty Latina detective fell in beside him.

"Mr. State's Attorney. We need a few minutes. It's not good news. Is your wife up yet?" Johnson asked.

"Joyce? She sleeps late on Saturdays, but you know me. Gotta read the papers early. Why does that matter?" Alarm began creeping into the prosecutor's voice.

"Is there a room we could speak for a few minutes, Tom?" Johnson asked.

Cavaretta hesitated a moment before he led the officers into his living room, glancing up the stairs. He wanted to check on Jennifer; he hadn't spoken to his daughter this morning, and she usually got home long after he went to bed.

As he led the police into the living room, Cavaretta tried to reassure himself. It was bad, but not personal. One of his people caught in a DUI, maybe a hit and run death. It could be handled.

Johnson cleared his throat before speaking.

"Tom, Mr. State's Attorney, this is detective Sylvia Ortiz and her partner, Mike Halloran."

"Halloran, I heard your testimony in the Hit Squad trial. Nice work on that." Cavaretta grasped the detective's hand. "Nice to meet you, too, Detective Ortiz." The two detectives nodded, and silently deferred to their boss.

Even though thrown off by this early morning invasion, Cavaretta was still polite, still the politician. He motioned the three cops to the sofa and chairs. Johnson remained standing; so did his subordinates.

"Tom—there's no easy way to say this. There was a homicide this morning in Old Town. I'm very sorry to inform you that the victim our people found was Jennifer. I'm sorry, very sorry. She was a wonderful girl, a joy. I know, I..." The words stopped coming.

Cavaretta stood stock still for a moment, his mouth open, then slumped onto the sofa, looking first to Halloran, then to Ortiz.

Ortiz managed to murmur, "I am so sorry, Mr. Cavaretta."

Halloran stood mute, his eyes looking beyond the prosecutor to the photo of his daughter proudly placed on the mantle over the white marble fireplace.

"Are you, are you sure, John? How can you be sure it's Jenny? I haven't been upstairs yet, but..." Cavaretta stopped.

He knew. Johnson would not make a mistake on something like this.

"I saw the body, Tom. I'm very sorry. Her purse was in the front seat under her. It's your car. Our people are all over this. I assure you. I know

I don't have to tell you this. Mike Halloran and Sylvia Ortiz are two of our very best detectives. We'll find this guy. You have my word."

Cavaretta was nodding at the superintendent. His mind was swimming. Jenny was supposed to go to the club with him this day for lunch. Jenny loved to work out at the Union League Club downtown.

He wanted to run upstairs to wake her, to tell her about this incredible mistake that was happening. He wanted to give his daughter, his only child, a hug. He gave her one last night when she left the house with Annie Doyle, her best friend. But Tom Cavaretta knew he would never hug his Jenny again. He knew. Then he heard his wife stirring upstairs, and he froze for a moment, knowing how Joyce would be devastated, torn apart.

Joyce was a good woman, an accomplished woman, a strong woman, but a mother more than anything else, and in the past few years, the best friend in the world to her daughter.

As her husband rose and tried to compose himself, Joyce Cavaretta swept into the room, elegant and charming even this early in the morning.

"John, so nice to see you. Has Tom even thought to offer you coffee?" Joyce Cavaretta spotted the two detectives and turned to Ortiz. "Hi. I'm Joyce Cavaretta, and you are?"

"Sylvia Ortiz."

Joyce Cavaretta turned to Halloran.

"And who is this tall, handsome Irishman?"

" Mike Halloran, ma'am."

There was an awkward silence for a second or two, before Tom Cavaretta rose and put his right arm around his wife's shoulders.

"The police have some bad news, dear. Horrible news--Jenny, Jenny..."

He faltered. Joyce Cavaretta threw her hand to her mouth. She looked up the stairs. She slowly began to shake, then sob softly. She dropped to the couch, her husband joining her and wrapping both arms around her.

"What happened, John?" Joyce asked, her eyes lasering in on the top cop.

"She was found murdered, Joyce. In Old Town. We don't know how or why or who did it? But we *will* find out. I know you need some time. I will be in contact again in a few hours. There will be a squad out front until your security arrives. Anything you need..." Johnson started backing out of the living room. Ortiz and Halloran were a step ahead. Halloran paused in the doorway.

"Our condolences. We're gonna find this guy."

Ortiz shot him a glance. Johnson nodded. The three officers left the house in silence.

Just before Johnson got into the back seat of his car, he turned and looked Halloran right in the eye.

"You *are* gonna get this guy. Right?"

"We will, boss," the partners said in unison.

CHAPTER 6

Just a few minutes away from the State's Attorney's home, Halloran and Ortiz pulled into the Dunkin Donuts at Narragansett and North to discuss the case.

The Pakistani proprietor smiled broadly at Halloran. Cheated out of his swim, caffeine-less and confronted with a heater case of unprecedented proportion, Halloran grunted out his order. Two large black coffees. Seconds after he paid and grabbed his morning fuel, Ortiz walked in. Several male heads swiveled in a booth to follow her entrance.

"Okay, what's the game plan?" Ortiz asked, slipping into a booth across from her partner. She knew that in the three minutes it took to get here, Halloran had been making mental lists.

"Well, the first question is do we split up today or try to do all this together. I say we got two cars; let's go two ways," Halloran said.

This was a time to split their talents even though he knew that he was better with her than without her. Her instincts and ability to pick up on nuances in an interview were a fine complement to his finely honed interrogation techniques.

The fact that most suspects were male and not blind to Ortiz' charms sometimes opened doors he never dreamed would open. That these mopes were stupid enough to think Ortiz would look twice at them always amazed him. But that's what keeps the streets safe: stupidity.

"So how about I go back to the Area and take a look at what the forensic techs picked up. You go to the autopsy. I know you love that shit," Ortiz said.

In fact, Halloran did not mind a trip to the Stein Institute, informally known as the county morgue. It was a quiet place run by smart and dedicated doctors. For the life of him, he couldn't figure how the docs there gravitated to this branch of medicine. Jane Powers explained that the work was steady, and the patients didn't complain. No malpractice lawsuits so she didn't have to take a second mortgage to pay pricey insurance.

"Fine. I'll head to the post. Then we should have a better idea what we got. I'll double back to the Area then, and we'll compare notes. Later we hit Ranalli's to see if we can find the caller."

"Sounds like a plan," Ortiz said, getting out of the booth and heading for her car.

This case is going to be a ballbuster even if the guy walks into police headquarters at 35th and Michigan and confesses today, Halloran thought. *The brass and the press are going to be all over this.*

***

Mike Halloran had always been the biggest kid in his class. Raised in Edgewater on the North Side, he measured in at 6'5", 230 by his senior year at Gordon Tech, where he made All State as a rugged tight end.

Halloran started the fifth game of his freshman year at Illinois and was honorable mention All-Big Ten his sophomore year. But his career-ending knee injury and subsequent surgery forced him to drop out of school. After months of physical therapy, he regained his mobility but grew increasingly restless. So, he booked a trip to India, a good starting point to satisfy his wanderlust. With the nest egg he'd set aside from his construction work, he was set for an extended trip. His parents worried but they had a full-grown adult now, and headstrong.

From India, he island-hopped to Australia until he ran out of dough and had to bartend. Then he took off to South Africa, working a few months as a hospital orderly, and finished his travels with a tour of Europe. After three years on the road, he had matured and returned to Chicago in early 1986, resolved that college was not for him. He took the police exam three weeks later. Four months later, he was taking notes at a desk in the police academy.

***

A half hour after leaving Ortiz, he pulled up to the morgue, or more accurately, the Robert J. Stein Institute of Forensic Medicine, a nondescript grey concrete building on Harrison in the midst of the ever-expanding West Side medical complex.

After flashing his badge to get by security, he passed the red metal door marked in black letters "Body viewing room." Couldn't get lost here, he mused. The first floor was where the action took place at the morgue. The autopsies were performed there, the bodies identified. In a corner room, he found Powers in her surgical scrubs.

"Hey, Doc, I didn't want to miss the cut," Halloran said by way of greeting.

"Just for the Bears' starting tight end slot. You could've wiped out all Ditka's records, big fella."

"Maybe if you'd done the cutting on this knee, I could've had a chance."

"During my residency, maybe, but I'm a little less delicate with my patients here. You here on the Cavaretta case?" Powers looked up from the lifeless body of Jennifer Cavaretta.

"Yeah. Got to move on this one, Jane. What's it look like?"

"Well, this is no mystery. He stuck her once, and she bled out in a matter of minutes. Cut to the right carotid, she probably was only conscious for 50, 60 seconds before the blood stopped going to her brain."

She went on to say what Halloran already knew. The toxicology tests would take weeks and would show if she was on any drugs, which Halloran doubted. And, she added, there was no evidence of recent sexual activity or assault.

"How about the blood alcohol?"

"Already done. Maybe two beers over three hours. It was .03 BAC. She could have driven home, no problem."

"Yeah, until shithead got her. Hey Jane, you been doing this for a couple decades. How many ice pick murders you seen?"

"I have few firsts, but this is one. That's a lot of dead bodies over a quarter century. This asshole either knew what he was doing, or he got lucky with the first shot at the carotid."

"He ain't gonna be lucky for long. Could she have called out, screamed?"

"If he had slashed her with a knife, he might have cut her windpipe and cut off the outcry. But this wound missed the windpipe, so she could've screamed. But I'm not so sure she got much chance."

"Why?"

"See this bruising around the mouth and what looks like a bruise around the wound?"

"Yeah." Halloran leaned forward over the body.

"My thought is this: He jabbed her with the ice pick, thinking it would kill her quick, but maybe first she screamed or tried to, and he clamped his hand over her mouth hard to stifle her. And this bruising around the wound—that was because he kept the pick in. It punctured the right carotid, but because he left it in, the blood started leaking out and filled subcutaneously."

He'd seen and heard enough. "Thanks, doc. Can you fax me your report, and let me know when the tox results get in?" Powers was already pulling the sheet up back over the body.

As he walked out the front door, he was hit again with the peculiar stench of the place. It smelled like the dentist office when the drill had been whirring for a while, the scent of burning bone, calcium under stress, the stress that came from a saw opening a skull.

CHAPTER 7

Syl Perez had excelled at the Police Academy, graduating fourth in her class. After a strong run on patrol with several commendations, she passed the detective exam. A year of stellar work as a dick on burglary led to her assignment to homicide, the rising star paired with the veteran Halloran.

Just after she made detective, she married Joe Ortiz, a prosecutor, and dropped her maiden name while keeping her ethnicity. They bought a Cape Cod in Edgebrook and started having kids after Joe went into private practice.

Before she left home, Ortiz glanced in the hall mirror. *Not bad,* she thought. *Still fit after three kids and one Caesarean. God, Johnny was hard. She turned in the mirror and appraised herself. Yeah, better put on some makeup, honey, it's going to be a long day. She quickly applied blush, mascara, and a thin coat of lipstick. Enough.*

Twenty-five minutes later, she walked into the canyon of desks at Area 3. She found the forensic techs spreading out some of the evidence from the murder scene.

"Hi, Syl. Jesus, is this one hot. I've had two calls from the Chief of D's and one from the First Deputy," forensics technician Jack Gallagher said.

"Lay it out for me, too, will you, Jack?"

"We got an old ice pick. I dusted it but couldn't raise a print. It's a pretty rough surface. There were some reddish hairs on her blouse that didn't appear to be hers. There was a crushed Camel unfiltered in the car. Ashtray looked like it had only been used to put out that butt. A half empty water bottle in the rear. We bagged it and sent it to the lab with the butt. We dusted inside and out and got a few usable prints. Oh, and found a small baggie of grass in the gutter not far from the front passenger side door. Strange, huh?"

Syl took it all in. Gallagher went on to describe what else they had gathered around the car. Nothing else spiked her interest. Syl thanked Gallagher, then crossed the room to inspect a stack of supplemental reports that were the results of the canvass the beat cops conducted shortly after the body was found.

Methodically, Ortiz went through each report. No one saw anything. The white-haired woman who had pointed the beat cops to the Cavaretta car only came out after hearing a scream. She only got close enough to the car to see the body and the ice pick sticking in the victim's neck.

Syl hadn't expected much, and that's what she got. Halloran called her on her cell. He was in the parking lot, checking out an unmarked car, anxious to compare notes and get to Ranalli's, and then talk to Anne Doyle, the victim's friend. Ortiz joined him in the lot, slipping into the shotgun side.

"Only one small surprise in the autopsy," Halloran said. "The rest you probably suspect." He told her about the precision of the wound. Ortiz nodded.

"To say that is curious is an understatement. How many ice pick murders you investigated, Mike?"

"I'm with Powers. It was her first and mine, too. This is my virgin ice pick investigation. Is that a double entendre, with a phallic overtone?"

Halloran grinned. Ortiz smiled.

"Chief of D's reached out to the other Areas to get their best people," Ortiz said. "A task force is shaping up. And right now, we got zip—no suspect, no motive. Nada. You don't want to hear all the names. Don't worry too much. They're mostly good."

"I'm sure. Fill me in on the way."

CHAPTER 8

Ranalli's had a patio where yuppies congregated in warm weather and a pleasant pizza joint atmosphere inside, nestled in the shadow of the Lincoln Park Towers, the old Four Torches apartment complex. The restaurant had been owned by the Ranallis for more than 25 years and catered to mostly single young professionals who came in to eat, have a few beers, and repair to their nearby condos. It had a bar, but it really wasn't a pickup place. When the manager, Ed Meinert, heard the rap on the front door at 1 p.m., he was a bit annoyed. He was just checking the bar's inventory before the joint opened at 2.

"Yes, what is it?" Meinert asked, cracking the front door to see who the intruders were.

Halloran and Ortiz both flashed their badges. Not rehearsed, but usually effective.

"Oh sure, officers, what can I do for you?" Meinert's tone amped down a bit as he swung the front door wide. Ortiz turned once inside and Meinert practically bumped into her.

"There was a murder across the street, on Lincoln Park West, late last night or really early this morning. We need to talk to any of your employees who were here last night after closing in case they might've seen something."

"Of course. There were just me and Betty and Swede here after we closed. They'll be in any minute."

"It's Betty we'd like to talk to first, but since you're here, did you see anything unusual last night about closing time? Anyone unusual?" Halloran asked.

"Well, it was pretty quiet. Nothing unusual."

"What time did you leave?" Ortiz asked, looking beyond Meinert into the empty restaurant.

"We close at 2, but I left about 3:20 a.m. I had to get up early to take the wife and kids to the in-laws this morning. Betty, the night manager, and Swede cleaned up and restocked, probably left about 3:45 or so."

Just then, a hefty, bleached blonde about 50 walked in, lots of makeup and a tight red sweater.

"Betty, these are police officers investigating a murder, and they'd like to speak with you." Betty Kotowski's eyes widened, and then spoke.

"Sure, officers, what do you need?"

"What time did you leave here last night?" Halloran asked.

"Am I a suspect, officer?" Kotowski eyed Halloran, a smile creasing her makeup.

"What time, ma'am?" Halloran was used to an occasional flirt; the job attracted it. He smiled, but not encouragingly.

"About 3:50, 3:55."

"Did you call the police from that pay phone outside?" Ortiz asked.

"No. No, I just left a few minutes after Swede, and went right home," Kotowski said, looking first at Ortiz, then at Halloran. "Why?"

"Look, miss, we're investigating a murder. You're not a suspect in the murder, but you are a strong suspect in the phone call. We have your voice on tape and can do a voice print comparison. It's a felony to lie to the police. Do you want to do this the easy way here, or the hard way back at the station?" Halloran asked.

Betty Kotowski winced; she looked like she'd been slapped.

"Okay, I didn't want to get involved, but I thought the police should know that there was a woman screaming, ya know. Don't throw me in jail 'cause I did the right thing."

"Nobody wants to throw you in jail, but we do need to ask a few more questions," Ortiz said. "Did you see anyone on the street after you heard the scream?"

"No, I just turned to use the pay phone. I'd left my cell in the car, ya know?"

"How about as you walked out the front door—see anything?" Halloran asked.

"Not a soul."

"Did you see this woman?' Ortiz asked, pulling the photo of Jennifer Cavaretta she had pulled from the Illinois Secretary of State's files.

She studied the photo for a minute, then said. "I don't think I ever saw her, that night or any other night."

By this time, Swede Olson, the bartender had joined the small group and had overheard the last few questions.

"And this is Swede," Meinert said. The pair of cops shifted their gaze to the new addition. Olson spoke first.

"Well, I left about 3:30 and I didn't see anything or hear anything."

"See this woman?" Ortiz took the photo from Kotowski and handed it to Swede.

"Nope," he said.

"What about earlier in the night, see anything, hear anything?" Ortiz asked.

"Not a thing," Swede said,

"Anything comes to you, give us a call," Halloran said, handing over his cards as Ortiz did the same to all three.

Back in the Crown Vic, Halloran fastened himself in just as Ortiz's cell phone went off.

"Yeah, Ortiz here. Oh, yes, Mr. Cavaretta. Uh, yes, thank you. Yes, that would help. Let me get a pen."

Ortiz motioned to Halloran, who handed her a pen and a pad of yellow post-its. She scribbled down the phone numbers and addresses of Anne Doyle and Tom Reynolds, Jennifer's boyfriend. The State's Attorney said his daughter had been with both of them Friday night.

"Thank you, sir. Yes, we will keep you posted. And, uh, sir, I'm very sorry." Ortiz snapped her cell shut.

"It's 'Sorry for your troubles,' you're supposed to say," Halloran said.

"Don't feed me any of your bullshit Irish wake rituals. The boyfriend lives over there." Ortiz was motioning with her chin at the nearby Lincoln Park Towers.

"The boyfriend knows. It would've been good to catch him cold. Cavaretta called him."

"Yeah, would've been nice, but only if he whacked her," Halloran said. "Let's pay a visit to the boyfriend."

"Ya think Cavaretta thinks we should've gotten that information on the boyfriend and Anne Doyle from him when we there with the Supe?" Ortiz asked.

"I think if we'd started asking those kinds of questions there, we would've been stepping on the Supe's toes."

"You're right. I'll take the lead with Reynolds, okay?"

"Lead on."

CHAPTER 9

Standing at 30 stories across the street from the Lincoln Park Zoo at Armitage and Clark, the Lincoln Park Towers had long been a favorite for the city singles. Young professionals liked the convenience to downtown and the busy nightlife in Old Town and Lincoln Park.

After badging the doorman, the two detectives rode the mirrored and wood-paneled elevator up to Tom Reynolds' modest studio apartment on the 8th floor. Both Ortiz and Halloran took one look at Reynolds' red, swollen eyes and knew he was a grieving boyfriend, not an ice pick-wielding killer.

"Mr. Reynolds, this is Detective Halloran and I'm Detective Ortiz." She flashed her badge as they walked into the sparsely furnished apartment. Reynolds stepped back from the door and then followed them in. Halloran walked over to the balcony's sliding door as Ortiz began to speak.

"We are sorry for your loss, Mr. Reynolds. Tom, isn't it? Can we call you Tom?" Ortiz asked.

"Sure." Reynolds looked and sounded very young to Halloran.

"First of all, how long had you been going out with Jennifer?" Ortiz asked.

"About 7 months I've known her, and we started dating right after St. Patrick's Day." Reynolds sank into a stained plaid sofa that looked like it might have trailed him from college. He grabbed a Marlboro Light and lit up. Halloran noted the cigarette brand.

"How would you describe your relationship? Friends, dating, serious?" Ortiz asked.

"Well, I was crazy about Jenny." Reynolds was tearing up. "She was great, just great. Smart, funny, sensitive—great, just great. But I guess dating would best describe it."

"I know this is hard, but we will be as brief as we can. When did you last see Jenny?" Ortiz noticed Reynolds' auburn, dark red hair, similar to the strands found on the body.

"Well, we had met Annie and some others from law school at Gamekeepers and had a few drinks. We'd left about 2 and came back here. We had a glass of wine and were watching the tube. I maybe had a little more than she did, and I drifted off on the sofa here.

"I woke up about 6 and she was gone. I always walk her to the car—she never stayed overnight—I just..." Reynolds stopped, took a drag on the cigarette, crushed out the cigarette in a Budweiser ashtray, then stood up and ran his fingers through his thick auburn hair.

"If I hadn't fallen asleep, she..." and the slightly built young man began to sob, his shoulders heaving.

Ortiz came up and put a hand on his shoulder.

"Take your time, Tom, we know this is hard." *This guy is either the greatest actor since Jimmy Cagney or he has no more to do with this murder than I do,* Halloran thought.

"No, I want to help. I know Mr. Cavaretta wants me to tell you everything I know. So, go ahead."

"I know this may sound strange, but is there anyone who might want to harm her, who was out to get her?" Halloran asked.

"Jesus, no. I'm sure you know how wonderful she is by now."

"Well, actually, why don't you tell us a bit," Ortiz said.

"I would describe Jenny as beautiful, but my dad called her 'cute as a button.' She had a presence that turned heads when she walked into a room. Everyone loved her, wanted to be with her." Reynolds caught his breath, turned away and wiped his eyes.

He went on to say how she had been the class president at Oak Park-River Forest High School, played soccer and been good enough to make the suburban All Star team in the Pioneer Press.

"She'd gone to Duke but didn't much like it. She deserved to be at Northwestern," he said suddenly. "Some people may have thought her father's clout had helped get her in, but she was freaky smart, a 3.6 GPA at Duke and a 169 score on the LSAT (Law School Admissions Test)."

Reynolds said he loved Jenny, but was never sure it was reciprocated, describing it as 75-25 relationship; he liked her more than she liked him. She was a year older and in her second year of law school.

"We met at a political party on St. Patrick's Day, and she started asking me questions immediately. When she found out I was at Northwestern Law, too, she started giving me a hard time. 'Why would anyone want to be a lawyer? If you're a defense attorney, you have to stand up and represent some scumbag. And prosecutors are in bed with the cops. And divorce attorneys, corporate shills, personal injury-ambulance chasers—how about it?' "

Reynolds laughed at the memory, then groaned.

"It's an honorable profession, I told her. Then I asked what she was. A flight attendant? In sales?"

"'Oh, I'm in law school,' she said, and then laughed so hard I didn't know what to do. Before the night was over, I asked her out," Reynolds recalled. "Everyone loved Jenny."

"Well, thank you," Ortiz said. "Don't take this wrong-- we have to ask--did she ever do drugs?"

"God, no. She was so straight. She's a light drinker; she's very aware of who her father is." Reynolds was slipping into the present tense as so many victims' friends and families do, a subconscious effort to keep them alive.

"Did you see anyone on the street that night who might've been tailing her, stalking her maybe? She was very attractive," Halloran asked.

"No. Nobody, but we were in here for at least an hour before I fell asleep. But there was a kind of creepy guy at the bar who stopped Jenny for a second on her way back from the john."

"Who was that?" Halloran asked.

"Oh, I don't know. Jenny said it was just a guy she'd met at school. Said it didn't matter when I asked. She only spoke to him for a second."

"Creepy, how?" Ortiz asked.

"Guess it was the tattoo I could see peeking out from his long-sleeve shirt. Not many law students with tattoos. It looked like a claw snaking out of his shirt onto his inside wrist. I noticed it 'cause he had his elbow up on the side table, a cigarette in his hand, so the shirt had edged up a bit, showing the tattoo."

"Did she tell you his name?" Halloran asked.

"No, she just stopped for a second. We were all having a good time. When I looked back a few minutes later, he'd left."

"How old?" Ortiz asked.

"I didn't get a good look; his back was to me. But maybe 40?" he said.

"Thanks, Tom. White, black, Hispanic?" Halloran asked.

"I think white," Reynolds said.

"Oh, yeah," Ortiz said. "One other thing. Did Jenny smoke?"

"No, never. She was death on that. I never smoked around her."

Halloran cleared his throat.

"Tom, did Jenny usually have the top buttons of her blouse open?"

"Geez, no. Why?"

"No good reason. Just a question."

Before the detectives left, they each gave Reynolds their cards, instructing him to call if he thought of something that might help.

At the security desk, they asked to see the video of the morning of the murder. It showed Jennifer leaving at 3:52 a.m. No one in the camera's view but her.

Back out on Armitage, Ortiz and Halloran walked to the squad before speaking, then stopped before getting inside. Halloran leaned against the passenger side door and looked at his partner.

"So, Mike, who's Camel unfiltered is it in the car?"

"Good question. Let's make sure the lab works that up for a profile ASAP. And whose dope was that?"

"Another good question. And with this case, we'd better not hear any bullshit about a backlog at the lab," Ortiz said.

"And the guy at the bar, we gotta look at that harder," Halloran said. He pulled his cell and called chief of detectives Mallory. Mallory had made it clear he wanted to be kept abreast of any development. Halloran told him about the cigarette butt, and its lack of ownership. He asked the chief to use his clout to expedite the DNA test on the cigarette.

"Chief, yesterday would be great on that, huh?"

"I'll call the director over there right now. We'll get the results forthwith."

Halloran withheld the questions he had about the grass found in the gutter. Chances are Mallory already knew. Truth was, Halloran didn't know quite what to make of the dope.

"It doesn't sound like the dope was our victim's. Could've been our guy's, but is he using or selling? It looked like a full lid, so it could be a dealer who dropped it," Ortiz said.

"Yeah, it's too early on this. Let's not get tunnel vision. Right now it looks like a robbery, but the question might be: Was it made to look like a robbery? We don't want to outsmart ourselves on this. What busts my Irish ass on this is--an ice pick murder? Where's the pattern with that?"

"That MO bothers me, too, but what bothers me more is there is one wound. One wound and he hits the artery. Pretty precise for some thug looking to boost a purse or car."

"And here's a $50,000 car, too. Why didn't he shove her out and take the car?"

"Beats the shit out of me," Ortiz said.

"Well, I don't want to do that," Halloran grinned. "Let's go back to the Area and see what they've come up with."

Just as they were about to get into the squad, Halloran's cell went off. The number belonged to Frank Marone, the Sun-Times crime reporter.

"I gotta take this."

After Ortiz rolled her eyes at her partner, Halloran walked out of earshot before he hit the button to connect. After a number of heater cases, Halloran knew the media could be useful. Ortiz told reporters to call News Affairs, but she knew her partner had helped out a reporter or two.

"Halloran," he said, as if he didn't know who was calling.

"Mike, it's Frank Marone. Big one, huh?" Halloran could almost see Marone talking out of the side of his mouth, looking around.

Now out of earshot of his partner, Halloran spoke more openly.

"I got nothing so far, Frank. But I could use a little help. We're on background, right? Do a clip search for me and see if you get a nexus between ice pick, murder and carotid."

Background was media code that Halloran knew well. He would talk as long as he never saw his name in the paper and any attribution went to the usual suspect, "sources close to the investigation."

"You saying the State's Attorney's kid was killed with an ice pick to the neck?"

"I never said that. But you're a smart guy. You got a keen sense for the obvious. A firm grasp of the axiomatic, as you erudite guys in the media might say."

"But I wouldn't be wrong going with the ice pick as the murder weapon and wound to the carotid artery?"

"If I were you, I wouldn't lose any sleep over that."

"Thanks, Mike. Any suspects? Close to an arrest? Anyone in custody?"

"Call me when you get anything on that nexus," Halloran interrupted and then disconnected. Marone would never run out of questions.

He knew that the murder weapon would come out eventually but probably not immediately. The circle of those who knew the details was widening rapidly. Probably a scoop for Marone.

As he returned to Ortiz, he found out how wide.

"Yeah, right. About 15 minutes away. We'll be there, Lu." Ortiz was snapping her cell shut. "The task force. We're invited."

Lt. Charles Fagan, commander of Area 3, had formed a task force of the top detectives recommended by Chief Mallory to investigate the Cavaretta homicide. Its first meeting was in a half hour. Halloran groaned.

"A clusterfuck. Christ. But we knew it was coming."

CHAPTER 10

Built on the site of the old Riverview amusement park, Area 3 had been thrown together in the mid-1970s as a state-of-the-art police station/courthouse. But now it was showing signs of age, and the ghosts of the freaks that made up the Freak Show at Riverview seemed to keep resurfacing daily in the procession of pimps, prostitutes, petty thieves and various other perpetrators who found their way into the two-story, red brick building.

On the south side of the building was the entrance to the branch courts, one felony courtroom and one misdemeanor courtroom. Just east of the courthouse door was the entrance to Area 3, which the newspapers called the Belmont Area station, and so did half the cops.

Dicks came in through the north entrance and ascended the stairs to a sprawling room on the second floor dotted by desks. There were a few interview rooms where suspects and witnesses were questioned. Sticking out of the cinderblock walls of the two interview rooms were two giant steel eyebolts where the dicks handcuffed suspects to the wall.

In recent years, unobtrusive digital cameras had been installed to capture the details of each interrogation of suspects in any murder case. The Chicago Police Department had fought this in the state legislature, but a wave of false confessions coupled with heavy media pressure had carried the day to make taped interrogations the law in all homicide cases.

Most detectives knew they could outsmart the suspects; a few dinosaurs still thought a closed fist, a gun thrust into a suspect's mouth, or a telephone book to the temple were fine interrogation methods.

Those methods, unfortunately, had resulted in confessions from guilty men being suppressed by judges and the cases either being thrown out or retried later. Halloran had come on the force in the waning days of the rogue cop. He found it incomprehensible that these old warhorse dicks would rather beat it out of a guy than simply spend a little more time and energy and brainpower to outsmart them. He'd heard the stories, and he knew some of the allegations were true.

In the heat of an interview, Halloran was not above lying, threatening, cajoling, humiliating, ingratiating or any other technique he could think of to get at the truth. Many a night, he had slammed his meaty right hand flat on the table so hard that the smack reverberated throughout the second floor. It invariably got the suspect's attention, but it never got a case tossed.

Lying to get the truth was a time-honored, perfectly legal interrogation technique, the courts had ruled. When he told Kotowski he had her voice print, he knew the science was mixed and the courts skeptical. But the threat prompted her to come clean.

He laughed to himself as he drove north on Western to Area 3 when he thought of the effect he had and the woman's quick confession.

"What's so funny?" Ortiz asked as they pulled into the Area 3 lot.

"Zilch. But before we go in there and find out how much smarter everyone is than us, whattya think about the ice pick?"

"I think we should find who makes them and where they are distributed," Halloran said.

"Who would even use one nowadays and for what?"

"Well, if we're getting help, maybe someone can chase that while we go talk to the Doyle girl," Halloran said.

"Okay, let's face the music."

In the second-floor conference room, Fagan was just walking into a room filled with mostly aging white guys with 9 millimeters and .357 magnums on their hips.

Halloran and Ortiz joined Fagan and the other 10 detectives who had been picked from all the Areas. With him and his partner, it was a baker's dozen of dicks, Halloran mused.

"Good, Halloran and Ortiz, come on in." Fagan interrupted his spiel when he spied the two detectives. "Why don't you tell us what you've been doing, and then we'll tell you what we know."

Halloran ran through the brief details of the crime scene, the autopsy and the interview with the boyfriend. Ortiz jumped in with a few words about the boyfriend's demeanor and the time link on the security camera.

"No way he's the guy," Ortiz opined.

"Well, let's keep all our options open," Fagan said. *Sure, Lu, cover your ass and look like you're in control at the same time,* Halloran thought. Fagan stood up and approached the blackboard after the two detectives had finished.

"Okay, here's our to-do list." Fagan began numbering the obvious. Check the ice pick for who makes them and who sells them; check with the lab for any DNA hits on the bottle or cigarette butt; check to see if there were any usable prints taken from the car; make sure Reynolds got printed for a comparable and swab him for DNA; check the victim's phone calls; interview the State's Attorney and his wife; check with the lab on the hair found on the victim.

By the time he'd finished, Fagan had a few dozen items on the to-do list and divvied them up, two to each detective team.

"Now I know you are the lead detectives, so is there anything else you can think of now to add here?" Fagan turned to stare at Ortiz and Halloran.

"You just about covered it, Lu," Halloran said. Ortiz nodded.

Neither Halloran nor Ortiz had any intention of sharing everything about the case or everything they thought had to be done. They'd take the help the department was imposing on them, but it was their case. Some of this stuff, like checking on ice pick manufacturers, was just grunt work anyway. Besides, the partners were sure that the reddish hairs on the victim would turn out to be Reynolds'.

Halloran and Ortiz would return to interview the State's Attorney and his wife, but not this day, they agreed. They also were assigned to interview Anne Doyle, Jenny's good friend who was with her at Game-keepers the night she was killed. It would be a long drive.

"She lives in Lake Forest? What's her daddy do, own a bank?" Halloran asked.

"Beats me. But we'll find out."

Minutes later, heading west on Belmont to catch the Kennedy Expressway, Halloran and Ortiz chewed over the troubling details of the case.

"So, okay. It looks like a robbery or made to look like a robbery. M.E. says no sexual assault. But how do we explain the blouse?" Halloran asked.

"Well, let's walk through it. We know she leaves the apartment about 3:45. The boyfriend usually walks her, but this time she solos it, lets him sleep. Probably figures it's just a block--what can happen? So, she's walking to the car, and someone spots this good-looking girl, well-dressed, approaching a Jag. Alone. Prime target, right?"

"Okay, but she has a whistle on her key chain and pepper spray in her purse. And yet she uses neither, right?" Halloran said. "No one reported hearing a whistle. This is the State's Attorney's daughter. She was weaned on crime. She knows the city. She sees some creep and she gets prepared."

"Well, maybe the guy had a gun and told her to shut up and get in the car. I don't think she'd go quietly if he just showed the ice pick. Do you?"

"No. I think she's smart enough to smooth-talk him for a minute until she gets a chance to grab the spray and zap the fuckhead. Maybe she never got the chance."

Halloran groaned as he pulled onto the Kennedy.

They were in the teeth of the evening commute. Ortiz hated it, but Halloran skirted the traffic by taking the shoulder until they hit Montrose and the traffic halved as it split to the Edens, and the Kennedy headed to O'Hare. Traffic eased a bit just past the Peterson Avenue exit.

"Powers tells us there are no signs of a struggle except the bruising around her mouth. Does he clamp his hand on her mouth to keep her quiet and force her into the car? Was there a gun? If so, why didn't he just pop her with his piece instead of using an ice pick?" Ortiz asked.

"Damned if I know. So, okay. Try this: They're in the car now. He tries to get in her blouse. She resists. She screams. He muffles her and picks her. He grabs the money and credit cards and splits."

"It works, mostly. But what are the chances he gets the carotid on the first swing?"

"Well, if we think it's just a street crime by Mickey the mope, then we think he gets lucky. But still, you would think in his frenzy he would give her a couple more whacks. How about if he knew where the carotid is?"

"You think we got a mad doctor turned killer, huh?"

"Well, it could explain why she didn't make an earlier outcry. What if she knew the guy?" Halloran asked.

"Okay, let's look at that for a minute," Ortiz said. "Some guy she knows waits in the dark for her to emerge from Reynolds' place, then strikes up a conversation with her, and then whacks her. Only if there is a jilted lover does it work for me. This lady ran in some pretty lofty circles--River Forest, Northwestern Law School, the leadership of the Democratic Party."

"Yeah, there's problems with it, all right. With the little we got, it's a bit of mental masturbation, right?"

"Hey, I'm happily married. When those guys called you a jagoff last week, I told them you broke the habit last month." Ortiz' eyes twinkled as she tossed one of his bad jokes back at him.

"You eat with that mouth?" Halloran countered. "Your children know their mommy uses that kind of language? Does Joe know you discuss my private, victimless sexual activities?"

They lapsed into silence as they passed Lake-Cook Road as the Edens became U.S. 41 and was no longer an expressway. In 10 minutes, they were at Deerpath, and exited to head to the Doyle home on Melody Lane, just off Waukegan Road.

"Who owns these houses? Whatta they got—12 kids?" Ortiz said as they passed $2 million homes with circular driveways, towering shrubs, and four-car garages.

"Long way from Pilsen bungalows, eh, Senora Ortiz?"

"And Edgewater two-flats."

In a moment, they pulled into the long circular driveway of the Doyle estate. They could see the pool house in the rear as they pulled up to the front door, an 8-foot dark oak entrance with glittering brass doorknob and knocker. A surveillance camera hung a few feet over the door.

Halloran ignored the doorbell and pulled back the heavy knocker and rapped twice. The detectives could hear it reverberate through the house.

After a few seconds, the massive door swung open, and a tiny Hispanic woman stood there in a black uniform with an immaculate white apron.

"We're here to see Anne Doyle." Ortiz held her gold detective star up.

"Please, come in. Mister is expecting you. Please to follow," the maid said in an accent Ortiz suspected had origins in Oaxaca.

"Mister?" Halloran mouthed. Ortiz shrugged. The floors were glistening dark cherrywood, covered every few feet with Oriental rugs—Isfahans, Tabrizes, a Bokhara, Halloran noted.

As the parade reached the library, the maid announced the two detectives and stepped aside at the entrance.

"Officers, how are you? I'm Ed Doyle, and this is my daughter, Anne." He shook Halloran's hand and motioned Ortiz into the office.

Doyle was a small, somewhat dainty man in his early 60s, grey hair, close-cropped. Seated on a small red leather sofa was Anne Doyle, her face flushed and eyes teary. Dressed in designer jeans and an off-white Irish sweater over a pink blouse, Anne Doyle looked up from her hands, then walked up to the officers and extended her right hand.

"Thank you for coming, officers. Can we get you something? Coffee, a Coke? Something stronger?"

"I'm Detective Halloran and this is my partner, Detective Ortiz. We're sorry for your loss. We'd like to ask you a few questions about Jennifer, about last night," Halloran said.

"Nice to meet you, detectives. I'll answer any question you have. But how about something to drink first?"

Halloran opted for water; Ortiz, a coffee, black. The maid soon materialized from the hallway to take the order and disappeared. Halloran's eyes drifted to a picture on the wall of Ed Doyle and President Reagan, a grip-and-grin taken in the library in which they were sitting.

"For all your help, Ed. Best of Luck, Ron," read the inscription.

Ed Doyle slipped behind a massive walnut desk, sinking into a dark brown leather chair that almost swallowed him. He motioned the two detectives to chairs opposite him and by the side of the sofa.

"We are just devastated by this. Jenny was a wonderful girl, so bright, so pretty, so full of life. Who would want to hurt her?"

"Daddy, I think that's why they're here. To ask some questions. You don't know who did it yet, do you? I've been watching the news."

"Well, we have a few leads but there's no one in custody," Ortiz said. "How long did you know Jennifer?"

"Since college. Duke. We met on the same plane going there as freshmen. Hit it off and been friends ever since."

"You were with her last night at Gamekeepers. Did anything unusual happen? Did you sense anything was bothering her?"

"God, no, nothing was bothering her. She was very happy. She had just aced some big test."

She sucked in some breath, bit her lip. The eyes welled up with tears.

"Tom said she had stopped to speak to some guy at another table. You know who that was?" Halloran asked.

"No, I asked Jenny 'cause he was pretty old, maybe close to 40. I mean, old for that bar, you know?" Anne stared at the two detectives she now realized were closing in on or had passed 40. "Not really old, you know, just older than us."

"That's fine. What did she say?" Ortiz asked.

"She said that he was just a guy she'd seen around school or something and he had talked to her a couple of times, not hitting on her, I thought, just talking."

"She mention a name?" Halloran asked.

"No, no name. It was just a quick conversation."

"Can you describe him?" Ortiz asked.

"I didn't really pay much attention to him. A white guy, slim, maybe 40-45. Short brown hair, not too grey yet. Had a tattoo on his wrist of some sort, like maybe a snake or the end of a rope."

"He look like a student or professor?" Ortiz asked.

"Not really. Too old for a student. Nor a professor--he didn't have a tweed sport coat on, ya know."

"What did he have on?" Ortiz asked.

"I really only glanced at him. I don't know, maybe jeans and a long-sleeve shirt or maybe a sweatshirt."

"Would it have been normal for Jennifer to have the top buttons of her blouse undone?" Ortiz asked, switching gears abruptly.

"No, not really. That's hardly her style."

At this point, the maid came in with the drinks. She put the glass of ice water in front of Halloran on a silver coaster. Ortiz' coffee was served in a delicate China cup on a floral Hensley saucer.

As the detectives sipped their drinks, Anne Doyle volunteered what a "sweet, loving, beautiful" young woman her friend was. Ed Doyle broke in.

"You think you may know who did this to Jenny?"

"It's still very early, Mr. Doyle. We have a team of our best detectives working on this. We have no reason to think we won't get him," Ortiz said.

"Who left the bar first?" Halloran asked.

"I did. I got home a little after 2," Anne said. The detectives glanced at each other, silently nodding they had no further questions.

"You've been very helpful. Is there a cell phone number you can be contacted at on short notice?" Halloran asked Anne.

After getting several numbers, including her cell, Ortiz and Halloran thanked the father and daughter. Anne led them out. As they passed the kitchen, they looked out through a huge plate glass window into the back yard where an Olympic-sized pool was covered for the winter.

Outside, Ortiz looked to make sure the door had closed behind them.

"So, this is how the other half lives."

"You mean the other 1/25th of one percent, don't you?"

As Halloran drove off, he passed a Lexus SUV stopped at the curb along Melody, a bleached blonde at the wheel with a cell phone pressed to her ear. In front of her, a Mercedes 500 had stopped and the woman driver, dressed in tennis whites was walking back to the Lexus.

"Christ, we must be the only people in Lake Forest driving an American car," Halloran said.

"That's because we don't live here."

As they headed back to the city into the teeth of the reverse commute, Ortiz' cell buzzed to remind her she was supposed to make a call.

"Oh, Jesus--the State's Attorney. Cavaretta wanted a call."

"What're you gonna say? We got next to zip right now. A guy she said boo to at the bar. No name, general description. I think all I feel good about so far is it wasn't the boyfriend or the best friend."

"I don't know what he wants. That's what I'll find out if I can call him." A little irritation had crept into her voice. It was now 7 in the evening, and they'd been at it nonstop for 12 hours. With nothing to show.

"Mr. Cavaretta. Detective Ortiz. Yes, I'm sorry, I just got the message."

Then she listened, nodding, taking a few notes, the cell tucked between cheek and shoulder.

"No, sir, I wouldn't say that yet. I don't think you can necessarily say that. We are working on a couple of leads, a few people who may have had contact with her. But I would not categorize anyone as a suspect. Not yet. Yes, sir. I will call as soon as there are any significant developments."

As soon as she disconnected, Halloran looked right, and lifted an inquisitive right eyebrow toward Ortiz.

"Well, he gave us her cell phone number so we could trace her recent calls. He means well, but I assume that that's been done by now. It was on the to-do list. He mentioned how he thought it might've been a car-jacking, and he was blaming himself for giving her the Jag for graduating from college."

"I am saying this sincerely. My heart goes out to the guy. But I hope we don't have him calling us every few hours for an update. He's going to be disappointed. And I don't want to disappoint the highest-ranking law enforcement officer in the county. You?" Halloran deadpanned. Then he cast a grin her way.

As they approached Area 3, Halloran shook his fingers at his partner. "I'll handle the paper."

"Night, and thanks partner. I owe you," Ortiz said and headed for her van.

CHAPTER 11

Back at Area 3, he checked in with Fagan. The silver-haired lieuten-ant peered over his granny glasses at several reports and quickly walked Halloran through what the rest of the task force had been doing.

The usable prints from inside and outside the car had come back to the victim, the State's Attorney, and Reynolds. Cavaretta's prints were still on file because he was printed as a young Assistant State's Attorney. Jenny's were on file from her summers working for her dad at 26th Street. Reynolds had freaked a bit when he got printed hours earlier.

The DNA from the water bottle and the cigarette butt were being worked up and would be put into CODIS (Combined DNA Index System), the FBI's national databank of known profiles established in 1990. The lab guys at the Illinois State Police crime lab on the near West Side were working overtime to get this done.

Halloran gave Fagan a brief recap of the conversation with Anne Doyle. He also reassured Fagan that they'd called Cavaretta back.

"Mind if I run out for five minutes for some lunch, Lu?" Halloran asked, glancing at his watch, which said 7:45 p.m. As soon as he'd said it, Halloran realized it might come across as a mild complaint and regretted it.

"We're all putting in the time, Halloran. Save the brainpower it takes to come up with that crap and use it to figure out who offed the girl." Fagan looked up from a stack of reports on his desk.

"Be back here ASAP. I want to see those supps before I leave." Supps were the supplemental reports that detectives typed up, following the initial incident report that the beat guys file to launch the mountain of paper, or computer work, which followed any murder investigation.

Ortiz said she'd owe him. He'd never taken typing. He had gone through school before the computer revolution made typing as much a skill as reading or basic math. Still, after more than 20 years as a dick, he was a pretty fast hunt-and-pecker. He looked at the keys, but he still pounded out about 55 words a minute. Ortiz' fingers flew across the keyboard at 95 words a minute.

But that could wait. First, he made a quick run to a Subway sandwich shop a block away.

He inhaled his turkey sub before he'd reparked the squad back at the station. As he returned to the Area 3 squad room, he spied Assistant State's Attorney Mary Catherine Egan talking earnestly with Fagan. He hadn't seen Egan since the end of the Hit Squad trial last year. The high-profile trial of cops killing drug dealers had been memorable for both as they won and flirted.

At 5'10", Egan saw eye to eye with most cops, and with her heels on, she looked down on many. *There was a subliminal message here,* Halloran thought. Tonight, she wore a black silk Christian Dior business suit, the skirt falling to the middle of her kneecaps, with three-inch black heels to accent her athletic and nearly perfect calves. *A fashionable dominatrix,* Halloran thought. The auburn-haired prosecutor always turned heads and short-circuited conversation when she walked into a police station.

And as the supervisor of Felony Review for the past year, Egan had walked into quite a few stations lately. Not long before her promotion, Halloran had testified in a high-profile case Egan was prosecuting.

Halloran's thoughts flashed back to how after a long night of tedious pre-trial preparations, he suggested that he and the attractive prosecutor a dozen years his junior grab a drink at Jean's, the gin mill of choice at 26th Street. It turned into a memorable night for both.

In the ensuing year, Halloran had learned she'd been promoted to head of Felony Review, in charge of 26 veteran prosecutors who approved any felony in Chicago, except minor dope cases.

It was no surprise to see that Egan had been chosen to quarterback the Cavaretta murder.

"Hey, Lu. Good evening, counselor," Halloran said as he stepped into Fagan's office.

"You two know each other?" Fagan asked.

With 13,000 Chicago cops and 900 Assistant State's Attorneys, it was hardly a slam dunk they would know each other.

"Yes, of course. Nice to see you again, Detective Halloran," Egan said, smiling and extending her hand. "We've worked together before, Lt. Fagan."

"Worked well, I hope," Fagan said.

"Seamlessly," Halloran said, returning the lawyer's smile.

"Good to hear. The three of us might be spending a lot of time together," Fagan said.

"Enough to get this right. Right?" Egan looked to Halloran and flashed a brilliant smile.

Halloran nodded.

"Absolutely." Fagan missed the eye-lock between cop and prosecutor.

CHAPTER 12

The 11-7 midnight shift was just clearing the Area 3 squad room by the time Halloran had finished briefing Fagan and Egan.

Area 3 encompassed the Loop, the Rush Street area, the Gold Coast, Streeterville and Lincoln Park. A lot of dough and heavy hitters in that small chunk of real estate on the North Side. The Area also covered less ritzy neighborhoods, like Andersonville and Ravenswood.

It was well after midnight when Halloran had finished and printed out the supps for Fagan. Egan had left without a word; Halloran had failed to notice, his concentration rooted in pecking away at the reports. Then he began leafing through the other supps the rest of the task force had filed. Nothing jumped out at him. He walked the printouts into Fagan's office.

"She any good? Awfully young. And not too tough to look at," Fagan said.

"Yeah, good and pretty tough. And yeah, she's okay to look at."

"Okay? Who you dating? Demi Moore?"

"Demi's a little long in the tooth for me, Lu."

"Yeah, and Egan is a little short in the tooth for you."

"Ease up, Lu. I'm a professional. You know that."

"Remember that. Now go home and get some sleep. We reconvene here at 8:15 in the ayem."

Out in the parking lot, Halloran took a deep breath. A late fall rain had swept the city. It smelled sweet, clean of the exhaust fumes that permeated the air during the day at the busy intersection of Belmont, Lincoln and Western, just east of the station.

Halloran needed a beer. He headed southeast on Lincoln toward Armitage, returning to the scene of the crime. But he was on his way to Ranalli's for a pint of the Guinness he had seen on tap there.

He slid his Jeep into a bus stop at Wisconsin and Lincoln, just 100 yards or so from where Jennifer Cavaretta had taken her last breath.

What a waste, he thought. Just then, his cell went off.

"Halloran."

"Detective, this is Tom Reynolds. I don't know if this is important, and I was too embarrassed to say it at first, especially in front of your partner."

"Say what, Tom? This is a homicide investigation. You can't hold back."

"Well, it's hard, but I want you to catch this guy. I know, well, I guess, that is..." Reynolds said, embarrassed and still hesitant.

"Look, Tom, you can tell me, whatever it is. We need any detail, no matter how small."

"Well, Jenny and I were not sleeping together. But that night, we were making out and we were doing a little petting, nothing heavy. But, but..." Reynolds faltered.

"But you had your hands in her blouse. Is that it, Tom?"

"I feel like I'm sullying Jenny. I, I..." Reynolds started crying.

"And that's how maybe her blouse was open a few buttons, you figure?"

"Yeah, I don't know if it's important, but I thought I should tell you, you know?"

"You did the right thing, son. And this stays with me, and my partner. It's important to know because we were looking at a possible sexual assault that went awry. This is important. Thanks for the call."

Halloran shook his head and smiled at his phone. Good to know, but tough for Reynolds.

Outside he walked back to where the Jag had been parked. He wanted to get a feel for crime scene in the silence of the night, for the solitude the cul de sac offered. There was a streetlight 75 feet away from where the Jag had been parked, but you couldn't read a newspaper by the light.

No thunderbolts of insight hit Halloran, so he decided to forget the Guinness and jumped in the Jeep for the 15-minute drive home. He headed for North to pick up the Drive.

"It's four o'clock in the morning, all the people have gone away. Heading north on Lake Shore Drive, tomorrow is another day," Halloran sang to himself as he pulled into the indoor parking at his pink stucco high rise at 5555 N. Sheridan.

After Halloran's mother had died, old man Halloran--William Dudley Halloran--had moved into the ancient Edgewater Beach Apartments, the grande dame of lakefront high-rises, which had gone up in the early 1920s, the residential twin to the old Edgewater Beach Hotel. After his father had died, Halloran had moved in. It felt like home.

He was the perhaps the youngest resident. But it had a pool, now under repair, a sprawling fenced-in garden, and an Oriental rug the size of a handball court in the baroque, marbled lobby, and indoor parking. As Halloran stared out the window of his 14th floor apartment, he gazed down at the Drive and the park and the darkened lake.

"I'm gonna find you, shithead. That was a nice girl you killed."

CHAPTER 13

As Halloran headed west on the Ike the next morning, he spoke cryptically to his partner riding shotgun.

"The alphabet—you know A to Z. And it's the first letter-A-a vowel."

"Okay. Spit it out." Ortiz was used to Halloran's tortuous method of getting at something that was on his mind. They were headed to interview the Cavarettas.

"A, as in the last letter in Giancana and the first in Accardo." Halloran had been hesitant to bring out the mob card, but they were headed to River Forest, home to the late Mob boss Tony Accardo. Accardo had died naturally, not so lucky was rival Sam Giancana, who was found slain in his Oak Park home.

"You telling me—I hope not—that because the victim has an Italian surname, that because the name ends in A, a vowel, you smell a mob hit?" Ortiz had turned in her seat to face her partner, the seatbelt straining.

"I'm not saying that, no. But I am saying that we would not be running out the groundballs here if we didn't even consider it."

"I'm all for running out the ground balls. I'll run to first on a dropped third strike, for Christ sake, but Mike, don't bring up this mob stuff with any of the brass. They'll have your ass walking a beat in South Chicago if you even hint State's Attorney Cavaretta is mobbed up."

"With what we got so far, all I'm saying is we don't put blinders on, no tunnel vision."

"All right, but we go there only if we're led there. No questions even hinting at that with this family, right Mike?"

"Gimme just a little credit for tact."

As he approached the Harlem Avenue exit, Halloran made a mental note to fill up the Crown Vic when they got back to Area 3. It was said that the Ford Crown Victoria Police Interceptor could pass anything on the road—except a gas station. Halloran figured the beast got maybe 9 miles to the gallon.

***

Thomas Cavaretta slept fitfully that night. At one point, he awakened with a start, wondering if he had dreamt the whole thing. He walked down to Jenny's room, peered inside. The teddy bear with the pink ribbon around the neck was still on her pillow where she had left it Friday morning. He sat down on her bed. He wept quietly; he did not want to wake his wife. She was heavily sedated with prescription sleeping pills. He lay down on the pink comforter and pulled the bear to his face. It still smelled of her. The prosecutor cried himself back to sleep on his daughter's bed. He awoke with a start when his cell phone rang. He grabbed it from the bed stand.

"Hello," Cavaretta whispered. "Yes, detective. I'm up. No, it's all right. A half hour. Sure, I'll be here. She's sleeping but she will be up by the time you get here."

Cavaretta went down his spiral staircase to the hall leading to the kitchen. It was a nice house, not ostentatiously big at five bedrooms. As he passed the living room, he glanced at the picture on the mantle of the three of them at Jenny's college graduation in Durham. She was radiant, so was Joyce. Even the usually reserved prosecutor was smiling broadly.

"God, who would kill this precious gift to the world?" he wondered aloud.

He made a quick pot of coffee, enough for the detectives. Cops spent their lives drinking coffee, he knew.

Outside, the first frost had come overnight, and his bushes, wet from the night rain, had a brushing of frozen dew. He could see his breath as he bent down to pick up the Trib and Sun-Times on his driveway.

"Prosecutor's daughter slain," blared the Sun-Times. The Tribune story was over the roof, atop a Baghdad bombing story that ran down the right side.

He couldn't get past the third graph in the Tribune before he threw his right hand over his mouth, the tears welling up as he stood in his driveway looking at the papers.

"You gotta be strong for Joyce," he muttered to himself before he walked back inside.

"Who was on the phone, Tom?" Joyce asked, her pink Christian Dior robe wrapped tightly around her.

"Oh, I'm sorry that woke you. It was detectives Halloran and Ortiz. They're on the way over," Cavaretta said. "Did you sleep?"

"Have they caught him?"

"Well, they didn't say. I didn't ask. It was a very short conversation. I think they would've said if they had someone in custody. They'll be here in a few minutes."

"Is this a life without parole case?" Joyce asked.

"It could be. If it was in the commission of a robbery or a ra..." Cavaretta stopped short. "Or an attempted rape, it could be a death penalty case."

"Will you make that decision?"

"I would not be the one. It's a clear conflict of interest, but this is all a bit premature." Cavaretta was taken aback at his wife's abrupt questions. Her steely resilience still brought him up occasionally short.

This morning, this daughter of a congressman and wife to the State's Attorney, was ready for the detectives. She put down her coffee when the front doorbell rang.

"Come in, please," Joyce said as she opened the door. Cavaretta came up behind his wife and extended his hand as Ortiz and Halloran entered the foyer.

"Please join us for some coffee." Joyce led the detectives to the kitchen table.

'Thank you for seeing us so early," Ortiz said.

"What do you have for us?" Joyce Cavaretta asked before they were seated.

Speaking alternately, the two detectives detailed the interviews that had been conducted and the status of the physical evidence.

"And what are your thoughts about this tattooed man in the bar? Does he look like a suspect?' Cavaretta asked.

"We need to find him and talk to him. We think that with a sketch we should be able to find him. The sketch artist is on the way to Reynolds right now," Halloran said.

That may have been presumptive, but he felt comfortable telling the State's Attorney that after Fagan had reassured him he had already rousted the department's sketch artist to swing by Reynolds' that morning.

"Is there anyone who has a grudge against you?" Halloran asked.

"Me? You saying you think someone killed my daughter because they're mad at me?" the State's Attorney asked, his voice rising.

Ortiz shifted suddenly, casting a furtive frown at her partner. *You weren't going to go there, Halloran.*

"We're looking at everything," Ortiz broke in. "Your office puts thousands of people in prison. You must get some threats."

"Oh, yeah, sure. I get e-mails, letters, calls. The secretaries screen them and send them on to our Investigations Bureau to look into. I don't see Jenny's death as anything that relates to my job."

State's Attorney Cavaretta was getting a bit agitated, his brow furrowed. The thought that he in any way caused his daughter's death was incomprehensible. He had focused on the prospect that the Jag had led to a bungled carjacking.

"We don't want to leave any stone unturned,' Ortiz said, abandoning the baseball metaphor they had used in the car.

"Getting back to those threatening letters, sir. Could I get a look at those today?" Halloran asked.

"I'll call Ted Gillespie right now. He's our chief of investigators and lives in Bridgeport, so he's close to our Investigations Bureau at 26th Street," Cavaretta said.

"I know Ted, good man, please tell him I'll reach out to him in about an hour," Halloran said.

"One more thing, did Jenny carry much cash?" Ortiz asked.

"Not normally. But it kind of depends what you mean by much cash. I insisted she carry a $100 bill stashed in her wallet for emergencies. It made me feel better. She put it right behind her driver's license. I don't know that she used it often. She was a big girl. We didn't ask too many questions, but we worried..." Cavaretta stopped, caught his breath, then coughed self-consciously.

The detectives had heard enough. After promises to keep in touch, Halloran and Ortiz left. Outside, a camera crew from Channel 7 was just pulling up. Ortiz groaned, and Halloran walked quickly to the squad, head down.

"The inventory didn't mention the $100 bill, did it?" Ortiz asked.

"No way."

"Well, she could have spent it and not replaced it. Unlikely, the guy would've been digging behind the license after he whacks her and she's already screamed, eh? But just one more thing we may never know," Halloran said.

Back on the road, they sorted out the rest of the day. Ortiz was going to return to Area 3 to work the phones while Halloran would head to 26th Street to hook up with Gillespie. But first he called to check with Fagan to see what else may have turned up.

Fagan related that the profile on the cigarette had been worked up post-haste and run through both the state and the national DNA banks and turned up nothing. The lab DNA expert, Karen Svenson, had come in and run the tests herself. Fagan said they had determined there were dozens of ice pick manufacturers and hundreds of outlets that sold them. It would be a wild goose chase to further pursue that angle. Halloran dropped Ortiz at Area 3 and took off for 26th Street.

CHAPTER 14

Built in the same year the stock market crashed, the sprawling, grey, neo-classical Criminal Courts building has handled the worst of the worst Chicago area criminals.

The ebb and flow at the building each day is a show that can enthrall even the most jaded cop, reporter, judge, or attorney. It was called "the place where mothers go to cry."

Wide-eyed prospective jurors enter the hubbub each day and are quickly spotted and squired to the assembly room on the third floor of the 14-story annex, built in the mid-70s to handle the mushrooming traffic that all branches of the county government had suffered under as the war on drugs had doubled the number of cases.

In 1972, there were 5,000 inmates locked up in the County Jail and the old Bridewell House of Corrections, which housed misdemeanor defendants. By 2013, there were nearly 10,000 inmates scattered in nearly a dozen buildings, most of them new.

After flashing his badge to get through security, Halloran made for the top floor of the annex, which housed the Investigative Bureau and the Narcotics Bureau of the State's Attorney's four-floor suite of offices. There was no one at the 14th floor reception, so Halloran picked up the reception desk phone and called Gillespie's office, just a few dozen yards beyond the locked doors that led to the inner offices.

After a minute, Gillespie answered and came right out. Gillespie's office had a panoramic view of the sprawling jail complex and the industrial Southwest Side. Lining the east wall of his office were bookshelves with dozens of photos of a smiling Gillespie shaking hands with various police superintendents, mayors, senators, ballplayers, and even Sonny Bono. Gillespie is smiling, but some of the dignitaries appear to be grimacing as much as smiling.

For reasons best known to Gillespie, he had adopted a killer grip, a handshake that brought tears to the eyes of brave men, and an occasional cry of pain. As a young man, Gillespie had joined the Army, gravitated into Special Forces, and worked the border patrol in Korea for six months. He made it his lethal business to get strong enough to kill with his bare hands. The top of his middle finger just above the last joint had been lost in an industrial accident as a youth. He was built like an icehouse at 6' and 225. He was completely bald, had a bushy white mustache and a slightly menacing smile.

The trick with Gillespie, Halloran knew, was to get in quick with the hand all the way back and lock thumbs. Gillespie held his right hand like a Venus flytrap, halfway open and ready to maim. He had killed two men in the line of duty, both good shoots. The story went that Gillespie's remorse was not tied to the offenders' deaths; he regretted he did not get to use his bare hands to exact instant street justice.

Halloran was aware of the Gillespie grip but feared not. He had spent much of his high school and early college squeezing tennis balls and hand grips to strengthen his hands to catch a football; his own handshake was to be feared.

As he entered Gillespie's office empty handed, he plotted his strategy.

"Hey Teddy, how you been?" Halloran said, thrusting his right hand forward, getting the inside position all the way back in Gillespie's meaty paw. Before Gillespie could put full throttle into the shake, Halloran withdrew to point down into the jail complex.

"That the new Division 11?" Halloran asked, even though he knew the answer.

Gillespie turned, looked down to where Halloran was pointing, and said, "Sure, I think so."

Halloran quickly ran through the facts of the case for Gillespie, as much as he needed to know before asking to see the files of threatening letters and e-mails.

"We checked all of them out. Most of them come from guys that are still in the joint or are locked up in the loony bin out near Dunning," Gillespie said, referring to the Read Mental Health Center at Oak Park Avenue and Irving Park Road.

"How about when they get out?"

"We make sure the prison folks put a red flag on their discharge, so they let us know when the guy gets out. We talk to parole to track them, not just for Cavaretta, but the guys who are actually putting the bad guys in the joint, as well."

"Any jump out as you as credible, not just venting from the cell?"

"Not really," Gillespie said.

"Okay, I may have to get back to you, but I gotta run back to the Area to hook up with my partner," Halloran said. He grabbed the files in his right hand, avoiding the obligatory departure handshake. In a few minutes he hit the Dan Ryan on the way back to Area 3. Just then, his thoughts were interrupted by his cell. It was Ortiz. He explained nothing jumped out with Gillespie. Ortiz relayed how the sketch artist was struggling to come up with a composite based on Reynolds' recollection but hoped Doyle would add to the mix.

Just shit, Halloran thought.

CHAPTER 15

For more than 30 years, Mary Lou Daniels had spent day after day sitting in state and federal courtrooms, working for various television stations, sketching the faces and gestures of countless judges, defendants, prosecutors, defense attorneys, and jurors. It was never dull.

But after she retired and traveled a bit, she became restless, bored. So, when the Chicago Police Department came calling four months into her retirement, looking for a sketch artist, she jumped back in. She had always been on the fringe of law enforcement in court; now she was in it—sort of. But she did get a great deal of satisfaction when some child rapist was arrested based on her sketch.

She had just returned from the 12:15 mass at Queen of All Saints when she got the call from Fagan. It took her only 20 minutes straight southeast on Lincoln to get to Reynolds on what turned out to be a frustrating trip.

As Halloran was fingering through the last of hundreds of the threatening letters from Gillespie's files and various notes from support staff, Egan slipped into the squad room in a perfectly tailored, navy blue Chanel pantsuit, standing to the side of the seated officers.

"Sorry, Lieutenant. I had to arrange for someone to take a 10 a.m. call for me before Judge Williams," Egan said.

"You didn't miss a thing. We'll be getting two new dicks, Cook and Hillard, by noon. They're young, but good. They worked the overnight, so we're letting them get a little sleep. I trust few of you are well rested," Fagan said.

Fagan quickly went through the checks on the to-do list. There had been no attempts to use either of the credit cards missing from the wallet. He briefly summarized Halloran's conversation with Gillespie.

Fagan told Ortiz and Halloran to immediately hit 35th & Michigan. Mallory had given a "forthwith" demand to the two detectives to personally stop by and talk to the superintendent and him. Halloran ignored that for 30 minutes while he retreated to an interrogation room and thumbed through the last of the threatening letters. Nothing there, as Gillespie had said.

Back in the car. Ortiz turned to Halloran before starting the engine.

"So, were you good last night and go straight home?" Ortiz asked.

Halloran halved the question. "I was good."

Halloran got off the Dan Ryan just as they passed the shadow of U.S. Cellular Field, across 35th street from where Comiskey Park once stood. Most Sox fans called it Sox Park, it was a shorter and more familiar name. Ortiz was an avid Sox fan; Halloran found the game boring. As they rode, Halloran took a call from Daniels; as expected, Doyle had added nothing useful to Reynolds' vague description. Scratch sketch.

At headquarters, they took the elevator to Police Supt. Johnson's office. Sgt. Robert Dakauskas served as the superintendent's secretary, major-domo, and screener. He'd been the top bulldog at the gate for six straight superintendents over the past 20 years.

"Morning, Mike. And you must be Detective Ortiz. Please have a seat. The Superintendent will be with you in a minute. Chief Mallory is in there and Chief Bruner." David Bruner, the humorless quisling who ran Internal Affairs, was notorious throughout the department for being a ballbuster, and a snake. Ortiz and Halloran glanced at each other at the mention of his name, but kept their mouths shut. The walls have ears at headquarters, they knew.

The door to the superintendent's office opened, and Bruner walked out, eyeballing Halloran and Ortiz. Close-cropped grey hair, ramrod straight, he stepped briskly into the corridor. Halloran smiled when he saw a bulky sergeant turn the other way and duck into the john to avoid Bruner.

"The superintendent will see you, now." Dakauskas held the door open for Halloran and Ortiz, then closed it once they crossed the threshold.

Johnson had the corner office looking northeast to the Loop. He had a fine view of the skyline, but from the fourth floor, he couldn't see the lake, a small perk previous superintendents had enjoyed at the old office at 11th and State.

The superintendent was seated behind a sprawling and shiny dark oak desk, dressed in a blue pinstriped suit. He rose to shake the detectives' hands.

"Halloran, Ortiz. Where are we on this? I wanted to hear it straight from you."

Johnson knew in his heart that he had been chosen for the top cop job because of the color of his skin. But he also knew in his heart that he had worked his ass off at every step along the way and deserved it. Patrol officer, detective, sergeant, lieutenant, captain, watch commander, district commander, assistant deputy superintendent, chief of detectives, deputy superintendent. His was a steady rise through the ranks, wounded as a young patrolman in a shootout with the old Blackstone Rangers.

Not even the most racist white cop could say that Jack Johnson had not paid his dues.

Yet, he knew the mayor wanted to keep the community happy, so it helped to have a black face on the 10 o'clock news explaining why a cop had shot some unarmed young black boy.

Johnson had solved crimes as a dick and supervised the entire unit as chief of d's. He knew something about detective work, good and bad. So did Mallory. Johnson spoke first.

"I need to know where you think we can go on this. Tom Cavaretta and his family are fine people. We cannot let this go unsolved. The mayor has called me twice, first at home on the day of the murder, and again this morning. Tom is a friend of his, too."

Mallory cleared his throat and looked first to his boss and then at the two detectives.

"Run it through, what's been done and what is being done. This is just for our ears and does not escape this room. Charlie Fagan is a fine man, and an honest officer, but we all know he is where he is because he married the mayor's sister. So, I want to know what the lead detectives are doing in minute detail, as does the superintendent."

Johnson only nodded in the moments of silence that followed. Halloran spoke first.

"Right now, I got to lean to a street crime. Maybe a carjacking or robbery gone bad. But I am troubled by the weapon and how quick it was. An ice pick? Very strange. And one wound does it? Again strange. We're checking to see how many other carjacks or attempts there have been in the area in recent months," Halloran said.

He nodded to Ortiz. She took up the thread.

She detailed how Jennifer's cell phone records turned up nothing suspicious over the last six months. Home calls were the same, though the dicks had needed a little juice from Mallory to get Verizon to cough up the State's Attorney's phone records. The chief of detectives had explained to a retired district commander who now headed Verizon security in Chicago that he really did not want to get Cavaretta to make the phone call. The security chief understood immediately, and the records had been e-mailed in an hour.

Johnson stood up and turned his back to Mallory and the two detectives. The three glanced at each other as the top cop stood mute for a full minute before speaking.

"This is personal, detectives. I've known Tom and Joyce for 25 years. Tom was the godfather to my daughter. My wife and I went to Jenny's high school and college graduation parties. They've dined at my home, and I in theirs. Tom Cavaretta is color blind, but I am not. I know that a white girl killed is big news. The State's Attorney's daughter is bigger news, national news."

He turned to face the detectives.

"I've personally gone over your records this morning, detectives. Your work has been exemplary. You may be our department's two best detectives. We will see. I can tell you that this case is a career maker or breaker. If you solve this, if you find this monster who killed this beautiful girl, I *will* remember you.

"I know you will succeed. I have faith. Chief Mallory has faith. The full resources of the department are at your disposal. Call me if you have a problem. Here are all my numbers," he said as he shoved his card toward Ortiz and Halloran. "Oh, and how is it going with the lab, by the way?"

Johnson's speech had left Ortiz a bit stunned. Halloran had been at it for too long. He kept a poker face and hoped the promises were over so they could get back to their case. Halloran spoke first.

"Fine. We got a good relationship with Svenson there. She is personally supervising and ramrodding the work. No problem so far, and we don't expect one,"

"All right. That will be all," Johnson said.

And the meeting was over.

In the elevator crowded with brass, Halloran and Ortiz held their tongues.

Outside, Ortiz exhaled.

"Christ, feel any pressure, Mike?" Ortiz asked.

Halloran shrugged, then smiled.

CHAPTER 16

Back in their squad, Halloran and Ortiz rode along in silence as they hit the traffic on the jampacked Dan Ryan Expressway approaching Cermak Road.

Johnson's veiled promise of rewards for a job well done would have little effect on Halloran. He was exactly where he wanted to be: he loved being a dick, solving crimes, helping victims, something new every day. The best that Johnson could do for him would be to leave him alone. The worst, however, was the punitive transfer.

Right after he joined the force, he saw the punitive transfer in action. A popular, media-friendly, gregarious police superintendent had gotten a bit too big for his britches, at least as far as the erratic Mayor Joan Burke was concerned. One day, Jim Delorti was superintendent holding forth from a corner office at police headquarters in charge of 12,000 police officers, the second largest police force in the country. The next day, Mayor Burke, who the press wags quipped had "a whim of iron," promoted a more obsequious Polish commander to superintendent and sent Delorti to be the overnight watch commander in the far Southeast Side 4th District. Delorti, who lived in Jefferson Park near O'Hare, was not only demoted, his commute more than doubled.

Halloran wasn't ambitious, but he understood police politics--and he wasn't stupid. The brass could screw with you in a hundred ways if they wanted.

On the other hand, Ortiz had ambitions. There had never been a Hispanic female police officer make it as high as Assistant Deputy Superintendent. She aimed at least that high. Working on her Master's in Public Administration at Roosevelt University, she was on a fast track. She had scored third out of 100 in the sergeants' exam last spring. A boss in waiting.

But like anyone involved in city government, she needed clout, a Chinaman. Johnson hinted he could be that clout, someone who was on her side, who would promote her candidacy, look out for her. At 52, Johnson had maybe another 10 years on the job, if he survived the political tsunamis that regularly swept over the police department. Odds were 50-50.

"So where do you think that puts us in dealing with Fagan?" Ortiz finally broke the silence.

"It's a delicate situation, Syl. You have to play ball with the supe and chief, but you don't want to piss off the mayor's brother-in-law. I think we keep Mallory informed at every point, tell him the same things we tell Fagan. And we tell Fagan that. That way, we don't get our balls squeezed in some power play."

"My balls squeezed?" Ortiz laughed.

"Okay, my balls. Speaking of whom, I'd better call in to Fagan."

Fagan was busy and told them to just return to the Area, and they could get up to speed.

First, however, they got some carry-out from Negro Leon on 18th Street, Syl's favorite Mexican restaurant, smack in the middle of Pilsen, originally an old Czech neighborhood, but for recent generations of immigrants a Mexican stronghold.

Back at Area 3, the two detectives were not overwhelmed by a beehive of activity. The new guys, Ty Cook and Edgar Hillard, were working the computers to search for recent carjackings or other street crimes in Old Town, and the bordering DePaul, Gold Coast, and Lincoln Park areas. They could enlarge the search but most carjackings, in truth, happened in the "busier" districts, a euphemism for crime-ridden neighborhoods.

Unspoken for the most part, those busier districts were in predominantly black or Latino neighborhoods, Halloran knew. So did Ortiz, but they mostly avoided the subject.

"Hey, Mike, how's it going?" Cook stood quickly to extend his right hand. "We met last year on that bar stabbing on Webster. I was still in uniform. Remember?"

"Sure." Halloran lied as he shook the younger cop's hand. "How's it coming?"

"Got a carjacking three months ago, couple miles from your homicide in front of Welles Park. But the guy got caught. And the MO doesn't wash. He used a baseball bat. Aluminum. Probably borrowed his little brother's Little League bat. But he got busted and was in County Jail at the time," Cook said.

"Yeah, that's what they say at the jail in-take/out-take, but you should maybe double-check with records. You know how those layabouts at the jail are. He could've made bail, you never know." Halloran paused then added: "Good to have you guys helping out on this."

He did not like issuing orders to other detectives. He was not a boss, and they knew it. But he was the senior guy, and they also knew that. What they didn't realize was that Mallory had told Halloran and Ortiz in a very obtuse way that they should run things. Mallory's veiled suggestion was, in fact, an order.

Halloran mulled over the report, nonetheless. The carjack was also in broad daylight, and the car was a 1999 Ford Escort. If our guy was a carjacker who aborted his attempt when she screamed, he was after a nice car—the Jag. He put the thought aside.

"Syl, you think it would do any good to take another run –by phone —at Anne Doyle to see if she could come up with a better description of the guy in the bar who talked to Jenny that night?"

He caught himself as he mentioned the victim's name. He had crossed the bridge to familiarity with his victim. It helped cops stay detached by calling the victim of a crime "the victim." But Halloran had heard enough about Jennifer Cavaretta to develop a sense of her, to begin to like her memory, to make this personal. Catching himself calling her by her first name brought this home to him.

"Can't hurt to see what else she remembers. I'll call, but she was pretty vague with our sketch artist," Ortiz said just as Fagan walked up with some faxes in his hand.

"Come on in. Let's talk."

As Halloran and Ortiz followed Fagan into his office, several of the dicks lifted their heads from their computers to give them a perfunctory "How's it going?" Halloran shrugged. Ortiz lifted her eyebrows.

"No surprise here. The DNA on the water bottle was hers. No surprise. No usable prints on the car. Can't figure our guy had a clean sheet, so that leaves us with his wearing gloves—in October," Fagan said.

"Can't argue with that," Halloran said. Ortiz nodded, waiting for Fagan to continue. They both knew no prints proved nothing, certainly not gloves.

"Talked to Mallory. Says he wants you two to keep him informed. Got a problem answering to two bosses?" Fagan asked. He was seated and turned to begin looking through a sheaf of reports, purposely not to face the two detectives.

"Hey, it's a big case. So, we add another layer of protocol. We don't mind, do we Syl?" Halloran said, winking at his partner.

"I think I can learn a lot from both you and the chief, Lu. No problem at all."

Fagan rose to close the door to his office.

"I know you didn't notice, Halloran, 'cause you're a color blind Mick, but those two new guys, Hillard and Cook, are African Americans. They are very streetwise, made a lot of pinches on tac, worked undercover on some of the gangs, but they are mostly known at Area 4 for their prowess with the computer. I know you're good with that stuff, Syl, but Halloran probably still has a manual typewriter at home. Point is, use them to look for patterns on the computer. They should be able to help."

"Ease up, Lu. I've seen you hunting and pecking over the keyboard," Halloran said.

"Two fingers, 45 words a minute," Fagan laughed. "Now get to work."

CHAPTER 17

The next few days were spent chasing down leads that were thin at best and evaporated like the early morning mist over Lake Michigan.

Still running out the ground balls, Ortiz talked to Anne Doyle again about the man she saw talking to Jenny that night at Gamekeepers. She said she saw him only from the rear and could only say he was a medium built white guy, about 40 with a tattoo of some kind of snake or rope on his hand, maybe the right wrist. She never saw his face and only had glanced at him for a few seconds. No sketch possibility there.

The lack of developments hardly stopped the media from speculating about the murder. Television was the worst. There were stories about a mysterious suspect, not charged, the "latest" from the parking lot at Area 3—live at 10.

Marone was in for the long haul; no bullshit follow-up stories for him. Not his style.

Fortunately for the detectives and unfortunately for the family, the electronic media focused on the wake and funeral. The wake was held at the church because no funeral home could handle the expected crowd.

Whenever a person so young dies, the friends from grammar school, high school, college and in Jenny's case, law school, turn out in droves. They all looked lost, never having lost one of their own, stunned by the stark evidence of their own mortality. And then the parents' friends, colleagues, politicians, and hangers-on stopped by to pay their last respects, or merely to gape.

The line went down Lathrop Avenue and flowed for five hours through the doors of St. Luke's Catholic Church in River Forest, and past the dark oak coffin containing the remains of Jenny Cavaretta. It was an open casket, unusual for a murder. But because the wound had been so surgical, so minimally intrusive, she looked like she was sleeping, the neck bruise covered by makeup.

Johnson sent a group of undercover detectives to watch the crowd for anyone looking suspicious. It was a shot in the dark, but they were not getting any closer to solving this murder. Popular wisdom had it that if a murder isn't solved in the first 48 hours, the odds of finding the killer dwindle rapidly.

Halloran had to park more than two blocks away from the stately Tudor Gothic church, the turnout was so overwhelming.

Halloran showed up to pay his respects. He didn't normally do this for his murder victims, but this case was different. He was beginning to know Jennifer Cavaretta. He knew a lot more about this victim and her family than he knew about most. And the truth, the sad truth in most homicides, was that the victim was somewhere he or she shouldn't have been, doing something a little criminal, a little hinky.

A dope deal gone bad, a barroom fight, a drive-by shooting with one gangbanger shooting another. There were innocent victims, of course, but few as apparently innocent as Jennifer Cavaretta.

Retracing her steps that night led him to retrace her life. He got much of that from the State's Attorney and his wife, some from Anne Doyle, and a bit from poor Tom Reynolds. That guy will blame himself for the rest of his life, Halloran realized, for not waking up and walking her to her car.

After waiting for 90 minutes in line, Halloran finally got up to the coffin, which was surrounded by dozens of floral arrangements sent by friends and family of the Cavarettas.

He knelt by himself and gazed at the porcelain good looks of this once attractive and vibrant young woman.

He crossed himself out of habit, but he made a silent promise to Jennifer Cavaretta's lifeless form.

I am going to get this guy, Jenny. I promise, Halloran thought before silently rising. He stood and got back in the line leading to the Cavarettas.

"I'm sorry for your troubles," Halloran said, offering the standard Irish condolence when he reached the State's Attorney. It was much more old country than Irish American, but Halloran had learned the wake routine from his grandmother and his father. *What you said was not important; your presence was.*

"Detective Halloran, thank you so much for coming. We appreciate it, don't we, Joyce," Cavaretta said, holding on to Halloran's hand and half-turning to his wife. Joyce Cavaretta was being brave; there were no tearstains to mar her perfect makeup. She was just withdrawing from the embrace of an enormous white-haired woman in a floor-length mink coat, too early for the season.

"Mike, so nice to see you. So good of you to come. How are you doing?" she asked, reaching to grasp his right hand as her husband turned to the next mourner.

Halloran hesitated just a second before answering. He wondered if she was being perfunctorily polite or wondering how the investigation was coming. Or was she tacitly asking why he wasn't out there investigating? He chose his words carefully.

"Me? Well, I'm fine, but I wanted to come to say how sorry I am for your loss..." Halloran stopped. *They knew he didn't know their daughter in life, nor did he know them. So, why was he there?*

Joyce Cavaretta immediately sensed his discomfort, and just as quickly realized that she might have caused it. She was still grasping the right hand he had extended to her, then she squeezed it tighter and folded her left hand over his. She smiled and looked up into his eyes, tilting her head slightly to the left but keeping eye contact.

"I know Jenny is in God's good hands now, Mike. And Tom and I know that this investigation is in these good hands with you. Thank you for coming. I know you're busy."

Halloran nodded, grateful for the dismissal. She hadn't been wondering why the hell he was at the wake instead of catching the killer. She was glad that he had been thoughtful enough to stop by. The mother turned her attention to a woman behind him, who gasped:

"Oh Joyce, she was such a wonderful child," and threw her arms around Joyce Cavaretta.

Halloran heaved a sigh of relief as he rejoined the slow-moving line, now snaking out to the rear of the church.

Outside, he looked down the long line still waiting to come inside. He saw no one who looked out of place. The arsonist returns to watch the fire, but the murderer doesn't show at the wake. Still, the superintendent needed to let Cavaretta know that there was a police presence.

As he left the church, he checked his phone and found Marone had left a voice message. The reporter said that he could find no previous ice pick murders with a carotid wound. *No surprise.*

Just then, Becky Thompson spotted him from the Channel 7 van and gave chase.

"Halloran, wait up." In seconds, she ran him down. It would have been unseemly to run from her, so he stopped dead in his tracks.

"Becky, I didn't see you. How are you?" Halloran lied.

"I'm dying. That's how I'm doing. What do ya got? Give me something, anything. Who are you looking at? The boyfriend?"

"We're off the record here, but I can say 'Don't go there,' Becky. We got no reason at all to think the boyfriend did it. No reason."

Part of the delicate dance with reporters was at least to offer them some guidance. The good ones appreciated it; the bad ones didn't care about the facts or anyone or anything but their careers. Fortunately, they were few. Becky Thompson was not one of the few. She'd been around for a dozen years or more and Halloran sort of liked her.

"I hate this shit, coming out to cover the wake. God, I feel like a ghoul, but the desk sent me, and I've got nothing else. What bone can you throw me?"

"It's what you'd think. We are checking similar crimes in the area, carjackings, muggings, early morning attacks. But you could guess that."

"No, I couldn't. Can I use that, saying a source close to the investigation?" Thompson asked. She sounded desperate.

"Sure, why not?"

"You're the best, Halloran. Now I can bolt out of here, God help me, and go back to the studio."

Not bad, Halloran thought. *Two beautiful women in five minutes tell me how great I am.*

CHAPTER 18

Up before dawn, Halloran was in the pool moments after the night doorman, Walter, opened the locker room door. The pool had been under repair for a few weeks, but now Halloran returned to his daily routine.

Although the pool was only 21 meters long, the beauty here was that he usually had it to himself. So, instead of swimming laps, Halloran frequently swam in circles, going from corner to corner to corner to corner, and then kitty-corner to break the monotony.

Unlike competitive sports like football, basketball, or handball, you don't have to think about what you're doing when you're swimming.

As he swam, Halloran kept turning the case over and over in his mind. It still lacked focus. They had made no mistakes, but there was no one in custody, either. Neither he nor Syl was convinced that the murder of Jenny Cavaretta was a carjacking or street robbery gone awry.

If he wanted the car, why didn't he just push her out after he killed her? The street was desolate at that time of the morning, and even though she'd screamed, he would still have had time to get away. And if it was a street robbery, why did he leave the purse? He would have taken it and dumped it later after taking the money and credit cards. And was it just blind luck that he found the carotid artery with the first stab?

Out of breath and answers, he climbed out of the pool, dried off and headed back to his apartment.

It wasn't just Halloran and Ortiz who were striking out; the other members of the task force had been vainly chasing the scores of leads that were coming into the hotline the chief had set up on the third day after the murder.

The hotlines attracted more than the fair share of crazies, but there was the chance someone would call in with a legit tip. The Chicago Bar Association had put up a $25,000 reward, which was matched a day later by Northwestern University's School of Law.

In the three weeks since the murder, the story had been gradually dropped from page one to the metro front to inside the met section, to a brief.

When she saw the story disappear, Joyce Cavaretta granted an exclusive to the Sun-Times, which played it across the front page:

"Every night, Joyce Cavaretta puts a fresh rose on her daughter's bed, next to her teddy bear with the pink ribbon around the neck. 'It's a way for us to keep her memory sacred, fresh. We don't want to forget. We want to remember. And we don't want the public to forget either. Somewhere, someone knows something, and they should come forward,' the mother of Jennifer Cavaretta said."

The tabloid knew how to work this story. The Sun-Times had done scores of stories on the murder, but none with the words of the wife of the chief law enforcement officer in Cook County, the leader of the second-largest prosecutor's office in the country, behind L.A.

The story began on page one, then jumped to page three with pix of Joyce sitting on her daughter's bed next to the teddy bear. The story prompted requests for interviews by all the television stations. Joyce Cavaretta bravely gave all five stations their time inside her home. And then went on public television live in its studio where her husband had been interviewed numerous times.

Halloran had watched the live performance the night before. It got to him. *Why was this girl killed? He could not believe it was a street crime. Why didn't he grab the purse and take it with him?*

But if it wasn't a street crime, then someone had a grudge against her or had targeted her. It still could have been a rape gone awry, but Jenny Cavaretta probably would have been smart enough to spot a rapist or at least to talk him out of it. And why kill her? It was possible, but no profiles popped up that made any sense as a suspect.

Halloran had learned from Doc Powers what the toxicology report showed, and there were no drugs in Jenny's system.

Hillard and Cook had been by Northwestern to talk to Jenny's professors and a number of her fellow students. No one had remembered anyone matching the description of the tattooed guy from the bar. No one at Gamekeepers remembered anyone with that tattoo that night at the bar. No one remembered Tom and Jenny either.

And the interview of Joyce Cavaretta had been a one-time shot to keep the story out there.

The investigation was stalling. The media moved on.

CHAPTER 19

Tom Cavaretta had been patient, getting most of his briefings on the status of the investigation from Chief Mallory. Johnson also spoke frequently to the State's Attorney on other matters, but always tracked down Halloran and Ortiz for a briefing before talking to Cavaretta.

On the one-month anniversary of his daughter's murder, Cavaretta asked Halloran if he could stop by in the morning to give him a personal briefing on the investigation.

"Syl is scheduled to go before the grand jury on an old case, but she could get out of it, sir, if you need us both," Halloran had said.

"No, detective. That won't be necessary. I am sure you're up to speed. If you could come by at 11 a.m., I should be through with my testimony before the county board on the budget," Cavaretta said.

The request was a thinly veiled command performance, Halloran knew, but he had to hand it to Cavaretta; he was very polite, and the request could have been done through channels. *A very classy guy,* Halloran thought not for the first time, *but no one's perfect.* The State's Attorney's office was on the 32d floor of the Dunne administration building, which had been purchased at much taxpayer expense and angst from the editorial boards at the two newspapers.

From his office on the northeast side of the building at Dearborn and Washington, Tom Cavaretta had a clear view of Monroe Harbor. Outside his office, sentried like a pit bull with a smile and a tenacity for detail and precision sat Maisy Kennedy Morowski, his secretary for the past 20 years.

At the same time that he was leaving the U.S. Attorney's office and joined Keenan Levin, Maisy was leaving the mayor's office after the city's first black mayor was elected. There were enough doughy-faced Irish men and women, so Maisy was sent packing. Maisy's husband, Casey, had coached Tom on the high school baseball team, and the families had known each other for decades.

Tom snatched Maisy up as his secretary at Keenan Levin and never let go. She knew everything, and everybody, and she was fiercely loyal to Cavaretta.

"Good morning, detective, could I get you a cup of coffee, a Coke?" Maisy said after Halloran cleared security.

"No, thank you. Glass of water would be nice," Halloran said.

Maisy disappeared as Halloran peered around, taking in the office. Not the same ostentation of the monied law firms, but bureaucratically functional with some faux wood trim on the secretaries' cubicles and industrial strength grey carpeting.

After Maisy returned with his water, Halloran thumbed through Time magazine as he waited a few minutes before he was shown into Cavaretta's office. He was on the phone, smiling and nodding as he spoke to and stroked an Illinois Supreme Court Justice. He waved Halloran in and pointed to a seat in front of his desk.

"We know you'll do the right thing, and I wouldn't presume to try to influence you. No ex-parte from me, Madame Justice," Cavaretta said. He soon hung up after a few more pleasantries.

"Come in, Mike. Maisy took care of you, I can see. But how about a Coke or Sprite?" Cavaretta asked.

"Nothing, sir, thank you. Maisy, uh, your secretary already offered. Thank you. I wish I had something positive to report," Halloran said. Just then, Maisy walked in and announced:

"Sen. Duncan on the line from Washington, Mr. Cavaretta."

"Oh, sure, I forgot. One minute, please, Mike. I got to take this," Cavaretta said.

Halloran started to get up and leave, figuring any conversation with a U.S. Senator was surely something that the likes of a homicide dick was not intended to hear. As he picked up the phone, Cavaretta motioned Halloran down, like a dog being told to stay, but with a smile.

The State's Attorney spoke for about five minutes about the need for anti-gang funding, both preventative and better surveillance equipment for the street gangs that were becoming as electronically sophisticated as a teenaged clerk at Best Buy.

On the bookshelves Halloran eyed photos of Cavaretta with Jimmy Carter, Mike Ditka, George Foreman, and then-Mayor Richard J. Daley, the crown prince of Chicago when Halloran was a kid. The photo of Cavaretta and Daley was taken when Cavaretta clerked in the Corporation Counsel's office.

Amidst the plaques and diplomas was a photo of Cavaretta on election night that appeared on the front page of the Tribune with his wife in one arm and his daughter in the other. They were all three beaming. Halloran winced inwardly. He didn't need reminders of how Jenny Cavaretta looked in life. But the image was better than the images he had frozen in his brain from the crime scene, the autopsy and the wake.

"Thank you, Senator. I know you will. And please say hello to your lovely wife for me and Joyce," Cavaretta said. "Yes, yes, she is doing very well, and thanks for asking." Halloran couldn't hear the other end of the conversation, but he could guess that the senator had just asked how Joyce Cavaretta was holding up.

"So, Mike, I'm sorry for the interruption, but I had called him earlier. What can you tell me about where we are in the investigation?"

Halloran knew that Mallory had been briefing the prosecutor all along, but he went briefly through the progress, or lack thereof, thus far.

"Sounds like you are pursuing every lead, and I appreciate that. When you find this guy, I'll have to recuse myself from any decision-making. My First Assistant, Dick Dunne, will make that draw. Have you met Dick?" Cavaretta asked.

"Back when he was in Felony Review, we had a case together," Halloran said.

Cavaretta hit the intercom button.

"Maze, will you ask Dick to step in for a minute, please?" Cavaretta said.

Dick Dunne was a career prosecutor who fell in love with the office when he was a law clerk at 26th Street while attending John Marshall Law School. His had been a steady rise through the ranks, starting in appeals, then misdemeanors, a two-year stint in Felony Review, felony trial in the Markham suburban courthouse, back to 26th street as a deputy supervisor in Felony Review, then as the supervisor of Felony Review. He had tried big cases, including the murder of a Chicago cop.

At 47, he had spent 22 years as a prosecutor. Cavaretta had plucked him out of Felony Review and named him Chief Deputy, the No. 3 spot in the office. When Cavaretta's last First Assistant had been appointed to a judgeship, the State's Attorney moved Dunne up and he had become Cavaretta's strong right arm. Dunne was a blunt, but very bright prosecutor, who could tear apart a case and put it back together again. Raised in the 19th Ward, he was politically astute enough to see the shades and nuances involved in almost any high-profile case that wound up in the local prosecutor's purview.

"Mike, good to see you again. Been awhile," Dunne said, extending his hand.

"Dick, nice to see you. It's a little different here than midnights approving felonies, eh?"

"I was glad to hear Johnson put you on this," Dunne said.

Cavaretta walked around the side of his desk and joined the two men at his circular cherry-wood conference table. In quick order, Halloran ran the case for Dunne, who sat by Cavaretta's side, asking a few questions but mostly taking mental notes.

"You'll be dealing mostly with Mary Kay Egan, but keep me in the loop, too. If you think you got the guy or are close, call me. Anytime. I mean it, anytime," Dunne said. He then scribbled down his home number on his card right below his cell and slid it over to Halloran.

After a few more minutes, Cavaretta rose to signal the meeting was over. It was a subtle move, but unmistakable.

"Maisy, make sure we have all the numbers to reach Mike. We want to stay in touch," Cavaretta said as he subtly ushered Halloran and Dunne out. The alderman from the Second Ward was waiting to air a concern she had about a case involving a constituent.

Dunne retreated to his office as Maisy escorted the alderman into the boss' office.

Feet don't fail me now, Halloran thought as he slipped out to the elevator.

CHAPTER 20

On the ground floor, Halloran realized he was supposed to check his contacts with Maisy just as his beeper went off with Maisy's number on it.

Upstairs again, Halloran was greeted by a smiling Maisy, who asked politely:

"Detective, could you look at these vitals I keep for you," Maisy said, handing Halloran the card from her Rolodex. It had his cell phone, his office phone, his pager, and his home phone. And his address.

"Pretty thorough. You know where to get me anytime," Halloran said. "How long you been with the State's Attorney?"

"Give or take a month or so, 20 years. Not as long as his wife, but longer than just about anyone else," Maisy said.

"You knew Jenny well, then, too, I assume?" Halloran asked.

"I did. She was a wonderful child, young woman, I mean. She..." Maisy faltered for a second, her voice catching.

"Maisy. We're not getting anywhere fast. It's been a month. No one has used the credit cards taken from her purse. We're beginning to grasp. You got any thoughts on who might have had it in for Jennifer?" Halloran asked. He was leaning forward over the counter that separated her desk from the waiting area. Maisy thought for a moment, then said:

"No. She was so sweet. So nice. Prosecutors make enemies, cops make enemies, judges make enemies, but sweet Jenny..." Maisy fought a tear.

"Sorry to bring this up, to tear the emotional scab off. But let me ask you this: You say prosecutors make enemies. Gillespie showed me the threatening letters the State's Attorney has gotten since he took office. Remember any others? Calls, e-mails, earlier letters?" Halloran asked.

Maisy stood up wordlessly, holding her right index finger up. She started looking through a file cabinet drawer. She stopped at T, for Threat.

"I got this," she said, and slid a letter and an envelope stapled to it out of a manila file folder. "He got this while he was in private practice in between prosecutor jobs." Halloran looked at the postmark. It was from Joliet, and the return address had a prisoner's number. He began reading:

"Hey there, Mr. Big Shot Lawyer. Heard you made your bones and were now in private practice. Hung a few innocent scalps on your belt like mine and now you're getting rich. Don't get too comfortable, tho, asshole. I got friends and I got means, and what goes round comes round. Have a nice life but keep looking over your shoulder."

It was signed: "Eric Peterson, framed in 1982, thanks to you and your corrupt cop buddies." Halloran turned the envelope over and looked at the date stamp on the cancellation mark. It was from 1988.

"Got a house mail envelope, Maisy?" Halloran asked, holding the letter by one corner with his right index finger and thumb. Maisy pulled one from a slot on her desk.

"You think that's important?" she asked.

"Maisy, this may be the closest thing we've had to a motive since this case began. Yeah, you bet I think it's important," Halloran said. "And thanks for being so meticulous in saving things. Can I use your phone? This gets bad reception in these high-rises," holding up his cell.

"For privacy, you can use the one in the conference room. Follow me," Maisy said.

Maisy escorted Halloran down the hall and into a conference room with a long, oval, polished walnut table in the center with a dozen black leather chairs surrounding it. On a credenza at the far end of the room was a phone. Photos of State's Attorneys past stared down from the walls.

"Thanks," Halloran said. As Maisy retreated and closed the door behind her, Halloran dialed Syl.

"Syl, pull the sheet on Eric Peterson, convicted in 1982. And check the IDOC website to see if he's still in the joint," Halloran said.

"What's up, Mike? Who's Eric Peterson?" Ortiz asked.

"He sent a threatening letter to Cavaretta while he was in private practice. Name's familiar, but I can't make it just yet. I'm taking it over to Svenson to see what she can do with the envelope," he said. "I'll let you know more in a little while and let's do a LexisNexis search on Eric Peterson—back to 1980."

He then called Svenson.

"Karen, think you can raise a DNA profile off an envelope licked back in 1988?" Halloran asked.

"If Lincoln licked the envelope to send the Gettysburg address to Mary, I could raise a profile off it. What's up?" Svenson asked.

"I'll be over in 15-20 minutes and drop this off," Halloran said.

"Cavaretta murder?" Svenson asked.

"You got it."

"I'll get it," she responded. A six-inch pile of rape and murder requests would have to wait.

CHAPTER 21

With a PhD in microbiology from Stanford, Karen Svenson had a spotless reputation for efficiency and competence. Prosecutors loved her because she was death on cross-examination. No defense attorney could lay a hand on her.

She was wearing her white lab coat when Halloran showed up with the envelope Maisy had given him.

"Karen, how long to get a profile on this?"

Svenson knew about "heaters," too. The lab had been on the skewering end of several stories before Svenson arrived. As the technology of DNA evolved, almost on a monthly basis, the old technology became obsolete and as questionable as a pimp's promise. But Svenson understood that the Cavaretta case was the "white heat" of heater cases--the local equivalent of a presidential assassination.

"The actual work—I'll do it myself—takes 10 to 12 hours. It is a long, time-consuming and labor-intensive process. And you want this done right, right?" Svenson asked.

"You know the answer to that. What I need to know is when, what hour, might I hear from you? No pressure—okay, maybe a little—just give me a time frame, okay?"

"Well, it is now 1:30 p.m., and I have a class to teach tonight at 7, and then I have a life and a husband, and I will go home tonight. And so, I will be in tomorrow by 7:30, and you should hear no later than 12:30 p.m. Good enough?"

"You're the best," Halloran headed to the door, then turned. "I owe you."

A deposit in the favor bank.

***

Few of the inmates on the Illinois Department of Corrections website were smiling. Eric Peterson was the exception. He was cocky even with a death sentence hanging over his head.

Even though he had been out for nearly a year, his happy visage still lingered on the website. Ortiz hit the print button and got a printout of Peterson. With his date of birth of May 10, 1960, and name, she plugged into the CPD computer and got his sheet.

It was extensive and violent. First arrest as an adult came just a month after his 17th birthday for armed robbery. *His juvenile record was separate and would be harder to get at, but that might not matter,* Ortiz thought.

Between his first arrest and his conviction for a triple homicide, he had 18 arrests for charges ranging from possession of cannabis to aggravated battery. He was a month short of his 23d birthday when he killed a couple and their child and raped the woman. No indication that a rape kit had been done. When she looked at the record of which Felony Review prosecutor approved the murder charges, she found the name T. Cavaretta.

Kaboom.

Ortiz asked Detective Hillard to do a LexisNexis clip search on Eric Peterson. There were 39 stories that Hillard printed. The first hit showed a story after his arrest for the triple homicide, a 20-column-inch story in the Sun-Times. The Trib had a brief in the Sunday paper, then nothing until the trial began two years later.

The trial had been assigned to the Hon. James Duffy McShane, a former prosecutor who had sent more men to Death Row than any judge in Illinois history. Assigned as the first chair in McShane's court by the trial date was Tom Cavaretta. Ortiz read the story on the prosecutor's riveting opening statement.

Chicago Tribune

Jan. 13, 1982

By Lynn Meiners

In his last few moments on earth, Juan Perez was begging Eric Peterson to kill him, but spare his wife and child.

"But Eric Peterson would show no mercy that bloody October day last year. In fact, he may have punished Juan Perez for having the nerve to ask," Assistant State's Attorney Thomas Cavaretta said Monday in opening statements in the capital murder case against Eric Peterson.

In stentorian bursts, Cavaretta ticked off the events that led to the slashing deaths of Perez, 45, his wife, Angelina, 43, and their son, Pedro, 3. The three were found by police with their throats slashed on the second floor of their two-flat at 2113 W. 21st Pl.

Angelina also had been raped, the autopsy showed.

"According to the confession he gave police, he tied and gagged Perez, then cut off his ear and showed it to him with his wife and child watching, also bound and gagged. Why did he do that, ladies and gentlemen?" Cavaretta asked the eight-man, four-woman jury. "We can only surmise. I think it was because he enjoyed it."

At this point, Assistant Public Defender Agnes Stiller jumped to her feet to object.

"I'll allow it," McShane ruled.

Ortiz pulled up another story that appeared the day after Peterson left prison.

A reporter had asked Peterson how he felt.

"Angry," Peterson had said.

"What's the first thing you're going to do?" he was asked.

"I'm gonna be with my wife, if you know what I mean, drink some Glenfiddich, and have a great big steak," the story quoted Peterson as saying.

Ortiz put down the story and phoned Halloran. "We got motive and MO, Mike," Ortiz said. "And get this—Tom Cavaretta approved the charges against Peterson in Felony Review and then caught the case when it came to trial a couple years later. And before McShane. Lights out. Two-week trial and death from McShane.

"This old clip shows the defense tried to bar Cavaretta at trial, but since he hadn't taken the unsigned confession, McShane denied the motion," she said.

"And another link, the weapon—he cut their throats. Close enough. Ice pick, knife, throats? He got death, but he was pardoned by Gov. Riley. Unfortunately, the rape and murder sentences ran concurrently. And there's no record of any rape kit being done," Ortiz said.

"Yeah, sloppy work from Area 2. No surprise about no rape kit. They had three dead bodies and figured that's enough. But that rape was before CODIS, so any DNA wouldn't have made it into the system anyway," Halloran said. "Save those clips. I want to read them all."

The stories detailed how Gov. James Riley had pardoned 12 Death Row defendants in a desperate effort to establish a legacy in his scandal-plagued first and only term. The anti-death penalty crowd loved him; police, prosecutors, editorial writers and the general public were outraged at this usurpation of the judicial process. He had earlier declared a moratorium on the death penalty, which stood until the legislature—bowing to editorial insistence from the Tribune--eventually abolished it

Halloran took it all in. He had just left Svenson's office when he got the Ortiz call as he reached the ground floor in the elevator at the Illinois State Police Forensic Science Center, better known as the state crime lab.

Halloran started a to-do list in his mind. Hustling to the car, he got out a pen and started jotting down the checklist.

Prison records
Cavaretta talk
Check with Svenson. Hourly
Last known address for Peterson.

He started to jot down "*call Egan,*" but instead went to his recent calls list and hit her number.

"Counselor, I got a guy I like a lot," Halloran blurted out.

"Jeez, Mike, if you're coming out of the closet, I do *not* want to know about it." Egan loved to yank his chain.

"Mary Catherine Egan. Quiet, and listen to me."

Halloran went through the letter, the trial, the method of killing, Cavaretta's approval of the charges against Peterson, then catching the case at trial. He then told her about the threatening letter and DNA possibility.

"I like him, too, but it's not enough—yet. Does Svenson think she can get a profile off that letter? And what are the chances we get a hit with the profile from that butt?" Egan asked.

"Yes, and slim, but it's worth a shot. He's a violent guy with a vendetta. He thinks Cavaretta is to blame for all the screw-ups in his life," Halloran said.

"You get a match on the butt; we got a warrant. Without it, we need more. But you know that. Give me a call later."

Halloran pondered the last sentence: *Did that mean she wanted to get together again?* He hadn't been with her in months. But both had been extremely busy, Halloran with the investigation, and Egan with her normal court call in addition to staying in touch with the detectives and Dunne.

But thoughts of their relationship quickly disappeared like a fast cloud on a clear day. He focused on her remark that they needed more. Halloran knew he still had a work in progress, but for the first time in a month, he felt he was on the right track. His mind was swirling with possibilities.

After he disconnected Egan, he called Ortiz back.

"Syl, you still got that IDOC site up?" Halloran asked.

"Two seconds," Ortiz said, then, "Go."

"Somewhere there they list distinguishing marks or tattoos. See what they got," Halloran said.

"One sec--says scorpion on left forearm, wrist. Barbed wire across his ass," Ortiz said.

"Remember Tom Reynolds said that the guy Jenny was talking to in Gamekeepers that night had a tattoo with a claw on his arm near his wrist. Claw, scorpion stinger. Pretty similar looking in a darkened bar. Whattya think?"

"Yeah, and Anne Doyle described a similar tattoo, right? I'm liking this guy a lot now, too," Ortiz said.

"Yeah, I'm 20 minutes away. See if you can get the prison to fax us his prison records. Use your best bullshit. I doubt they can email it; last I checked, it was a no-go."

Without realizing it, Halloran had reached 70 m.p.h. as he headed out the Kennedy past North Avenue. *Slow down, pal,* he thought. But it was hard. This was falling into place. He called Cavaretta and got Maisy.

"That wasn't long, detective," she said.

"Is the State's Attorney available, Maisy?" he asked.

"He's tied up right now. Can it wait an hour?" she said.

"I'll be on my cell. It's important that he call as soon as he can," Halloran said.

"Should I barge in?" Maisy asked.

The word "barge" gave Halloran pause. This was not an emergency, he knew, but he wanted to talk to Cavaretta as soon as he could about the Peterson case, and whether he had seen or heard from Peterson since he got out

"As soon as the meeting is over will be fine," Halloran said.

The season's first snow was coming down as Halloran got off the Kennedy at Fullerton. The traffic was deteriorating, and there was no worse car on snow than the Crown Vic. It had to be one of the last cars in the world without front-wheel drive. Halloran was in a hurry to get back to Belmont, but he had to slow himself, and his driving, down.

I'm coming after you, shithead.

Shithead now had a name. Eric Peterson.

CHAPTER 22

One of the first things a detective does with a suspect in his sights is to run the guy's rap sheet--slang for arrest record, derivation unclear. His past would often dictate his future.

Ortiz saw Peterson's violent record with the quick visit to the Illinois Department of Corrections (IDOC) website, but she also called up his sheet. Somewhat to her surprise, she found an arrest in late July for possession of a pound of marijuana and a separate arrest earlier for domestic battery. The surprise wasn't that he was arrested for slapping his wife around or that he had dealer-quantity grass; she was surprised he was dealing just four months after getting out of the joint and being awarded $156,000 as a settlement from the state for his years of incarceration.

Lawyers at Northwestern's Center for Wrongful Convictions had filed the paperwork for the payout, according to a Tribune story found in the clip search. But most of the work had been done by Peterson, who fashioned himself a "jailhouse lawyer" in prison and then did some of the research at the school's law library, the story said.

Reading further to an earlier clip prior to his release, she found a gossip column item about Peterson marrying Joan Pritchard, the Midwest coordinator the People Against the Death Penalty. The ceremony took place in Stateville's spartan nondenominational chapel.

Ortiz went through her file until she found Anne Doyle's cell phone number.

She punched the numbers quickly.

"Anne. This is Detective Ortiz. I have a quick question: Did Jenny spend much time in the law library, and could this have been where she met the guy from the bar?"

"Well, sure. She studied a lot there. They all do. And I guess she could've met him there. She never said. Why do you ask?"

"Just chasing a hunch. Thanks." Click.

The nexus between victim and suspect deepened. Jenny Cavaretta, of course, spent time in the law library that Peterson apparently frequented. And the bag of dope found near the Jag could have been a careless drop by Peterson the dope dealer as he fled, Ortiz reasoned.

Pulling the report on the drug bust, Ortiz found that Peterson had been pulled over after blowing a stop sign last summer near Pritchard's home. The arresting officer smelled the distinctive odor of marijuana when Peterson opened his window, and ordered Peterson out of the car. A subsequent search turned up a one-pound brick of marijuana and a box of baggies under a blanket in the back seat.

As she read, Halloran walked into the squad room. Ortiz related how Peterson had researched his settlement at the law library, and perhaps that was where Jenny had met him.

"But didn't Hillard and Cook check out the library?" Ortiz asked.

"You think those Northwestern commies over there would really give this guy up?" Halloran said. "To cut the school a break, maybe Peterson had already done a lot of the work in the joint while waiting to get sprung. I know Hillard and Cook checked with her teachers, but maybe they weren't told to check the library?"

Before Ortiz could unload the growing list of connections Peterson had to the victim, Halloran's phone went off.

"Halloran," he said. "Oh, Maisy, sure I could, but do you think you can call me on the land line? The cell's connection comes and goes in here."

Ten seconds after he gave her the number on the desk by Ortiz, the "bell" or land line phone rang. It was Cavaretta.

"Yes, sir," Halloran said, still unwilling or unable to call the State's Attorney by his first name, especially in a squad room filled with big ears and acidic senses of humor. "We are taking a hard look at Eric Peterson. Anything stand out in your memory about him?"

"Sure, I remember Peterson. It was my first homicide case on Felony Review," Cavaretta recalled. "Sort of a thin case with a girlfriend with a motive to lie, an unsigned confession. I talked to him at the station, but he lawyered up, talked briefly to the girlfriend and she verified some of it, so I ran it up the ladder and the supervisor that night agreed with me, and we approved the charges. Then I caught it later at trial. What are the chances? Years later, when I was in private practice, he sent me that letter that Maisy--great secretary that she is--kept on file. I never thought much about it. He was on Death Row. You think he could've done this?"

"It's still early, but I'm sure going to find him to talk to him. I dropped the letter at the crime lab for DNA. But I can tell you that we're all over this," Halloran said.

"Good, good. Keep me informed of any developments. I'll mention it to Dick Dunne. Thanks, Mike."

As Halloran began reading about Peterson, he found that after he was convicted and sentenced to death, the case had been appealed, and despite the paucity of evidence against him, the conviction was upheld time and time again.

The case caught the attention of Northwestern and the anti-death penalty crowd. One of the recent clips had a photo of Peterson after his release being embraced by Pritchard at the gates of Stateville. She was a homely woman, scrawny, with pockmark scars and stringy, dishwater blonde hair. She looked happy in Peterson's arms.

Happy until he started slapping her around, Halloran thought.

Halloran began looking through the documents that the prison had faxed. Peterson had been a model prisoner the last years of his imprisonment. Halloran pulled out a 1994 letter to the Illinois Prisoner Review Board from a Dr. Anthony Moretti, asking it to consider paroling Peterson.

"Dear Board Members, many years ago, when I was working at the Audy Home in Chicago, I came across a troubled young man in Eric Peterson. My wife and I took Eric into our home as a foster child for several years until he reached the age of 17, when he left us. I would like to say on Eric's behalf that he should be given another chance because he has had a hard life but has an inner good. I found him to be extraordinarily bright and willing to learn. He helped me occasionally, and I found him to be a quick study, virtually soaking up facts and treatment like a sponge. He wanted to take a correspondence course to become a nurse. But he got in more trouble as an adult (17+), and that never worked out. He has corresponded with me since his most recent incarceration, and I believe he has changed for the better in prison.

Sincerely,

Anthony A. Moretti, M.D.

Halloran picked up the phone and dialed information to get Moretti's number.

As luck would have it, he apparently was still alive and practicing at Rush University Medical Center. After a few transfers, he got the physician on the phone and introduced himself and asked a few perfunctory questions before getting to the key question he was interested in.

"Doctor, can you tell me if Peterson ever asked questions about the carotid artery?" Halloran asked.

"Not that I can recall. You aren't reopening the Ramos case, are you? The prison found no evidence that Eric was involved in that."

Halloran then recalled the conversation from a month prior with Frank Marone about the stabbing death of an inmate named Ramos at Stateville in 1986.

"No, no, this is a separate investigation, doctor. We have no jurisdiction in that old case. Just curious, thanks, doc. I appreciate your help. I know it was a long time ago. This is an ongoing investigation, so keep this conversation to yourself, okay?" Halloran said.

"Is Eric in trouble?" Moretti asked.

"He has not been charged with a crime. But beyond that, I cannot say. Your cooperation is appreciated."

He next called Stateville. He reached a clerk in the records department who put him on hold while he located the Ramos murder investigation file. When the clerk had the file before him, Halloran started probing.

"Can you tell me what Ramos was killed with?"

"It was a sharpened spring from one of the beds, it says here."

"Anyone ever charged?"

"No one. Looks like inmate Eric Peterson was questioned, but there were no witnesses, so --case closed."

"Say anything in there about why you looked at Peterson back then?" Halloran asked.

Paging through the prison records, the clerk found a list of disciplinary actions taken against Peterson.

"I got a January 1986 report of an altercation in the shower with inmate #9122055. It said the inmate—that would be Ramos--made sexual overtures to Peterson, then punched Peterson from the back when he refused him."

"Does it say there how he died?"

"Penetrating neck wound is all it said."

"How many?" Halloran asked.

"Doesn't say."

Good enough, Halloran thought. *A pattern.*

CHAPTER 23

A graduate of the University of California/Berkeley, Joan Pritchard had joined the Communist Party of California, then embraced the anti-war movement, and years later the anti-death penalty zealots.

A friend from college introduced her to the People's Lawyers LLC in Chicago, a group dedicated to review and eviscerate Death Row cases in Illinois. Pritchard started there as a secretary at first, then as a legal researcher. While keeping her day job, she branched out from the firm to found People Against the Death Penalty.

One of the weakest cases the firm came across was the conviction of Eric Peterson. One of the People's Lawyers' attorneys, Oliver Hemphill III, found lots of problems with Peterson's arrest and conviction. First and foremost, Peterson's unsigned confession could be folded into the dozens of other allegations of coerced confessions at Area 2. Then when they went to talk to the girlfriend who implicated him, she recanted. That was good enough for a post-conviction petition, and that got them a hearing after years of going up and down through the courts.

Pritchard had written Peterson and sent him books on transcendental meditation and Hinduism. He wrote back to thank her and to tell her how he chanted "om" in his cell to find peace and enlightenment. She wrote back that she would chant at the same time of the night, so they could connect in cosmic oneness. In lengthy missives, she told him of her time in an Indian ashram, how it had been so transforming.

Hemphill had been Peterson's best man a few years back when Pritchard married him in prison, much to the chagrin of her parents, who opted to stay at their retirement condo on Sanibel Island.

When Hemphill told Pritchard the news that Peterson had been freed, her reaction was stunned silence. Then tears. Only she knew what she was crying for—either joy or fear.

Whatever her thoughts, she had been at the gates at Statesville when they opened slightly and out popped Peterson, smiling and flashing the V sign for victory, or perhaps he thought-- vindication.

On the way home in the back seat of the limo, Peterson had stuck his hand down her pants. She was shocked but allowed it; he was not gentle on the ride home. After the reporters and cameras had all cleared out of Pritchard's condo and the lawyers had gone away, Peterson started drinking and asked if she had any grass. After a few drinks of Glenfiddich, he tore her clothes off and took her anally bent over the living room couch. It was a first for the 50-year-old former spinster. After he passed out following his third assault, she limped into the bathroom and cleaned the blood off her legs. She cried herself to sleep.

In the first few weeks, he had been very sexually demanding. No orifice was safe, and she wondered about AIDS. Then as he got a renewed feel for the city and his new celebrity, he stayed out more and longer. One night in June, he came home stoned and demanded oral sex. When she balked, he backhanded her into the wall.

"Suck, bitch, or die," Peterson commanded.

She complied, then slipped into the bathroom and called 911 from her cell.

By the time the police came, Peterson had gone out for more vodka. Pritchard's right eye had swollen shut when she opened the door for the police. But she had changed her mind by this time and told the police she had slipped coming out of the shower, striking her eye on the bathroom sink.

Under a law passed while Peterson was safely in prison, a police officer could press domestic battery charges even if the victim refused if the officer saw fresh signs of abuse. The ringer that had closed her eye was enough evidence for the cops, so when Peterson came walking into the apartment, the cops grabbed him, and cuffed him. They recognized him and were happy to haul him down to the station.

The incident left Pritchard wondering if her new husband had truly embraced the teaching of Gandhi or had used her.

The case was still pending as Halloran and Ortiz approached Pritchard's condo at 2000 W. Race St. Hillard and Cook were right behind them. Halloran drove slowly past the six-flat and pulled into the alley between Race and Ohio. The lights were on in the kitchen of Pritchard's apartment.

"Ty, you and Edgar set up in the rear. Be quiet. Don't do a thing but sit. I'm pretty sure we got the element of surprise, but this asshole is smart, violent and he's been around. Don't take any chances," Halloran said into his radio while eyeing the kitchen window.

Halloran watched in the rear-view mirror as Hillard parked behind a garage out of sight of the condo. Halloran circled around onto Hoyne, then parked down Race a half block west of the apartment building.

The six-flat had been rehabbed from scratch and sold as condos recently. The large oak front door had been refinished and brass address numbers hung at an angle above the door's small square window. A six-foot wrought iron fence surrounded the front of the building and curved east around the Damen Avenue side, with an intercom and buzzer system attached to the front gate. Halloran radioed Hillard and Cook to let them know he was about to ring.

A few seconds after Halloran rang the bell, Joan Pritchard's voice came across the intercom.

"Hello, who is it, please?" she said. Ortiz stepped up.

"Hello, Miss Pritchard. This is Detective Sylvia Ortiz. I'd like to come up and ask Mr. Peterson and you a few questions."

"If it's about my case, officer, I want the charges dropped," Pritchard said, an edge to her voice creeping in now that she knew it was the police outside.

"That's part of it. Can we come up, please?"

"Who's we?" The initially sugary voice had now turned all steel.

"I'm with my partner, Mike Halloran. Please buzz us in."

"Just a minute. I was on the phone with my mother when the doorbell rang. She's an invalid so I can't keep her on hold." Pritchard disconnected from the intercom with a click.

Just then, Halloran saw Peterson come flying down the front stairs at a gallop, into the lobby and disappear down a hall, heading to the side exit.

"He's on the run," Halloran shouted.

CHAPTER 24

Racing after Peterson, Halloran grabbed his radio from his lapel, and called out to Hillard. The signal was bad, and he just got static. He started running toward Damen, just in time to see Peterson sprinting toward Ohio. Leaning over the six-foot locked gate, Halloran yelled into the darkness and connected with Hillard.

"Ty, Edgar. He's on the move. Cut over through the gangways to Ohio."

Halloran ran first to Damen, and then toward Ohio, but the bum knee and age had taken their toll on his speed; Peterson was putting distance between them. Ortiz was right behind her partner.

Hillard and Cook sprinted though a gangway toward Ohio. They met Halloran a couple doors west, just in time to see Peterson getting into a grey Buick LeSabre a half block away. Hillard was the fastest of the four, but missed getting to Peterson by a few seconds. The Buick took off with a screech of the tires, heading east.

"Ty, you drive west to Hoyne, then go north. See if you see him. We'll take a U and see if he heads back east on Grand. We'll call it in, and be on the radio!" Halloran yelled.

He wheeled and raced back to wind up neck and neck with his partner. As Ortiz scrambled into the shotgun seat, Halloran jumped into the squad, started it up and hit the siren and flashing emergency lights. He screeched into a U as he spied the Buick fly by a block south, heading east. It was dark, but Halloran's headlights illuminated the driver for a split second. It looked like Peterson.

"I think that's him." Halloran floored the Crown Vic. Its huge engine roared as he took off in pursuit. Ortiz was on the radio, calling in the chase and asking for help. She also asked for a trace to see if Pritchard owned a grey Buick LeSabre.

As soon as he turned east on Grand, Halloran spotted the Buick weaving through heavy traffic two blocks ahead. When the Buick hit solid traffic in both directions, it veered to the right and jumped the curb and up onto the sidewalk. A teenaged boy holding hands with his girl saw the car coming and pulled his girlfriend off the sidewalk and into the gutter on top of him an instant before the Buick flashed by.

As it approached Ashland, it passed all the eastbound traffic backed up at the light, jumped back off the sidewalk, then swerved left, side-swiping a CTA bus.

Halloran veered into the oncoming traffic, his siren blaring, lights flashing. The oncoming traffic had all stopped, so he lurched back into the middle of the street just as Peterson slammed into the bus. The traffic in the intersection had stopped dead as Halloran roared into a sliding stop parallel to the Buick and just a few car lengths away.

"Mike, watch it. He's got his window..." Ortiz said. But before she finished, a hand came out of the driver's window, a gun spitting bullets at the two detectives. The squad's passenger side window exploded into a thousand shards of flying glass.

Halloran threw open his door and rolled into the street, pulling his Browning .380 from his holster as he hit the ground. He leaped to his feet in a crouch, thrusting the gun across the roof of the squad.

But Peterson had already slammed the Buick into reverse and had just sideswiped a Volvo in the middle of the intersection.

Halloran squeezed off three quick shots, two going through the rear window. But the Buick plowed over the curb and through a Shell gas station, heading east on Grand. Halloran jumped back into the car to find Ortiz slumped sideways, holding her left hand over a bloody wound that was oozing blood just above her bulletproof vest.

"Mike, I'm hit," Ortiz whispered.

Halloran ripped the radio off his coat and yelled, "10-1, 10-1, officer down. Shooter eastbound on Grand from Ashland. Armed and dangerous. Grey Buick."

Halloran quickly reached over to undo Ortiz' seatbelt, and pulled her close, gently.

"You'll be fine, partner, just a nick. I'll get you to Stroger. Fix this right up."

Halloran was lying about the wound.

The blood was flowing quickly all over the front of Ortiz's coat. Halloran had to think fast. He ripped open her coat to get a better look and saw a bullet entrance wound the size of a dime. Then, he got back on the radio.

"This is Halloran. I'm taking my partner to Stroger myself. She's got a chest wound. I'm five minutes away, at Grand and Ashland. Give me some traffic help," Halloran pulled his partner close, and she moaned.

"Tell Joe to take care of the kids. Tell him..." Ortiz faltered.

"Tell him yourself. You're going to be fine, partner." Halloran said. He jammed half of his right middle finger into the gurgling wound to stop the flow of blood. Ortiz moaned again and clamped her left hand over Halloran's probing hand.

With his left hand, he awkwardly threw the car in reverse, backed up with a screech, and again used his left hand to slam the car into drive to race south on Ashland, his lights and siren still on. Blood was dripping into his right eye from a gash on his forehead from flying glass. He jumped into the northbound traffic as he approached Lake Street and then veered back into the southbound lanes to avoid the oncoming traffic.

By Madison, he started getting support. Squads had shut down the westbound and eastbound lanes of Madison and the southbound lanes of Ogden as he raced toward Stroger Hospital, the county hospital that had the busiest emergency room in the state. The blood dripping into his right eye was blurring his vision. He closed that eye, squinting at the road with his left eye.

At Jackson, a field lieutenant pulled in front of Halloran in a marked squad with his lights flashing and sirens wailing. They both raced southwest on Ogden.

As Halloran passed Harrison Street, he spotted a line of squad cars and wagons that had blocked all lanes of Ogden in a line that steered straight into the emergency room entrance. Ortiz' grip was lessening, but he could feel her pulse in the wound. His finger could feel the tip of the bullet that was lodged perhaps five inches above her heart.

After he screeched to a halt in front of the emergency room door, Dr. Tula Kocoras, head of the emergency room, threw open the passenger side door and jumped into the front seat, staring down at Ortiz and quickly sizing up the situation.

"Keep your hand right where it is. Don't move it until we have her on a gurney and inside. You hear, officer."

"Right. Let's go."

Kocoras and a young resident gently quickly pulled Ortiz out of the front seat as Halloran lifted his stricken partner with his left arm while holding his right hand in place.

They lifted Ortiz onto a waiting gurney and Halloran rushed into the emergency room with the two doctors and a dozen nurses, still holding his finger firmly in place in the wound.

Dozens of police officers lined the entrance, grim and ashen as they stared at Halloran and Ortiz, flanked by the growing parade of doctors and nurses. Once inside, they wheeled the gurney into a curtained stall, then Kocoras grabbed a handful of gauze pads.

"Now, slowly take your finger out," Kocoras said.

Ortiz tightened her grip as Halloran began to take his finger from the hole in his partner's chest just as Kocoras stood ready with gauze pads to press into the wound. Ortiz opened her eyes as he withdrew his hand and stared at her partner.

"Thank you," she mouthed.

"You're good, Syl. You're good. Doc Kocoras here's the best."

For Halloran it was an oath of faith he was taking for his partner's benefit; he'd never heard of Kocoras before but had read her nameplate.

"You've been hit. Go have one of the nurses look at that cut on your forehead," Kocoras told Halloran. "We'll take care of her."

A swarm of doctors and nurses surged into the gap Halloran left, hooking up IVs to Ortiz as a nurse pulled the curtain closed and Halloran was shut out. Another nurse took Halloran by the arm and guided him into another stall nearby.

"That might take a couple of stitches," she said, dabbing the head wound.

"How is she?" Halloran demanded.

"Too early to know for sure, but you're right about Dr. Kocoras. She's the head of the department. She's brilliant." The nurse was a redhead, about 50, named O'Hara, freckles all over her hands and arms.

"How'd you know to stick your finger in there? Were you a medic or something in the Army?"

"Not hardly."

Halloran's mind flashed back to the time he worked as an orderly in Johannesburg and Halloran had seen a patient come in the emergency room with a tire iron sticking in the middle of his chest. The doctor had told Halloran later that the man would have bled to death if he had taken the tool out. But he didn't feel like sharing that tale with O'Hara.

Just then, a surge of police brass came pouring into the emergency room, Johnson in the lead.

"You hit, Halloran?" Johnson asked.

"Just a nick. Syl was hit—high in the chest just above the vest."

"Take good care of him," Johnson said to O'Hara, then looked at Halloran. "We'll talk later."

A resident came to take a look at Halloran and determined that a butterfly bandage would suffice, no stitches necessary. It was a distraction Halloran neither needed nor tolerated.

"Later, doc. Later," Halloran said.

CHAPTER 25

For 15 frantic minutes, the team of doctors and nurses labored over Ortiz at a fever's pitch. Finally, the curtains parted, and the doctors and nurses started wheeling Ortiz down the hall, with IV lines and flashing monitors being wheeled alongside the gurney.

From a bench in the ER, Halloran jumped up and rushed toward the gurney and Kocoras.

"She's stable. We're taking her to surgery. We'll know more in a short while," Kocoras told Halloran as she disappeared into the elevator with the gurney. He tried to see his partner's face, but it was blocked by the medical entourage.

Fagan walked up to Halloran and patted him on the back as the elevator doors closed.

"She's going to be fine. Don't worry, Mike. She's tough."

Halloran stood immobile, still staring at the closed elevator door.

"Say a prayer, Lu," Halloran said and turned to face his boss. "We catch that motherfucker?"

"Not yet, Mike. But it's been less than a half hour," Fagan said.

Halloran found a chair nearby and sunk quickly down, burying his face in his hands. The brass had gathered in the lobby and were whispering, but they knew enough to leave Halloran alone in his grief. Minutes passed like centuries for Halloran as he waited for word on his partner.

A half hour later, Kocoras emerged from the elevator and strode quickly to Halloran.

"She's going to be okay. Lost a lot of blood, but the bullet didn't bounce around inside, so it didn't hit any vital organs. If you'd waited for an ambulance, detective, she would have bled to death. Putting your finger in there saved her life. Where'd you learn to stop bleeding like that?" Kocoras asked.

"Remember the little Dutch boy and the dike? Seemed kind of logical to me. She need any blood?" Halloran asked.

"No, no. She's being patched up by one of the best surgeons in the country, Dr. Simpson, and she should be okay in a few weeks," Kocoras said.

Before Halloran could reply, Joe Ortiz came tearing into the emergency room wild-eyed, running up to Halloran.

"Mike, Mike. Where is she? She okay? What happened?"

"She's going to be okay, Joe. She's in surgery now. Doc Kocoras here can put your mind at ease."

Kocoras eased Joe Ortiz into a nearby office and sat him down, then closed the door.

Seconds later, Johnson, Fagan and Mallory approached Halloran.

"We need to talk for a minute," Johnson said, leading Halloran and his two subordinates into the security office.

For the next half hour, Halloran detailed the abortive arrest, the chase and the shooting in minute detail. The three supervisors said little, mostly nodding and asking a few questions. Then Johnson rose slowly and walked over to Halloran.

"Sounds like it was all by the book. Hope one of your shots found shithead," Johnson said, placing a hand on Halloran's shoulder.

"I hope," Halloran said.

Exhausted and frustrated with nothing to do but wait, Halloran brooded about Peterson.

You'll pay for this asshole. I'm gonna get you.

CHAPTER 26

Lining up the loci marks on the DNA profiles, Svenson was sure she had a match. But to be sure, she again carefully compared the profile from the envelope to the profile from the cigarette. She fed the data into the computer. Seconds later the machine belched out the figures, the ones that always appeared in the newspapers.

The odds were 14 quadrillion to one that the person whose profile was on both the cigarette and the envelope was anyone other than Eric Peterson. She had meticulously done the comparison, then did it again to double-check. Still clutching the printouts, she grabbed the phone as she entered her office, then walked around to her chair as she dialed Halloran's cell. It had taken 13 hours in all, then another hour to redo the math, double check the comparisons, and finally to print it out. She had worked with Halloran enough to know he wouldn't be putting that kind of pressure on her if he didn't feel he had the right guy. Now she couldn't wait to tell him he had been right.

When she called Halloran's cell, he was being questioned by Johnson, Mallory and Fagan. She left a message to call; it was urgent. She waited for several hours, thinking it was strange that Halloran wouldn't immediately respond.

Unbeknownst to her, Halloran was walking the halls of Stroger, waiting.

Waiting.

CHAPTER 27

After escaping through the gas station, Peterson drove just two blocks east on Grand before ditching the car. It had two bullet holes in the rear window, and he was sure that every cop in Chicago now had his license plate and description. He wasn't sure why the two cops hadn't continued the chase, but he reasoned that he might have hit the woman cop riding shotgun. *Tough shit,* he thought.

At Noble, he turned right and parked in the Burger Baron lot as two squad cars went racing west on Grand. He opened the trunk and grabbed his canvas bag. It contained a change of clothes, a Canadian passport, toiletries, and $15,000 in cash. He had prepared for the day the cops might come calling.

After he shoved his .357 magnum into his coat pocket, he got out and looked very much like a yuppie on his way to work out.

A middle-aged black nurse in her crisp white uniform was just walking to her car, carrying a bag with a cheeseburger and fries. She was pulling out her car keys as she approached her Dodge Caravan.

"Cold enough for you, sister?" Peterson asked. The parking lot was dimly lit, and the nurse immediately sensed something was wrong. Janet Grant didn't answer but quickly looked for help.

"Be cool and you won't get hurt," Peterson said, coming up behind her quickly and pulling out the revolver to motion her to the van. Grant's eyes grew wide when she felt the gun press into the small of her back.

"Please don't hurt me. I got babies at home. Please don't hurt me."

Peterson ordered her into the driver's seat, then clambered into the rear seat and crouched down. He ordered her out onto Grand and told her to drive east at the speed limit. Between the seats, he thrust the gun into the nurse's ribs.

"Turn left on Ogden and get on the Kennedy, and don't get cute if you want to see those babies again," Peterson ordered. "How much gas you got?"

"I just filled it up before I stopped for the food. Don't be hurting me, Mister. I'll do whatever you want."

"That's the spirit. Stay on the Kennedy until it blends into the Edens and continue north to Milwaukee. In other words, just go straight. And don't be eyeballing me in the rear view, bitch."

For the next hour, they rode in silence, except when Grant asked if she could eat her cheeseburger. He reached into the front seat, split the burger in two and ate half, handing her the other half as she drove.

Just past Kenosha, they approached the Wisconsin Highway 20 exit, and Peterson ordered her to turn off. She drove four miles west down the mostly empty highway before he ordered her to turn north up one of the deserted county side roads. Grant started pleading for her life.

"Mister, I didn't get a good look at you. No way I could pick you out of a lineup. You white folks all look alike to me. I got three babies, and they got no daddy. Just me. Don't kill me, mister."

"Relax sister. In the joint my best homies were niggers. I'm a white nigger my damn self. I ain't gonna kill you. But I need your car. Pull down that road and into that field."

They were in the middle of nowhere with only one farmhouse a mile up the road.

"Get out and lie face down on the ground," he ordered. He looked around in the van for something to tie the nurse up. Finding nothing, he ordered her to take off her stockings.

Grant sat on the snowy ground and leaned to the side, then rolled down her white pantyhose. She handed them to Peterson, keeping her eyes on the ground, even though it was nearly pitch black.

He ripped them down the middle and then ordered her to lie face down and put her hands behind her back. Peterson tied her hands behind her back with one length of stocking and then tied her ankles together with the other. He pulled tight on the binding on her wrists until she cried in pain.

"I think I just shot a cop who was trying to send me back to the joint, but I got no reason to kill you. You might freeze to death out here, but that won't be my fault. Good night, nurse."

He hopped back in the van, checked her purse and found $185 in cash, a credit card and a debit card. He walked back to Grant and stood over her. She thought he was going to kill her. It was still a possibility.

"What's the PIN for your debit card, Ms. Grant? And don't think about lying because I will drive back from Racine and shoot you in the head if you give me bullshit."

"It's 1231, the last day of the year, when my first baby was born."

"I believe you, but if you're lying, I'll come back and there are gonna be three orphans in Chicago tonight."

She wasn't lying. Peterson withdrew the maximum $300 at a Racine ATM and used her credit card to top off the gas tank. In six hours, he was in Minneapolis. And the next day, he had crossed into Canada aboard a Greyhound headed for Toronto, using the Canadian passport he had bought back in Chicago, near 26th and Kedzie, ironically just a few blocks west of the county jail complex. He was now Harry Peters from Vancouver.

CHAPTER 28

In the Stroger ER waiting room, Halloran spent the next few hours with Joe, pacing and awaiting word. His mask down, Dr. Thomas Simpson appeared shortly after midnight and assured Joe that Syl "pulled through the surgery like a champ." Once cleared by the hospital, Joe and Halloran joined a sleeping Syl in a cramped hospital room where monitors beeped and IVs snaked out of her arms.

Shortly after 7 a.m., Syl awoke, still a bit groggy. She forced her eyes open to see her two best men standing red-eyed in their bedside vigil.

"Jesus, Joe, do you know what lengths this guy went to just to get his hand in my blouse?"

Joe laughed; Joe cried. He knelt next to his wife and kissed her hand. Ortiz winked at Halloran. He grabbed her big toe and gave it a tug.

"You're gonna be fine if the first words out of your mouth are to give me shit." Halloran patted Joe on the back and left.

Joe rose and followed him into the hall.

"Mike, the doc told me she would have died without you plugging the wound. I can never thank you enough." Joe Ortiz held Halloran by both biceps, tears welling in his eyes.

"Enough. She's my partner. You're my buddy. Go to your wife." Halloran then turned and walked slowly down the corridor and out of the hospital.

Back in his squad car, he found his cell on the floor of the front seat, covered with blood. He wiped it off and saw there was a message for him. He hit the message icon and listened.

"Mike, it's your guy," Svenson laughed in her message. "You were right, big guy. Congratulations."

After he got home, Halloran took off his bloody clothes and showered, he called Svenson back. By now the news of the shooting had reached Svenson as reports of a cop shot ricocheted through the city. She answered on the first ring.

"That's real good news, Karen. Thanks. What are the numbers?"

"Are you all right? I heard Syl's going to make it. The numbers? Try 14 quadrillion to one. I guess you know you got the right guy now."

"Yeah, Karen, Syl's looking like she's going to be okay. I really appreciate it and the numbers are great news."

"Don't worry, Mike. You'll get him. I know you."

Halloran rang off, her last words echoing in his mind. He would rather have him handcuffed in an interview room than getting the well-wishes and vows of confidence from Svenson, as much as he appreciated her support and hard work. Before he hit the rack, Halloran grabbed a cold IPA from the fridge and looked out at the city, wondering where his prey was.

***

At about the same time, Janet Grant had freed herself and found refuge at the home of a Racine County farmer, shocked to see the mud-splattered, shivering nurse at his front door. The first thing she said was: "Can I use your phone to call my kids?"

Part II:

The Chase

CHAPTER 29

By the time Halloran arrived at the Area headquarters the next morning, the heavy hitters were already there: Mallory, Fagan, Egan. No word yet on Peterson.

Once Halloran related the DNA hit to Egan, she called Cavaretta, then Dunne. Then she began filling out the paperwork for a warrant. Peterson's picture was already being broadcast all over the country. His photo was in CPD's Daily Bulletin distributed to every cop in the city. In addition, last night Fagan had notified ISPERN (Illinois State Police Emergency Radio Network) to look out for the Buick and Peterson. But by 4 a.m., a patrol car had found the Buick in the rear of the nearly empty Burger Baron lot.

The FBI was also notified in case he had already fled the jurisdiction, cop talk for leaving the state. And within hours, Egan had secured a federal warrant for unlawful flight to avoid prosecution (UFAP) through her contacts at the U.S. Attorney's office. That would go to Interpol. But she knew it might be for naught, depending on where Peterson was found.

Even though he knew that all that could be done was being done, Halloran felt helpless, useless and a failure. Fagan picked up on his gloom and called Halloran into his office.

"Mike, it was by the book. You did what we do every time we go in. Don't beat yourself up over it. Sometimes they get by us. We'll get him--and soon, is my bet."

Halloran nodded and exited Fagan's office. He was thinking of all the places Peterson might go, and wanting to go to each place to stake it out, to grab him up himself. He broke away from his thoughts to interrupt Egan's paperwork in the prosecutors' office just off the squad room. At the station, they were professionals.

"Madame prosecutor, can we get a court order to get a wire on Pritchard's phone?"

"Yeah, no problem, detective. But first we're gonna get a fugitive warrant," she said, not looking up from her computer screen. "How's the head?' she asked, pointing to the bandage on Halloran's forehead.

"It's nothing." Halloran excused himself when his cell phone went off, answering it with a "hold on" as he made his way down the stairs and out into the parking lot.

This needs privacy.

CHAPTER 30

Outside, Halloran looked around to make sure he was out of earshot of anyone in the parking lot, then said, "Yeah, Halloran here."

"Mike, this is huge, huge. I hear you got a warrant for Eric Peterson for the Cavaretta murder." It was the Sun-Times' Frank Marone, breathless.

"Jesus, that didn't take long."

"So it's true. Unbelievable. What ties him to it?"

"It's what we in law enforcement call evidence," Halloran said. He seldom would reveal details, unless it served his purpose, but he would confirm. And that was all Marone usually needed. This time he might need a little feeding, a little leading.

"I heard it was his DNA on the cigarette in her car." It was not quite a question, but close enough.

"Your hearing's good, Frank. So is your source. Who is it? Mallory? Fagan?" Halloran asked. He liked Marone, and he knew he wouldn't give up his source. It was the reason Halloran would speak to him at all.

"You know I can't go there, and I know you know I won't. But the DNA link is good, right?" Marone wanted to hear it again from another source, and maybe get a bit more. The more informed the re-porter sounded, the more likely a conversation might ensue with other, richer details.

"You're halfway there," Halloran prompted.

"Halfway? Whattya mean?"

"You got the hit on the cigarette, right? But where did the other half come from is what you should be asking."

"From CODIS, I assume," Marone said. Halloran paused as he eye-balled a detective exiting his car and slowly making his way out of the parking lot, talking on his cell.

"You know what they say about 'assume' being synonymous for 'making an **ass** out of **u** and **me**,'" Halloran answered as the detective entered the station.

"If not from CODIS, from where? I know he didn't give you a sample even if you somehow suspected him."

"If you went back into Peterson's old file and looked at who approved the felony charges back 20 years ago, you would find out it was a young prosecutor named Thomas Cavaretta, who later handled the trial."

"Holy shit. That's great. But where did the DNA hit come from?"

"You know how some inmates got nothing better to do than send threatening letters to judges, cops and prosecutors, even reporters?" Halloran asked.

"You got the DNA off a letter Peterson sent to Cavaretta? That's unbelievable. From his saliva? How old was the letter?"

"Frankie, me lad, I think you have enough for a good little story. I got another call coming in."

"Just one more quick question. Anyone else got this?"

"You're my guy. Bye." Halloran hit the end button.

As it turned out, Marone did have the story to himself. The Tribune didn't know about it until the Sun-Times 3-star edition hit the streets at 11 p.m., and moments later, the Trib's city desk. A last-minute scramble by the Trib night staff failed to recover the story. After whacking cops and prosecutors for years, the Trib's sources were few and far between.

Halloran smiled when he walked up to the honor boxes the next morning at Bryn Mawr and Sheridan and read the headlines.

"Con killed coed," blared the Sun-Times.

"Mideast Peace Accord Near," yawned the Tribune.

CHAPTER 31

"How's Syl, Mike?" yelled the midnight desk sergeant when Halloran walked into 19ᵗʰDistrict on his way up to Area 3 on a cold January morning, two days after the shooting.

"She's going to be okay. Thanks, Sarge."

"I hear you saved her life," the sergeant said to Halloran's back as he disappeared up the stairs without replying, content to let the desk sergeant think he hadn't heard him.

Syl had been upgraded to good condition within 24 hours. But Halloran wanted to get back to work after another fitful sleep. As he hit the second floor, he spotted Fagan on the phone, gesturing as he spoke to Mallory.

There was a stir in the squad room that morning that had been missing in the grinding work that led to the warrants, both local and federal. There was still much high fiving about solving the case, but no talk about letting Peterson slip through their fingers. And the solution of the crime was tempered by Ortiz' gunshot wound.

Ortiz and Halloran had followed procedure, and Fagan understood and sympathized. That said, it didn't cover the partners or the department with glory, despite the solid and incisive detective work that led to the charges.

Halloran was nursing a cup of black vending machine coffee when his cell phone went off. It was Cavaretta.

"Mike, this is Tom Cavaretta. Good morning," the State's Attorney said.

"Good morning, Mr. State's Attorney." Halloran's response was a bit muted, not wanting to let his fellow detectives know he was talking to the head prosecutor. But Fagan had been standing close enough to overhear.

"First, I want to say how concerned my wife and I were to hear of the shooting. I hear Sylvia is recovering rapidly. That's great news. But I also wanted to thank you for the outstanding work you and your partner did in finding who did this. And I wanted to assure you that no one thinks that you or Syl did anything wrong when Peterson eluded you. I've talked personally to Supt. Johnson on this matter."

"Thank you, sir."

"Keep me posted, Mike." Cavaretta had said his piece, then hung up.

"I heard your end. What was his?" Fagan flopped down in the chair next to Halloran.

Halloran recounted the conversation nearly verbatim, then said, "nice of him."

"Mike, look, I'm not going to let you beat yourself up for the next month or two over this. You did a tremendous job on this. We'll catch this guy. Let's say you had followed asshole instead of taking Ortiz to Stroger. She'd be dead. That you would never forget. Let it go. You—we—did nothing wrong and everything right."

"I know, Lu. I know, and thanks. But that shithead is still out there and here we sit."

Over the next two weeks, the case stalled and Halloran stewed. He caught a few new cases that he worked with Hillard, but checked daily with the feds to see if there were any hits on the warrants. His contact in the U.S. Marshal's office assured him if there were, he would be the first to be called.

It was Feb. 6 when Halloran showed up at the Stein Institute to watch Jane Powers perform the autopsies in a particularly grisly double homicide. As he entered, an elderly Hispanic man was being helped out the door by a younger woman, presumably his daughter, also sobbing.

"Mi hijo, mi hijo (my son, my son)" he said between gasps. As they made it out the front door and into the parking lot, Powers was coming out to greet Halloran.

"Mike, good to see you. Back to the old grind. Great job on the Cavaretta case. Your partner back home? Any word on your perp's whereabouts?"

Halloran had his routine down now, thanking people for their kind words, but thinking that unspoken was the notion that Peterson had slipped through his fingers. He knew Powers was sincere. He said Syl was improving, and Peterson was still missing. She led him past the door marked "Body Viewing Room." Halloran always wondered what the deceased's family thought when they entered that room. *Must have a terry cloth rug in there to sop up all those tears,* he thought.

The two autopsies were painstakingly slow; Powers said she'd fax the reports to Area 3.

He needed to stop at the range to take his monthly practice to keep his shooting eye sharp. As he pulled out of the lot and headed west toward Damen, Halloran realized he was just a few blocks away from Pritchard's condo. He decided to take a run at her before the range.

Halloran parked a block away on Damen, just north of Race, and stared up at Pritchard's apartment. As he watched, a young man in a Bears stocking cap emerged from the third-floor apartment and started descending the back porch stairs. Halloran jumped from the car and walked quickly to the wrought-iron gate on the side of the six-flat.

"Hey, pal, open the gate, okay." Halloran flashed his badge at the man.

"What's the problem, officer?" He walked over to open the gate, stepping aside wide-eyed.

"Just checking some basement doors in the area to see if there's been any tampering. There's been some burglaries, and we think they're gaining access through the basements." Halloran lied, which saved him the trouble of picking the lock.

"Anyone hurt?"

"Nah, comes in when people are at work. We'll catch him. Thanks. You can be on your way."

"Uh, yeah, Glad to help." The man opened his garage door and pulled his black BMW 318i out into the alley and disappeared.

Halloran unsnapped the security strap off his gun in the shoulder holster. He was pretty damn sure that Peterson wouldn't be dumb enough to return here, but there was the slight possibility, and there was a small army of dead cops who bet the wrong end of slight possibilities.

From the third-floor porch, he peered in the kitchen window, but saw nothing except a small butcher block table with two wooden chairs on either side. On top of the table were the morning's Tribune, some envelopes and bills, and a postcard lying next to a set of keys.

Halloran put his hand across his eyebrows to shield the glare and peered in to get a better look at the postcard.

It read:

"Joan Pritchard
2000 W. Race
Chicago, Ill.
U.S.A."

The message read simply: *"Wish you were here. All's fine."* It was unsigned. Above the message, the card read: "New Delhi, India." The date was smeared.

Halloran jotted down a few notes, then knocked on the door. In a few moments, the door opened just enough for Pritchard to stick her face out.

"Detective Halloran, Miss Pritchard. I'd like to ask you a few questions."

Pritchard pressed forward and tried to close the door. Halloran's left foot was too fast, as he slid it between the door and the frame.

"You got a warrant?" she screeched, still holding the door tight against her shoulder.

Halloran gently but firmly shouldered the door open.

"We don't need a warrant to ask a few questions." Halloran stepped inside, peering beyond Pritchard down the hall and into the dining room.

"You fucking pig. Get out of my home."

"Have you heard from your husband? I'm assuming he's not home."

As he spoke, Pritchard turned her back to step between Halloran and the kitchen table, lifting up the Tribune and moving it over on top of the postcard and envelopes.

"I'd hardly tell a Nazi like you."

"You don't mind if I look around, do you?"

"Yes, I do mind, you asshole."

But Halloran was already walking into the dining room, then the first bedroom, then the second bedroom, then the front room. He glanced at the portrait of Gandhi.

"Where's your warrant?"

"We need a warrant if we're searching your house, and I'm just asking a few questions. I can come back with a warrant if you like."

"Yeah, I like. Now get the fuck out of my apartment. I have no idea where my husband is, and now you can see he isn't here."

"You familiar with the law called obstructing justice?"

"Yeah, I'm familiar with that, and I'm also familiar with the law that says a wife doesn't have to testify against her husband. And you should be familiar with the 4th Amendment barring illegal searches. So, hit the bricks, you stupid fucking Mick pig."

"Your mother know you talk like that?" Halloran started heading toward the back door.

"My mother is dead. Get out."

"Yeah, and my partner almost was, thanks to that scumbag you married. Now, lady, this is real personal. And if I find you're helping him, you're gonna do some prison time and cozy up to some of those poor innocents you love so much."

He closed the door behind him.

India?

CHAPTER 32

Driving back to Area 3, Halloran twisted the new information in his mind. He wondered how Peterson could have wound up in India, figuring the only reason Pritchard would have moved the paper was to prevent him from seeing that postcard. He called Egan.

"Do we have an extradition agreement with India?" Halloran asked.

"And how are you, too?" Egan laughed. She was sitting in her goat's nest of an office at 26th Street in the northwest corner overlooking the old Division 1 complex, which was built more than 85 years ago at the same time the courthouse was constructed.

"India? I'm flattered you'd think I know that, but I can find out. Why?"

Halloran gave her a quick rundown of the encounter with Pritchard and her surreptitious movements with the newspaper to cover the postcard from India. Egan said she would have to do a little research, that it was not the most common question that came up at 26th Street.

Within an hour, Egan was back to Halloran.

"We do have an extradition treaty with India, but we might still have a bureaucratic hassle trying to extradite on this. Are we just guessing at this point, based on the postcard?"

"Yeah, but the way she moved to cover up the postcard makes me think it was a prearranged note to let her know he was okay. Maybe a signal to send money. I don't know," Halloran said, then before hanging up, added, "I'll look over the recent MUDs to see who she's been on the phone with."

The Multi Unit Distance (MUD) records detailed all the calls into and out of Pritchard's phones since a month before the escape and since. The record printouts were kept in a folder on Fagan's desk.

Once he got back to Area 3, Halloran started sifting through the sheets and stopped at an entry from two days after the escape. It was a 20-second call to the home phone from London, a likely intermediary point if Peterson was fleeing to India. Then he looked over the transcripts from the consensual overhear they had secured on her home phone. They revealed little of the message left on her answering machine.

"Hi. It's me. The package arrived safely. We are all in fine shape here and looking forward to our next vacation. Hope things are better there. We all send our love, and you can send some, too." It wasn't Peterson, but a female voice, perhaps a fellow traveler on the anti-death penalty circuit.

There were few absolutes in law enforcement. Everyone would agree that Jack Ruby killed Lee Harvey Oswald, but beyond that, most cases were built on an accumulation of evidence—motive, opportunity, physical evidence, third-party admissions, eyewitnesses, confessions. There were few Jack Ruby cases.

After hearing Halloran update the case, Egan called the U.S. Marshal's office to get a rundown on how she could get a fugitive out of India. The Marshal had to check with the State Department. It would take time, she was told. Tom Cavaretta is not going to want to hear that, she told them. Cavaretta was on a first-name basis with the U.S. Attorney in Chicago, she added. That got the fed's attention.

Stirring the federal bureaucracy into action was not that tough once you invoked the clout of the U.S. Attorney's office in Chicago, which had perhaps the highest profile of any office in the country over the past 30 years. When the feds called from Chicago, Washington listened.

The next day, a State Department functionary who had a title like Deputy Assistant Liaison for South Asia Affairs called Egan and told her that the contact in India would be Deputy Consul General Christopher Prentice Grimshaw III in New Delhi.

CHAPTER 33

Every time Halloran took a winter walk along the lakefront, he thought of the Lou Rawls song, "Dead End Street" and its lyrics about the Hawk, the cruel, biting winter wind.

His thoughts then turned somewhat illogically to Elvis' "The Ghetto: On a cold and grey Chicago morning...in the ghetto."

For all of his life, Halloran had been hooked on the beauty of the lake. In recent summers, from July on, the lake had been as warm and clear as the Caribbean. He loved swimming along the lakefront from North Avenue to Oak Street and back. The Drake loomed in front and some of the great old high-rises, the originals built in the late 1800s, drifted by slowly as he swam.

On this cold Sunday morning the temperature hovered in the low teens, pretty cold for a March 4. He parked his car next to the Cardinal's mansion at North and Astor and walked through the tunnel underneath the Outer Drive. The smell of urine drifted up, the legacy of some drunk or homeless wretch with nowhere else to relieve himself.

As he gazed at the still frigid lake, he wondered where Peterson was now. It had been more than two months since the shootout and escape. In February, Egan had procured a search warrant for Pritchard's place, the second one, and this time they seized her computer. Between the murder in October and Peterson's escape in December, there had been searches for hotels in London, Berlin, Athens, New Delhi, Calcutta, Darjeeling Kathmandu, Colombo and Bangkok. Curiously, there were no searches for flights and no bookings.

Halloran figured that he had not planned to leave via plane. If the cops got wise to him, Peterson knew his chances of leaving from O'Hare or Midway, where there are cops every 25 feet, were nil.

The State Department informed Halloran that Peterson had not used his passport to leave or re-enter the country.

That did not preclude, of course, the possibility that he had gotten a passport in someone else's name. *Christ,* Halloran thought, *you could buy a Social Security card down on 26th Street for $50 any Sunday.*

Checking almost daily, Halloran found that the State Department had not informed the feds that there had been any correspondence from any Interpol or local police on the whereabouts of Peterson. And he had not used his passport anywhere in the world that tracked entry electronically.

Halloran pondered the prospects as he trod along the bike path toward Oak Street. He had caught new cases, and he still had to testify in court at least once a month, but it was the Cavaretta case that haunted him. As he leaned into a fierce southeast wind, he realized he was just a few blocks away from where Jenny Cavaretta had been impaled with the ice pick. It had been nearly five months since the murder and more than two months since Peterson escaped. As he turned to walk back to his car, he muttered, "Fuck."

A young couple approaching and holding hands stared at the cop.

"Sorry, it's personal," he said.

Indeed, it is, he thought.

CHAPTER 34

Just a month after their daughter's death, the Cavarettas had escaped for 10 days for a cruise on the Mediterranean. They flew to Athens, then rented a limo for a quick trip to Corfu. There they boarded the Aegean Queen cruise ship for a tour that took them to Cyprus, Crete, and Capri. Not in that order.

They played bridge, ate wonderful seafood, lounged around the deck and read best sellers. But they were a somber pair. After they returned, Joyce re-immersed herself in her charities and boards. She was on the Public Library Board in River Forest. She continued to tutor third graders at the Bradenton School in the heart of the West Side ghetto. Her friends worked hard to keep her busy; she needed little help with that. But she smiled more than she laughed, and it was a sad smile, no matter how hard she tried to mask her pervasive sorrow.

Meanwhile, Tom Cavaretta's job kept him as busy as he wanted. The law school speeches, the community groups, the advisory committees, the budget hassles--they all filled in whatever little time was left over after he tended to the meat-and-potatoes, life-and-death matters that were the daily fare of the State's Attorney.

Still, every day when he walked into his office at either the Dunne Administration building or his 26th Street office, he walked by the photo on his bookshelves of his smiling, beautiful daughter, holding her diploma the day she graduated from college.

On this early mid-March morning, he had just finished discussing the St. Patrick's Day Parade float with his political aide, the nasty, snide, fiercely loyal and Machiavellian Maria Montalbano.

As Montalbano cleared his doorway, he picked up the intercom and summoned Maisy.

"Maze, see if you can track down Mike Halloran and see if he would be available to come to 26th Street tomorrow around 3," Cavaretta said. "And Maze, tell him it's just him, not him and Ortiz, I need to see."

When he arrived at 26th Street, Cavaretta entered through the same rear door as the judges did, just across from the ancient Division I cellhouse of the County Jail. The sheriff's deputies never made the State's Attorney or the judges walk through the metal detectors; that was for lesser mortals, like the ever-dangerous press. In truth, the deputies just liked to hassle the Trib, City News, and Sun-Times reporters whose beat was the Criminal Courts building.

From his vantage point on the 11th floor of the jail and court complex's administration building, Cavaretta could see as far west as the Hilton standing alone on the western horizon in Oak Brook. In between, there were thousands of two-flats, three-flats, and humble clapboard homes that were built in the early 20th Century. Just north of his office were the Mexican strongholds of Pilsen and Little Village.

In his office, Cavaretta displayed photos of himself with the President, various governors, the mayor, and with some golf and fishing buddies from the old neighborhood. Over a plaque from the Urban League naming him Man of the Year 1997 was encased in glass his father's .45 caliber semi-automatic that he had worn at Normandy. When the father passed on, his will designated it to Tom.

Cavaretta hated guns, but he had mastered how to handle the ancient pistol on several trips to the FBI's North Chicago firing range. Cavaretta reasoned he should at least know the feel of a handgun, the weapons that kept him in the business of imprisoning those who used them to threaten or end the lives of others.

The kick from the .45 had startled him the first time he fired it, despite the warning from the bulky FBI instructor. He fired two clips, and actually hit the target with six of his last seven shots. By his fourth trip to the range, he had mastered the feel and accuracy of the weapon.

As he sat behind his desk, Cavaretta counted out one hundred $100 bills, the money he had withdrawn earlier in the day from the account he had set up for Jenny's law school tuition. His jaw was set as he placed the money back into a manila envelope on his desk.

"Detective Halloran is here to see you, Mr. State's Attorney," Maisy announced. "Thanks, Maze. Send him in."

Halloran walked in to find the State's Attorney standing at the west end of his office, looking down on the sprawling jail complex that had housed as many as 10,000 inmates at a time.

"It's bigger than a lot of towns in Illinois, Mike." Cavaretta waved out toward the jail buildings that stretched from 26th Street to 31st Street. "When I first prosecuted a case here 25 years ago, it was half that. The growth is narcotics, all narcotics."

"It's the money the drugs bring. You're right there," Halloran said. He was standing awkwardly waiting for the prosecutor to ask him to sit down.

"Precisely, Mike. Right on target. Can I offer you a Coke, 7-up, coffee?" Cavaretta asked, turning from the window to shake the detective's hand.

"Coke would be fine." Halloran was unsure why he had been summoned but figured it was the prosecutor's office, his play.

Cavaretta took out a caffeine-free diet Coke for himself and handed Mike a regular Coke.

"You don't want one of my sissy Cokes, do you, Mike?" Cavaretta said, holding the golden Coke can high while handing the detective the standard red can.

"This is fine, thanks."

Cavaretta motioned Halloran to sit on a large leather chair opposite him as the prosecutor then settled in behind his desk.

"So, Mike, is it your belief that Peterson has fled to India, by way of London?"

"Well, it's a leap, I admit. But I believe it's a good bet." Halloran then recounted briefly the postcard, Pritchard's furtive movement to cover it, and the phone call from London a few days before the postcard, and most recently the Internet searches they had found on the computer.

"So, how do you suppose he got to London?" Cavaretta fiddled with his fountain pen as he questioned the detective, twisting the gold cap between his right forefinger and thumb.

"My guess is it was him that hijacked the nurse's van a couple of blocks from the crash that night. She vacillated when we asked her to pick him out of a photo array, though she said she thought she might be able to pick him out in person if she heard his voice. Then after he dumped her near Racine, he drove to Milwaukee or Minneapolis, then caught a bus to Canada. No record of his renting a car. From Toronto on to London, then India."

"In a perfect world, what would you do to bring Peterson to justice?"

Halloran thought about this for a few moments, wondering just where the State's Attorney was going with it. Cavaretta sat there twisting the pen, waiting, watching the detective.

"In a perfect world--I find shithead myself and drag him back here by the balls. We try him. He gets nailed, and he gets the needle to heaven the week I get my first pension check."

Cavaretta smiled at the detective's colorful scenario and put his gold fountain pen down. He leaned across the desk tightlipped.

"Detective, in our business, we know the world is far from perfect, but I have a proposition for you, a proposal that might serve both of us well. As you know, I had high hopes for my daughter. I had hoped she would be a fine lawyer, perhaps a prosecutor for a while, then marry well, have children, and have a fine legal career while deftly balancing the needs of her family. In many ways, she died before her life really began.

"My hopes, of course, ended last October at the hands of Eric Peterson. I am half Italian, half Irish. The Irish half says 'Don't get angry, get even.' The Italian half says simply 'Get even.'

"I want you to find that animal and bring him back."

With that, Cavaretta pushed the envelope with the $10,000 and a credit card with both their names on it across his desk toward Halloran, who stared at the bulging envelope.

"I am asking a favor of you, a big favor. I've spoken with Supt. Johnson, and he's agreed to give you an extended paid leave of absence from the police department. All on the QT. This would be a gentlemen's agreement between you and me. I have there $10,000 and a credit card that I want you to use as you see fit to find Peterson. Stay in the best hotels, eat the best food, fly first class, but find that murdering scum. And when you do, bring him back."

His intense brown eyes had gone cold, his voice lowered with intensity as he stared at Halloran.

"I had put away more than $150,000 for Jenny's law school, and an equal amount for her wedding. There was a trust fund set up for grandchildren. I will never use that money, but I want you to use whatever means you need to find Peterson and bring him back. I will use all the power that I can muster with the White House and with our senators to make this happen if you find him and we run into any international complications."

The State's Attorney then detailed how he had personally researched and found the law dealing with international arrests and extradition a murky area. The U.S. Marshal and the FBI had both assured him that if Peterson somehow arrived at an American Embassy or Consulate anywhere, he would be taken into custody, and the embassy and the State Department would deal with whatever red tape had to be cut and ruffled feathers had to be smoothed to bring Peterson back.

He told Halloran how both federal agencies reminded him of the years-long battle it took to bring murder suspect Ira Einhorn back to Philadelphia to stand trial. Cavaretta finished his caveat, then stopped for a moment, leaned back and stared into the detective's eyes.

"What do you say, Mike?"

Halloran cleared his throat and opened the envelope, briefly riffling the stack of hundreds. His eyes strayed from the money to the photo of a smiling Jenny Cavaretta perched in a frame atop a cabinet behind the State's Attorney. He leaned forward slightly and put the palms of his hands on Cavaretta's desk.

"I know I let you down by letting him slip away the first time. It will not--I repeat-- not, happen again." Halloran's face flushed crimson at the thought of Peterson's escape and his partner's near murder.

"Mike, I'm not a cop, but I've been engaged in this stuff for many years, and neither I, nor anyone in authority at the police department, believe you are responsible for Peterson's escape. It could have happened to anyone. And the truth of the matter is that 99.9 percent of the detectives would never have figured out he did it in the first place.

"The further truth and the essential fact is that you are reputed to be the best detective on the force. I believe it. So, I say –go detect. Find him, bring him back, and don't worry about time or money or legal niceties. Is it a deal?"

"Yeah, damn right it's a deal. I appreciate your confidence, Tom, and tell your good wife I won't disappoint her either," Halloran said, unconsciously calling the State's Attorney by his first name for the first time.

"She knows you won't, Mike. She knows you won't. And I do, too. I will keep in touch with you by email. Right now, I have feelers out with the Secret Service for credit card use anywhere in the world by a Harry Peters. That is the name on a forged Canadian passport the feds believe Peterson bought in Pilsen, at one of those fake document joints," Cavaretta said.

Cavaretta said the federal authorities had put a red flag with the credit companies for any charges from any of the locations found on the searches on Pritchard's computer. His contact promised a call—day or night—for any hits out of New Delhi, Agra, Calcutta, Kathmandu or Darjeeling.

"We don't know where he's going for sure, but India's a big place and this might help," Cavaretta said.

"Thanks, anything will help," Halloran said.

With that the two shook hands on a deal that both knew might skirt the far limits of the law.

CHAPTER 35

Walking through the Criminal Courts building with $10,000 in cash, Halloran was acutely aware that a fair number of the people he was passing entering and leaving the building would gleefully blow him away for half the money he had in the envelope.

He subconsciously felt for his gun, much the way he did in the morning when he patted his back pocket to check for his wallet.

Beneath the Indian Consulate in the Wrigley Building, Halloran double-parked on Lower Michigan, ran into Citibank to deposit the cash, and then went up to the consulate to pick up his Irish passport. (He held dual citizenship thanks to a quirk in the Irish law that granted him an Irish passport because his grandmother immigrated from County Galway in 1893.) He would travel Irish, not American.

A svelte Indian woman in a maroon sari with gold trim stood behind the counter at the consulate and passed his Irish passport back to him.

"Enjoy your trip, Mr. Halloran. Have you been to India before?" Gita Gupta asked.

"Yes, but it's always a pleasure to go back."

"You have seen the Taj on your last trip?"

"By full moon. It's a rare treasure," Halloran replied.

Gupta laughed.

"You are a most knowledgeable tourist. Enjoy."

It had been a quarter century since he had been in India, and he was sure much had changed. But he was equally sure that much remained the same.

Back in his car with passport in hand, he tried Egan. After getting her voicemail three times, he left a brief message about the trip, but then decided to make the 20-minute drive back out to 26th Street, taking lower Wacker Drive.

The sheriff's deputies were changing shift as he pulled into the employees' lot at the courthouse complex, so he got a good parking spot, no small bonus. At the courthouse entrance, he flashed his badge at the deputies, who nodded at him and went back to their discussion of the Sox chances this season.

As he got in the elevator to go to Egan's 13th floor office, a young black man about 21 with corn rows and a goatee got on with him. He was about 5'8" and wore leather Nikes. He looked at Halloran smiled, then shook his head looking down at the ground, then up at Halloran.

"Man, if I had your size, I'd be in the NBA," the youth said, laughing.

"Man, if I had your skin, I'd be in the NBA," Halloran responded.

They both laughed. Then the elevator doors opened at the Public Defender's floor.

"How tall are you, big man?" the youth asked as he exited the elevator.

As the doors began to close, Halloran said, "Five foot, seventeen and a half."

He found Egan at her cluttered desk just slamming the phone down.

"And how are you today, detective?"

"Better than you, I'd guess."

"That? That's nothing. The PD is always hassling us to agree to a continuance. So, sometimes yes, but not when a case is two years old, no way."

"Counselor, got time for a late lunch at Nuevo Leon?"

"Geez, Mike, bad day. I just wolfed down a mangy salad from the ptomaine palace on the second floor, and I have to be in the grand jury in 15 minutes. Ever hear of calling ahead?" Egan said, no malice and eyes twinkling. The office was now empty, so she reached over and grabbed Halloran's right knee for a moment. Halloran spoke first.

"I solemnly swear that the testimony I am about to give before this honorable court will be the truth, the whole truth and nothing but the truth, so help me God. I called before and after I swam, and you were doing then what you were doing when I just walked in. Gabbing on the phone. I left a message."

"I wasn't trading recipes with a neighbor. It's been a busy day. But I got the message about this trip. And Dunne briefed me, but I want to hear all about the trip. How about a rain check?"

"I'll take that, but it may be a while. I may be taking off as early as tomorrow. Got my Glenfiddich bait, thanks to my partner's research, and the office is arranging the plane tickets," he said.

"You've got my email address, cell phone number, and I want to stay in touch while you're there—both professionally and personally." Egan took her hand off the knee as she spied one of her colleagues wheeling in an evidence cart.

"You got it, counselor, and I may need further guidance on this."

Egan's phone rang. She grabbed it, then waved at the departing Halloran.

On the way back to his car, Halloran reviewed his conversation with Egan. He wondered if there was a subtext. It was what he had always wondered in the 30 years he had been dating.

Does "no" mean "No, I'm not interested?" Or "No, I'm' interested but truly busy."

Enough, he thought. *I got a killer to catch.*

CHAPTER 36

In more than two decades of flying, Halloran silently envied and cursed those who pampered themselves in the large leather seats with the limitless legroom in first class whenever he passed them on his way to the cramped coach seats. But for this flight, he had taken the State's Attorney at his word and got a first-class seat to New Delhi, a logical starting point and the place where his contact at the embassy resided, Christopher Grimshaw. *Could it be any waspier? Halloran wondered.*

Settling into seat 5 B on the aisle, Halloran stretched his legs. His knees were two feet away from the seat in front of him. In coach, he was always sandwiched in with his knees right up against the seat in front of him. Almost without exception, the person in front of him would try to move their seat back but would meet the stiff and unyielding opposition of Halloran's knees.

But on this eight-hour flight on Air India to London, he would suffer no such hassles. He took out his favorite author, Michael Connelly, and started reading *Chasing the Dime.*

Somewhere over Canada, he guessed, the flight attendant appeared with a bottle of champagne. Dinner came somewhere over the Atlantic, a tasty sole dish, and they had Guinness. *God love the freedom-loving Indians who threw off the yoke of John Bull a generation after the Irish made him feel unwanted in the 26 counties,* he thought. After a long layover at London's Heathrow, Halloran boarded his 8-hour flight to New Delhi. He slept fitfully, but better than he would have if he had been in coach.

At Delhi, he passed quickly through customs, where his Irish passport with his India visa was stamped and his declarations inspected and initialed. After he picked up his sole bag, he was slowed briefly for a tedious inspection by an officious female police officer, who shook out every piece of clothing, including his underwear.

Then she repacked it casually and put a chalk mark on the bag before signaling him to the next checkpoint. He handed the declarations form to an immigrations officer, who asked the purpose of his trip.

"I've come to see the Taj and visit Varanasi."

"You will be too much enjoying Varanasi, Meester Halloran. It is best place." The officer grinned, then stamped the form. And in a few moments, Halloran was into the early morning light of Delhi, a teeming city of more than 12 million souls.

It was just past dawn, 6 a.m., but the morning traffic was thick with bicyclists, cabs, private cars, trucks, rickshaws, motorized three-wheeled rickshaws, and pedestrians bundled against the early morning chill. The stench of diesel fuel hung in the air like an early morning fog on Lake Michigan.

Halloran threw his bag into the back seat of a taxi, leaned back in his seat and directed the taxi-wala to the Ashoka Hotel, the magnificent red sandstone relic of the Raj in New Delhi. He had again taken Cavaretta at his word and booked into the fine hotel, where two decades earlier he had splurged on a beer in the hotel bar and then sneaked into the pool for a swim.

At the Ashoka entrance, a tall Sikh with a glistening beard, red turban and handsomely crisp white tunic opened the taxi door.

"Welcome to the Ashoka, sahib."

"Thank you," Halloran said as he grabbed his bag at the same time the Sikh made a move for it.

India, what a trip, Halloran thought. *Immutable.*

After checking in, Halloran was escorted to a posh room with a second-floor view of the sprawling grounds, flowering rhododendron and shimmering pool—Olympic size as he remembered it. After a leisurely swim, he unpacked and read some Connelly before an early lunch. By 1 p.m., it was back to a little Connelly before he crashed.

Nice, very posh, Halloran thought. *He closed his eyes to welcome sleep but thoughts of Peterson disappearing into the traffic on Grand Avenue dominated his thoughts.*

If you're here, you're mine. I'm coming, Halloran vowed before exhaustion overcame him.

CHAPTER 37

The chowkidar's tap in the hallway awoke Halloran at 3:45 a.m. At first, he was disoriented in the complete darkness. He had been sleeping for 15 hours.

After showering and dressing, he ventured out into the dimly lit hallway. Squatting flatfooted on their haunches in the hallway were five chowkidars, or night watchmen, who raised their hands in the prayer-like gesture of namaste, the Indian equivalent of "Hi. How are you?"

Halloran nodded to them and made his way down to the lobby. A sole clerk was at the front desk.

"Is the coffee shop open?"

"No, Mr. Halloran. It will open at 5:30 a.m."

Back in his room, he pored over his notes, but nodded off until 6. He read a little more Connelly for an hour, then found the coffee shop for a quick cup of very strong coffee before jumping into the empty pool as soon as it opened.

By 8 a.m., he had found a cash machine for some rupees and had caught a cab, asking the driver to take him to the "Amreekan Embassy." The driver turned out to have a fairly expansive English vocabulary and started telling Halloran of all the wonderful tourist sites he could show the visitor.

As they drove through the rush-hour traffic, Halloran was struck by the sheer number of people in the Indian capital. They passed a commuter bus, where young men in crisp white shirts, tight pants and slicked-back hair clung to the hang bars by the rear doors of a bus packed so tightly that Halloran doubted anyone could raise their hand from their side. *Good place for a pickpocket, he mused.*

Gliding into the embassy's circular driveway, he pulled out his photo of Peterson and began work.

"Have you seen this man? He's an old friend I think was here last month," Halloran said, thrusting the photo into the front seat.

The driver studied the photo. It was a picture of Peterson that had appeared in the Sun-Times at his lawyer's office shortly after his release from prison. Peterson was smiling and hoisting a bottle of Miller Lite in salute. Frank Marone had given Halloran an 5x7 glossy copy shortly before he left, a withdrawal from the favor bank.

"No, sahib, not seeing. But I help look." The driver's name was V.N. Kakar and looked a little like an Indian version of Lou Costello, but with the perfunctory mustache affected by Indian men. He held out his card to Halloran, smiling and nodding.

"Thanks—V.N." Halloran eyed the card. "I may call on your services." Halloran gave his newfound friend a generous tip, more than 50 rupees beyond the 250 rupees that showed on the meter. Walking up the polished grey granite stairs to the embassy's glittering glass doors, it was impossible to miss the stark contrast between rich and poor. A woman of about 50, perhaps younger, dressed in a dirty yellow choli, or blouse, and a tattered and stained maroon sari was sweeping fallen banyan tree leaves from the embassy's patio. She didn't look up as Halloran passed.

Inside, he was met by a young Marine, dressed in his perfectly pressed tan shirt, blue dress pants with red stripes down the side and a white cap. A .45 semi-automatic hung at his hip.

"Good morning, sir," the Marine said. His nameplate revealed his name was Carter, his two stripes on his arm showed he was a corporal.

"Good morning, Corporal Carter. I'm here to see Deputy Consul Grimshaw. He's expecting me. My name's Mike Halloran." The young Marine, maybe 22, phoned Grimshaw's office, then informed Halloran that Grimshaw would be right down.

"Help yourself to the water, sir. It's safe here." The Marine nodded to the water cooler against the far wall.

At this point, Grimshaw appeared, blue pin-striped shirt, red tie, tasseled brown loafers, tortoise shell glasses, and a reserved air.

"Hi, Mike, I'm Chip Grimshaw. Has Corporal Carter been entertaining you?" Grimshaw extended his rather small, freckled and aristocratic right hand to Halloran.

"Nah, we were just chatting. Good luck to you, corporal." Halloran shook Grimshaw's hand, restraining himself from inflicting any version of the Gillespie Grip. Grimshaw's soft hand delivered a flaccid grasp. No surprise.

"How is the cooperation with the government?" Halloran opened.

"At the highest levels, it's very urbane and sophisticated officially, but when you start getting into the lower levels of the government you become enmeshed in the bureaucracy," Grimshaw smiled as they arrived in his small but smartly furnished office.

"You made a point of saying 'officially.' I detect there is an unofficial, less time-consuming way that things can happen."

"Ah, yes, you detect--like a good detective," Grimshaw said. "This is off the record, but let me tell you a story that may be illustrative:

"Four years ago, the British were looking for an IRA bomber who had fled to India, via the overland route to Istanbul, then a tramp steamer to Karachi and another boat to Bombay. Scotland Yard badly wanted this man for the bombing in Omagh in Northern Ireland.

"No one understands the Indian bureaucracy better than the Brits. Hell, they created it.

So, the Brits tracked this Irish fugitive to Goa, shanghaied him to the British High Commission in Bombay, landed a helicopter on the grounds and whisked him away to a British ship in the Indian Ocean.

"The Brits pump more than a billion pounds into their former colony each year in foreign aid--we give away 10 times that. So, the Indian government turned a blind eye to this circumvention of their law. It was viewed on high here in Delhi as some minor transgression, a little international big-footing, you might say."

He took a file folder out from his top drawer and pushed it across the desk.

Halloran opened it and found the names and addresses of the American Consulates in Bombay and Calcutta, in addition to the American Embassy in Kathmandu.

"If for some strange reason, you convinced this Peterson to appear at one of the consulates or at the embassies—which is American soil-- and we became aware of his fugitive presence, our Marines would take custody, and we would make arrangements for him to leave the country."

Well, thought Halloran, maybe he had misjudged Mr. Preppy.

"I don't know that I have ever shanghaied anyone before, but this is the Orient, sort of, so there's always a first." Halloran winked at Grimshaw. The deputy consul smiled, rose and extended his hand.

"I believe we understand each other. Mr. Cavaretta has great clout in Washington, to coin a Chicago word."

Outside, V.N. Kakar stood leaning against his taxi, but snapped to attention when he spotted his fare and potential meal ticket.

"Any service, sahib?" V.N. said, smiling and saluting the tall, generous foreigner.

Halloran jumped into the back seat of the beat-up black and yellow taxi.

"I could use a little help, my friend," Halloran said.

"I am in the service business, sahib," Kakar replied.

A plan was soon hatched.

CHAPTER 38

There had been no confirmation from any source that Peterson had continued north beyond Racine. But the nurse had said he asked about how much gas she had. That made Halloran think he was heading farther north. And Cavaretta had said Peterson was thought to have bought a Canadian passport on the black market in Pilsen. So, it was just a hunch, he knew, but he needed to talk to someone at the Canadian High Commission, the former British colony's version of an embassy.

Thoughtfully, Grimshaw had called ahead to his Canadian counterpart, John Watts, to set Halloran up. Relations were mostly sound and collegial between the two neighbors, and this was a wink-and-a-nod situation where the Canadians would be happy to cooperate off the record, especially if an American fugitive was traveling on a fake Canadian passport.

Once inside the high commission, Halloran slid Peterson's photo across Watts' desk.

"This is all unofficial, of course," Watts said, smiling.

"Of course," Halloran said. Watts studied the photo for a few moments, then said, "not someone I've seen. But I can show it around a bit to see if he has been here."

"Well, that's the only other copy I have with me now, so I'd rather not leave it." Halloran, an electronic luddite, drew a smile from the younger Watts.

"Not a problem." Watts reached into his top desk drawer and pulled out a Nikon digital camera. He put the photo down on his desk and snapped a picture. Then he connected his camera by cable to his computer, hit a few keys, and out printed a color copy of Peterson's likeness.

"Pretty slick." Halloran took the photo back.

"I'll show it around and get back to you. Where are you staying?"

"The Ashoka."

"Shabash. First class. My favorite. When my mum and da came last year, I put them up there. They loved it," Watts said.

"Other than the Ashoka, is there a particular hotel or guest house that the Canadians prefer?" Halloran asked.

"Of the posh hotels, it's the Ashoka or the Oberoi. Of the lower tiers, you might find the Lodi Hotel clean and adequate if you were a pensioner. The young backpackers like several guest houses near Connaught. The Ringo or the Sunny are two of the favorites. They're right near the tourist office."

"Thanks for your help and let me know if you find someone who saw this guy." Halloran handed Watts his card with his room number at the Ashoka on the back.

Outside, a beaming Kakar stood ready by his taxi, which had a sign on the dashboard reading "Out of station," a stretch of the old British term for indicating one was not in one's office, perhaps in the field, at lunch or for extended casual leave.

With Halloran in the back seat, Kakar took off with great speed to Connaught Place to the Ringo Guest House, presumably named for the Beatle, but not for sure. As he approached the front desk, Halloran could see several young travelers sitting around a verdant courtyard reading, smoking cigarettes and exchanging war—or travel-stories.

At the front desk was a matronly and plump woman in a green sari, her love handles flopping under her white choli.

"Good morning, ma'am. I wonder if you might be able to help me. I am looking for my cousin, and I believe he might've stopped here several weeks ago." Halloran slipped the photo forward with a 50-rupee note under it.

The woman looked first at Halloran, then the photo. She also spotted the edge of the note sticking out under the photo. She swept up both with a flourish, palming the note like an alderman about to fix a zoning issue.

"Good morning, sir. We are having so many young people coming here. I will look at your picture, yes."

Mrs. Suna Battacharjii looked at the photo, then took it into the office to show her husband, who shook his head.

"Not knowing. I am sorry. So many tourists, you know." She was smiling and shaking her head from side to side in that peculiar sub-continental way to signal a slight befuddlement.

Halloran took the photo back, and then asked, "Do you mind if I asked a couple of your guests about him?" The rupee notes still fresh in her mind, she again wagged her head side to side.

"I am sure they not mind. They are most friendly young people." Halloran ambled over to a couple discussing a possible trip to Kashmir in the hotel's courtyard. She said it was still too cold there, and he insisted it would be lovely with the snow on the ground. She started winning the argument when she mentioned the quality of the roads and the bus drivers negotiating hairpin turns.

"Hi, guys. Sorry to interrupt, but I'm looking for my cousin. He might've stayed here. Mind taking a look." Halloran held the photo out between them.

The young woman, British, braless with a white kurta top and purple pajamas, had obviously gone native. Her jet-black hair was cropped short, and her ears had as many studded earrings as they could handle. She was probably 22. She took the photo and studied it for a few seconds.

"He maybe has a stubby grey beard and a foul mouth?"

"Could be," Halloran said. "I haven't seen him in a couple months, so yeah, maybe a beard, and he's my vintage, so grey. Yeah, he swears a lot."

The woman's partner, a short, squat Aussie, with dirty blond hair down past his shoulders took the photo.

"Looks like Dirty Harry, eh?" he said.

"I think you're right. About time you were right about something. You ever been to Kashmir?" she asked, turning back to Halloran.

"No, never been to Kashmir. Where did you see Dirty Harry and when?" Halloran asked. "I got 100 rupees for the right answer." He held the note against his chest.

"Easy C-note. Agra, the Taj, mate, or on the way there--to be precise --about two-three weeks ago." The guy leaned over and reached for the rupee note. Halloran pulled back and asked, "How long did you talk with him?"

"Man, he joined us in third-class. Foul mouth—fucking this and cocksucker that-- and a little on the grungy side for an old guy, you know?"

"Say how long he was going to stay in Agra or where he might be headed after that?"

"Asked us about Benares, Varanasi, you know. Asked about Calcutta, too, and Darjeeling. What a trip Calcutta is. Don't bother with that unless you want to pay a pilgrimage to Mother Teresa," the Aussie said.

"Full of shit, too. Said his name was Harry and he was from Vancouver. But when I asked him where he lived in Vancouver, he got all defensive and goes, 'Who cares where I live?' Well, I did. I know that very cool city and was just making conversation on the train. Later, when I saw him walking in front of us near the Taj, and called out to him, 'Hey, Harry' from across the street, and he didn't even turn around," she said.

"See any tattoos on him? My cousin has a pretty distinctive tattoo."

"Yeah, I got nothing against tats. Been thinking about one of those barbed wire doohickeys for my bicep. But he had what looked like a scorpion or dragon, snaking onto his lower wrist. Weird," Australia said.

Bingo, thought Halloran.

He leaned forward and dropped the 100-ruppee note on the lad's lap. As Halloran dropped his lucre, the young man pulled out a joint and lit up. He took a deep drag and passed it to his traveling companion. She shook her head.

"You?" He held the joint toward Halloran.

"No thanks, my man. I've always thought that expanding my mind would be like trying to inflate the Goodyear blimp indoors."

The girl burst out laughing. The guy scratched his goatee.

"Okay, cool," he said.

Cool is right, Halloran thought. *My man is here. But India was still a big place.*

CHAPTER 39

The Poorva Express makes the run from Delhi to Varanasi across the vast Indian state of Uttar Pradesh in just under 13 hours. Indian Airlines flies daily in less than two hours, but the hassle of getting a ticket is sometimes not worth the trouble, so counseled Grimshaw.

Since it had been several weeks ago that "Dirty Harry" had been inquiring about Varanasi, Halloran reasoned that Peterson probably had seen enough of Varanasi and moved on to Calcutta.

So, a three-hour flight brought him to perhaps the most overcrowded and depressing city in the world, one-third the geographic size of Chicago with four times as many people. At the Oberoi Grand, Halloran checked in, dropped his bag in his room, and went down to the lobby in search of the manager. In short order, he found Mr. Sharma, who welcomed Halloran into his office off the ornate Victorian lobby.

"I'm P.T. Sharma, acting manager of the hotel. How may I be of service?" The man sounded more like he was from Highland Park than Hyderabad.

"Whoa. Where'd you get that accent?" Halloran asked.

"Sounds like the same place you got yours. Chicago. I was born and raised in Hyde Park, then went to Michigan undergrad and back to Hyde Park for graduate school at the University of Chicago."

"I'm Mike Halloran. I'm a North Sider but I don't get lost in Hyde Park." It sounded so foreign to be talking about sides of town on the other side of the world, but Sharma loved it.

"Sox fan or Cub fan?" Sharma asked.

"I hate baseball. So slow."

"Please join me for a drink at the bar. My treat." Sharma didn't wait for an answer, leading Halloran into the dimly lit lounge.

"Beer. Whiskey?" Sharma asked. Halloran opted for a beer.

"We got Beck's, Bass Ale and Heineken," Sharma asked.

"Beck's is good," replied the American/Irishman.

Sharma ordered two Beck's and guided Halloran to a booth with a window overlooking the patio and pool.

"Now, my fellow Chicagoan, how can I help?" Halloran pulled out the photo and slid it across the table toward his host. Sharma's eyes flashed immediate recognition.

"This baadmash stayed with us for two days and left about three days ago. Very surly, got very drunk right here in this bar. But he had money and paid cash. Only good thing was he was Canadian, at least that's what his passport said."

Then this courtly Brahman grew slightly wary, his eyes narrowed, and he looked across at Halloran.

"Why are you looking for him?"

"Paternity case. He's got a lot of money, and I'm being paid to find him. Can't get into any more than that." Halloran was just tempted for a moment to level with this Chicago transplant, but he knew that the fewer people who knew what he was doing there, the better.

"I see. Well, cheers, and tell me how our city has been doing. I've been gone for three years."

Over three more beers, Halloran discovered that Sharma's sister was married to a State Representative and their parents still lived near 54th and Cornell in Chicago. They played a little of "do you know?" and found they knew a few folks in common.

Halloran made a judgment that it would not be wise to try to compromise Sharma with a little baksheesh in pursuit of information. But he wanted the manager's help and cooperation.

"Look, P.T., I won't try to bullshit you. You're too sharp for that. I can only tell you that I am here on an honorable mission, and this man is dishonorable, immoral, even truly evil. I would like a little help that I think won't compromise you."

What Halloran wanted and what Sharma acquiesced to was to see if there were any phone calls from Peterson's room that might give a clue to where he was headed.

They repaired to Sharma's office, and the manager sent a peon for the receipts from the days Peterson had stayed in Room 303. The name on the room bill was Harry Peters, the likely alias adopted by Eric Peterson, and not too clever either, Halloran thought.

"This guy registered as a Canadian, from Vancouver. He your guy?"

"He's a perpetual liar."

Sharma studied the bill. Peterson ate several meals and drank up quite a tab at the bar. There were only two calls. One was to London and the other was a call inside India, placed the day before he left. Sharma told Halloran he could not tell exactly where the call in India went to, except the number was somewhere in West Bengal.

"Can you call the number from this phone?" Halloran asked, holding up his cell.

"But of course. Our telecommunications have vastly improved in the past 10 years. That's why when you call for computer help in Chicago, the 800 number hooks you up to some helpful young lady in Bangalore. What a world."

Looking at the number Sharma held, Halloran dialed. It rang three times before a woman answered.

"Windamere Hotel. May I help you?"

"Hi. This might seem like a strange question, but where are you located?"

"No, not strange. We are just above the main mall right in the center of town on Observatory Hill. A vigorous walk up, my dear."

"I'm sorry. What town?"

"Why Darjeeling, of course. Do you need a reservation?"

"Well, I'm not sure I'm coming and don't want to commit just yet. Do I need one? I mean, is this your busy season?"

"Not really. Just let us know the day before you arrive. We will have room this month, for sure."

"Thanks." Halloran hung up and turned back to Sharma.

"How far is Darjeeling?"

"By plane, you can catch a small plane to Siliguri. Then it's about five hours by Land Rover, or eight if you take the narrow-gauge railroad. But I wouldn't recommend that—too smoky and slow. But what a beautiful place."

Mindful that he didn't want to risk his life on a tiny plane but see the scenery along the way, Halloran asked how long it would take by car to get from Calcutta.

"The scenery will not be so interesting until after Siliguri, but if you want to get a car and driver, I can arrange it, my friend. It would take maybe 18 hours to get to Darjeeling from here. It was the old summer resort during the Raj for the British to retreat from the Calcutta heat. Darjeeling makes the Grand Tetons look like molehills with powdered sugar on top. You'll love Darjeeling."

What I will love, Halloran thought, *is to catch Jenny Cavaretta's killer.*

CHAPTER 40

By sunrise, Halloran met the driver Sharma had found for him, Hira Lal (which means diamond ruby, he told Halloran), waiting in the lobby. Halloran jumped in the rear of a dated Land Rover before Lal took off from the Oberoi in a game of dodge-em, narrowly missing pedestrians, cows, rickshaws, buses and taxis. Halloran winced as Lal missed by centimeters a bicyclist pedaling to work, clutching his lunch in a sealed brass container. It was easier to look out the side window than watch the game of chicken unfolding in front of him.

Gazing out the window, he marveled as the sheer volumes of humans bustling to and fro. The air was thick with fuel exhaust belched out by overloaded and ancient buses, three-wheeled motorized rickshaws and aging taxis.

Lal whisked Halloran off to the American Consulate for his scheduled meeting with deputy consul William Prentiss. The nondescript grey building sat in one of the few nice sections of Calcutta.

On the 10-foot-wide strip of concrete that passed as a sidewalk leading to the Consulate, Halloran was besieged by beggars. A blind woman in a tattered blue sari held her empty hand up to Halloran as her armless, shoeless and shirtless son danced for baksheesh.

As he passed them, a man with elephantiasis wheeled his testicles, the size of watermelons, past in a wheelbarrow. He nodded to Halloran, who kept walking. A leper with filthy bandages around his fingerless hands sat on the sidewalk with a small copper bucket in front of him just yards from the entrance to the Consulate. Just before entering the inner sanctum of the Consulate, Halloran dropped 20 rupees in the bucket.

"Dhaniwad, sahib." The leper had a hole in his face where his nose once was. Halloran felt an involuntary shiver.

"Thank you, God," he murmured as he hurried by.

Inside the air-conditioned Consulate, a Marine who looked no older than 20 sat rigidly at a front reception desk. Halloran asked for Prentiss, who had been fully briefed on Halloran's mission. It was just a matter of seconds before the deputy consul appeared and greeted him with a firm handshake.

"Mike, nice to meet you. Coffee?"

Prentiss was about Halloran's age, with jet black hair. Tanned and fit, he was a head shorter than Halloran. Prentiss looked like he was ready for a suburban barbecue, dressed casually in a lime green polo shirt, khaki pants, and topsiders with tan socks.

"Black would be great."

"What do you think of Calcutta?"

"Every street looks like Michigan Avenue after the Bulls won the championship. It's a bit overwhelming," Halloran said.

"First trip to Calcutta then?"

"Yeah. Been to India before, but this is the first time in Calcutta. Old Delhi is crowded, but this place is incredibly worse."

"My first week in Calcutta, a couple of years back, I ran into an old Brit who stayed on after the Raj. Been here for 60 years. Summed it up a bit crudely this way: 'Too many fucking people, and too many people fucking.'"

Getting beyond the preliminaries, Halloran told Prentiss that he had good reason to believe that Peterson was in Darjeeling.

"Don't be surprised to see Eric Peterson here in the next 24 to 48 hours. I understand arrangements have been made. Is that right?" Halloran asked.

"How you get him back here is, of course, none of my business and don't want it to be. I am sure you will be persuasive or at least discreet. But I can say that if he were to show up here at the consulate, he would be on American soil. The deal that your very persistent Assistant State's Attorney, Ms. Egan, worked out with my boss at Foggy Bottom is that the Navy would have an Easy Rider SH-60B Seahawk helicopter land in our baseball field here in the consulate compound and whisk Mr. Peterson off to the U.S.S. Crommelin in international waters in the Bay of Bengal. From there, he will be taken to Guam and flown back to Chicago."

"And what about the Indian authorities?" Halloran asked.

"We have given this country tens of billions of dollars in foreign aid over the past 10 years alone. We're asking for a favor. They're pretending the conversation has not taken place. The wink and a nod are known in the East, too, my friend. Take this cell phone and call me anytime day or night to let me know you're coming. Punch 1 on the speed dial. That's me. Once you call. I can get the chopper here in two hours, 24 hours a day. This case has got a lot of heat."

"Kind of like this country."

"God lord, this? It was 91 yesterday. That's nothing. Try late June when it's 117 and so dry the dust hangs in the air so thick you can hardly make out the streetlights, just the bats."

"I hope I'll be long gone by then, but sounds charming," Halloran said. The two shook hands again, and Halloran walked out to find Lal parked nearby.

Despite going from one air-conditioned enclave to another, Halloran was soaked with sweat, picked up perhaps in the 50-yard stretch outside the Consulate to the Land Rover.

"Darjeeling," Halloran said.

Coming for you, shithead.

CHAPTER 41

Just past the village of Ghoom, Mt. Kanchenjunga lurched into view. At 28,169 feet, it's the third-tallest mountain in the world.

Hira Lal pulled the Land Rover over to the side of the road, adjacent to the narrow-gauge railroad tracks that led up to Darjeeling. It was time for Lal's tea. It was also time for Halloran to stare at Kanchenjunga across the wide valley, across verdant, stepped tea plantations. Lesser mountains branched out on either side, like the supporting cast spread out on the stage flanking an opera diva.

The air was cool and crisp, with the usual lingering smell of burning dung fuel in the air. Once they had started ascending from Siliguri, Halloran had noticed that the people began to look more Oriental. The strong influence of the Tibetans and the Nepali hill people could be seen in the faces of the children, beautiful even with their runny noses. The people here were also poor, but they carried themselves with a quiet dignity and their rosy cheeks shrieked vitality and well-being.

Pointing to Kanchenjunga, Lal said, "Lord Shiva is living there."

"Nice digs, fit for a god."

"Sorry, sahib. Digs?"

"Nothing."

Halloran was deep in thought as they neared Darjeeling. Halloran's plan was vague and had to be flexible. Halloran planned to strike up a conversation with Peterson, offer to buy him a drink at the bar, order Glenfiddich, then at the opportune time say it was stupid to pay the hotel when he had a perfectly good bottle of the stuff in his room. From there, he would set the trap to dupe his quarry.

The problem was Halloran had no idea if Peterson had made him in the chase that ended at Grand and Ashland. He thought it all happened too fast for Peterson to have gotten a good look at him when their cars screeched to a halt by the bus. Seemed a million miles and years away to Halloran.

But now Halloran had a two-week growth of beard and had not cut his hair for six weeks. He was looking a little shaggy. *At worst,* he thought, *I might be taken for a narc in Chicago by an edgy street dealer, but not here.*

Every time Lal rounded a bend and Kanchenjunga loomed up anew, Halloran was startled. The blue of the sky was stark, and the snow atop the mountains hurt the eyes, it was so white. Along the sides of the road leading to the hill station were hundreds of white Tibetan prayer flags flapping in the cool mountain breeze.

Pulling into Darjeeling, Halloran noticed the haphazard way the buildings were clinging to the hillside like grazing yaks. Little children chased metal rings down the street with sticks, a cheap amusement in a poverty-stricken land. In the middle of town, he spotted a sign that read "Himalayan Mountaineering Institute" and pointed down the road. Another sign read "Windamere Hotel" and pointed up a long series of crisscross stairs leading to the top of Observatory Hill. The Land Rover pulled up under the sign.

"Must be walking from here, sahib," Lal said, nodding up toward the hotel.

Halloran grabbed his bag and began a 75-foot ascent.

A smiling woman of about 50 dressed in a dark red sari, an emerald choli with a black shawl welcomed Mr. Michael Hanlon, the pseudonym Halloran had come up with on the spur of the moment when he made the reservation. He paid Pubitra Patel in cash for one night but said he might be leaving the next day for some trekking.

"I ran into a guy in Delhi who said he might be coming here. Just wondered if he might have arrived before me." Halloran then went into a short description of Peterson, figuring that there couldn't be too many Americans of his age in town.

"Oh, yes, Mr. Michael. He was with us for two days but has now gone trekking to Sandakphu. We expect Mr. Harry back tomorrow early afternoon. He left most of his things with us."

Halloran felt like jumping up and down and shouting, but said simply, "Good, he can tell me all about it. But do me a favor, don't mention I asked about him. I want to surprise him."

"No, no, Mr. Michael. Not mentioning, please." Pubitra showed Halloran to a small but comfortable room, distinguished only by the claw-footed bathtub and thick down comforters on the queen bed. No pool here, he lamented.

As Pubitra was about to leave, Halloran pressed a 200-rupee into her palm, saying cryptically, "I appreciate your help." He figured the small favor of not mentioning his inquiry was sealed by the baksheesh.

He put his bottle of Glenfiddich on the dresser next to a water jug and two glasses set atop a lace napkin.

After a lunch of rogan josh, white rice and a naan, washed down by the local beer, Tongba, Halloran stretched out on a lawn chair on one of two verandas overlooking the valleys on either side of Observatory Hill. Kanchenjunga had now disappeared in clouds that had drifted in and swallowed up much of the town below.

It was surreal as Halloran looked down at the clouds, like being in an airplane, floating above the town. After reading for a while, he headed down to the bazaar. Lal had checked in to the New Elgin Hotel, but the Land Rover was parked where he left it at the base of the stairs. Lal had already sold him on getting up before dawn to go to Tiger Hill to watch the sun rise and hit the Himalayas in spectacular fashion. It was overcast and a slight chill hung in the air, so Halloran bought a thick woolen sweater from a Tibetan woman squatting down on the road with her wares splayed out across an old Army blanket. Amazingly, he found one that fit and after some preliminary price jousting, settled at less than $20. A bargain for him and no doubt a good deal for her.

As he paid, a young boy of about 10 approached holding a Gurkha knife called a kukri.

"Chops off head of yak, sahib. Zap. Plop. For you, best price, 500 rupees for best kukri." It was a handsome curved blade, about 15 inches long, hefty, encased in a dark leather scabbard.

"Now why would I want to whack the head off a yak who did nothing to me?"

"Because you are Amreekan. And they love meat. Not like Hindus," the lad said.

"Your English is very good. Where did you learn it?"

"I am student at missionary school. The nuns are Franciscans from Canada. They never hit you unless you are very naughty. And then it is with love from Jesus," young George Gupta said.

"Some things don't change, my little friend. But I know that I can buy a knife like this for 100 rupees. Why would you charge so much?"

As he spoke, Halloran recalled how Peterson used a knife for the triple killing and an ice pick to kill Jenny Cavaretta. *A shank on inmate Ramos. Maybe he didn't need a gun. This would do just fine.*

Halloran took the knife from young George and started to unsheathe it.

"No, sahib. Don't take it out unless you will use it. Bad karma. If you take it out and don't draw blood, the blade will wind up turning on you. Old Gurkha legend."

With that, the boy took the kukri back and unsheathed it. He pricked his index finger with the razor-sharp blade and handed it to Halloran.

"Now, good karma. How about 250?" Halloran laughed and took the lethal-looking weapon from George. It had a good heft to it.

"Ever lopped off a yak's head with one of these?"

"No, no, sahib. That is just sales pitch. The angrez tourists love the image."

"You've sold me, my friend." Halloran pulled out 300 rupees and handed it to the boy.

"I have no change, sahib, but I get some. Just be waiting here one moment."

"That's all right. The extra fifty is for your drawing blood for my good luck and for telling me your name and age."

"George Gupta. I am 11. I am Christian. Hindu father, Christian mother. She won religious battle."

"At last, a good holy war with no casualties. Nice doing business with you, George." Halloran roughed up the boy's jet-black hair, then George ran off.

A kukri? Perfect weapon for this scumbag. He was set for tomorrow. For his long-sought prey.

When he repaired to his room after wolfing down a spicy goat curry, Halloran was met by the night maid exiting his room.

"Sleep well, sahib."

In his bedding, she had slipped a hot water bottle to warm up the countless comforters piled on his bed. She left a pitcher of tea on the nightstand. He could see his breath outside, and now, with the sun down, inside, too.

After he took a pull of Glenfiddich for a nightcap, He jumped into bed and grabbed Connelly to escape for a while. Lal had promised to be by at 5 a.m., and Pubitra promised coffee by 4:45 a.m. It had been a hard few days, and Halloran was exhausted.

Though it was only 8:15 p.m., Halloran turned out the light and listened to the eerie stillness of the high Himalayan night. He thought of his partner, his erstwhile girlfriend, his quarry. His life. It was a good life, he decided contentedly. Then drifted off to a sound sleep.

When he heard a knock at his door, Halloran leaped to his feet, uncertain in the darkness for a moment where he was. It was 4:45.

"Coffee, sahib."

That brought Halloran swiftly back to reality. He was tense and ready, then he realized why. He might just find his killer this day. He quickly dressed, forgoing the bath until later when he could no longer see his breath in the room. He gulped down his coffee, then exited to find Lal waiting on the verandah sipping tea, the more civilized breakfast drink in the epicenter of Indian tea country.

The sky in the east was just beginning to show pink signs of light.

"Think it will be good day to see mountains, sahib," Lal said.

Lal preceded Halloran down the steps in the darkness, shining his "torch" backward to make sure his boss didn't break his neck on the way to Tiger Hill.

A 10-minute drive brought them to a bend in a turn at the top of one of the Himalayan foothills. There were three other tourist groups already there, all Indians bundled up against the cold in thick coats and blankets. Halloran had just his new sweater over his button-down blue shirt.

As it got lighter, the group began to chatter expectantly. As the sun rose slowly into a cloudless sky, it shone over their heads and hit the far mountains first.

"There, sahib. That one, the orange one, is Everest. See the sun hits the tallest mountain first. Lal was pointing past Kanchenjunga.

And sure enough, there was one mountain among a series of peaks that turned orange while the rest surrounding it and in front were still whitish blue. Slowly, in a matter of minutes, all the rest of the snow-capped, bluish mountains then began to turn a shade of orange. Finally, almighty Kanchenjunga was hit by the morning sun, and its massive shoulders erupted into orange first, then a brilliant white as the sun rose higher in the morning sky.

"How far is Everest?" Halloran asked.

"About 150 kilometers." Halloran turned from Lal to face an elegantly dressed older Hindu gentleman who was wrapped tightly in a bright green scarf. "And Kanchenjunga may look close enough to touch but it's 50 kilometers across the valley."

"Thank you, sir." Halloran wished he had taken a camera with him but remembered that there were slides of this sight for sale in the bazaar. Now he had to remember to buy one.

The hill town was coming to life as they made their way back to the hotel. They passed a young man in a lungi and white t-shirt squatting down by a street spigot, brushing his teeth with a tree twig, the kind Halloran had seen for sale along the street in Delhi, six for a rupee.

After arranging for a hot bath to be drawn, Halloran had breakfast in the splendid old rustic dining room of the Windamere. They served him eggs over easy, with ham on the side, toast with mango marmalade and more coffee. Surrounded by tea plantations, Halloran felt a little guilty with his coffee, but hardly enough to forgo his morning ritual. Halloran was seated at a table by the window looking east, away from the bazaar and Kanchenjunga and across a series of tea terraces.

To kill some time, Halloran wandered around the town until 11:30, then started heading back to the hotel, winding his way through the roller coaster streets and back alleys. The 7,000-foot altitude and the walking had made Halloran a bit queasy, so he wasn't hungry for lunch. Nonetheless, he took up a spot in the dining room where he could see anyone coming up the path from the bazaar. He ordered a Darjeeling tea with lemon. Quite nice, he thought, feeling just a tad British.

Shortly after 1 p.m. a group started up the hill. Halloran leaned forward to get a better look. Three men and two women. The first two men were in their middle twenties, British, if he were to guess. Then coming up the trail, in short khaki pants, a Budweiser t-shirt and a sweater wrapped around his waist was Harry Peters, aka Eric Peterson, his scorpion tattoo in full view.

Gotcha, asshole. Now I just have to reel you in, Halloran thought.

Halloran watched as Peterson checked in at the front desk, spoke briefly to Pubitra, too briefly to have had a conversation about a stranger asking about him. He took his key, and marched off to room 9, just four doors down from Halloran.

After a few minutes, Peterson came out dressed in beat up Levis, a black sweatshirt and Nikes. He headed straight to the dining room and took a seat 30 feet from Halloran, overlooking the tea hills.

Halloran got up and casually walked out past the blooming rhododendron on the terrace and sat down on the verandah where he could keep an eye on the dining room door. He did not want to make contact until that evening. The more he controlled the conversation and the more limited it was, the less chance Peterson would get wise to him.

For most of the rest of the afternoon, Halloran kept what could best be described as "loose surveillance" of the prey he had been hunting for months. After lunch, Peterson had returned to his room and presumably took a nap, since he was in the room for two hours before he emerged later in the afternoon and set off for the bazaar. Halloran gave him a minute head start and then followed from a safe distance of about 200 yards. Easy to keep an eye on a white tourist.

When Peterson stopped to have a beer at the Hotel Sinclair, Halloran set up at a tea stall across the street and sipped some green tea for an hour from a rear booth. Peterson walked out with another westerner, then shook hands with him and took off back in the dusk toward the Windamere.

At the hotel, Peterson went to the bar and had a cigarette. Halloran watched from his room's front window with the lights out. By the time the sun set, Halloran walked back out and asked at reception when the buses and trains left for Siliguri in the morning, just in case his guy was thinking of leaving.

Now came a tricky part of the scheme, which was fluid and subject to change. He had gone over the details with Egan before he left. She had stressed: Don't do anything illegal; don't do anything the defense can use at trial; and don't get the Indian police involved "or we may have another Einhorn thing," referring again to the years-long struggle by Philadelphia to extradite Ira Einhorn from France.

The ideal scheme would be to somehow get Peterson to walk into the American Consulate on his own. But since Peterson was posing as a Canadian, why would he walk into the American Consulate? The reason had to be the same as for any other male who takes risk: money, drugs, or sex, or all three.

Halloran knew Peterson had a fondness for Glenfiddich. He also knew he would do drugs and had to still be horny after all those years in the joint. What was clear to Halloran was he would have to play Peterson, like any other shithead he was looking to outsmart. So, his plan was to wait until after dinner and then strike up a conversation with Peterson, and play it from there.

As luck would have it, Peterson was dining in at the Windamere. Halloran had coffee with dinner, but noticed Peterson was having what looked from the other side of the dining room like a Manhattan, the cherry on the stick being the tipoff. And he had another.

Perfect, Halloran thought. *Get drunk, asshole.*

Halloran waded through a perfectly tasty nilgai steak, a Himalayan antelope, with boiled potatoes and buttered carrots. The bill with tip was $6 American. He nursed a coffee while he pretended to read the Times of India newspaper.

After a while, Peterson got up and walked over to the bar, a short L-shaped job with 10 wooden stools with red leather seats surrounding it. A portrait of Queen Elizabeth stared down from atop the cash register. The Indian and British flags flanked her. It looked like the kind of pub where Rudyard Kipling might have tipped a pint of bitter--the place had been sitting atop Observatory Hill since 1882.

Halloran paid his bill, then sauntered over to the bar and plopped down three stools away from Peterson.

"Got Glenfiddich?" Halloran asked. Peterson's head jerked to attention. The bartender smiled ruefully.

"Not having, sahib. Two times in one night! We have JB, Bell's, Indian Whiskey."

"Yeah, I asked for the same stuff," Peterson said. "They got no class in India."

"I'll take Bell's straight up," Halloran said to the bartender. Then he looked to Peterson for the first time.

"American? Where from?"

"Close, but no cigar. Canadian. Vancouver. I get made for American all the time, so don't feel bad."

"Bartender, freshen my Canadian friend's drink up, will ya? You'll let me buy in pursuit of North American neighborliness, won't ya?"

"Hey, if I got a free drink every time I got made for an American, I'd be perpetually drunk." Halloran was now sure Peterson had not recognized him from the shoot-out that nearly cost Ortiz her life.

"Problem is we get taken down for what the government does, whether it's Vietnam, Iraq confiscatory taxes, throttling free enterprise or framing innocent dudes."

"That's kind of the way it looks from north of the border, too. Harry Peters," Peterson said, taking two steps and extending his hand. Halloran grabbed it but remained seated as he pushed the stool next to him out for Peterson.

"Mike Hanlon."

We're both liars, Halloran thought.

"How long you been in India?"

"Month or so. You?"

"A couple of weeks. This place is great, but Calcutta, hold onto your seat. Been there?"

"I'm on my way. Hear it's a trip."

"Yeah, never seen crowds like that, not even on St. Patty's Day in Boston. It's a place to pass through, not really visit, ya know?"

'You from there, Boston?"

"Well, sort of. My dad was Irish, from tinkers—gypsies, you know-- from Mayo. Mother an American from Boston. They split when I was three and they played ping-pong with me across the Atlantic for the next 15 years, half the time in Boston and half the time in Ireland. My brogue disappears in the States, and then gets resuscitated after a few weeks in Ireland. God help us," Halloran lapsing into a little faux brogue.

"And my Irish passport saves me some hassles."

For the next half hour, they made small talk about traveling and India and the Himalayas. Peterson recommended trekking up to Sandakphu. Halloran claimed his bad knee cashiered that.

Peterson bought the next round. Then it was Halloran's turn.

"Hey, instead of making these Indians rich, how about drinking my stuff? I got some Glenfiddich in my room. We can sit on the verandah and continue this rich bullshit."

"Can't argue with that."

As they adjourned towards Halloran's room, Halloran pictured the peregrine falcon swooping down on an unsuspecting pigeon.

Soon, I'll have you in my talons, and you will kill no more.

CHAPTER 42

Back in his room, Halloran grabbed the bottle of Glenfiddich and two glasses. The sun had set to the left of Kanchenjunga, and though still a bit cloudy, the sky was a spectacular orange set off by the white-capped Himalayan expanse.

"This must beat even the Canadian Rockies." Halloran settled into a rattan settee with dark red cushions next to Peterson and asked: "Been to Banff?"

"Never made it there, but I heard it's too cool."

"You come here on business or pleasure then?" Halloran asked.

"Sort of business, but I love Asia. Bangkok, Colombo, K'du, Bali. And there's money to be made, yeah."

"Money to be made. What are you into, man? Don't worry. I'm cool."

Halloran wanted to hint he played on the left side of the law to see where that took Peterson.

"See this?" Peterson asked, raising his sleeve to reveal his scorpion. "Got this from one of my homey artists in one of your joints in Illinois. Been out for a while, though."

"Looks pretty good for joint ink. I spent a little time in Leavenworth after a small disagreement with an MP, but I didn't want any artistry. Again, I've always been a little paranoid about diseases. No prison needle for me. No offense, man."

"That's cool. Hey, into anything you need help with?" Peterson asked, tilting his chin to the right and up.

"Maybe, maybe. I'm off to Calcutta tomorrow and then Colombo. You should see the star sapphires there. And cheap. You know these guys who smuggle blow in from Nigeria, Colombia, by swallowing that shit in rubbers? Stupid, man, and it can get the mule killed. And how you know they not gonna bolt on you?

"Now gems, stones, man. You can swallow $50,000 worth and shit 'em out the next day. And the man knows nothing, sees nothing," Halloran continued baiting, "they're so hung up on terrorists lately, you could smuggle an elephant in."

"Think about how many sapphires an elephant could swallow," Peterson chimed in, now on his eighth drink, by Halloran's count. Halloran held up his half-full glass.

"Here's to a little harmless larceny."

"I'll drink to that." Peterson reached over to clink glasses. Peterson was having a great time. Halloran was sober, calculating, and disgusted that he had to play this game to dupe this murderous scumbag.

"What about you, man? How come you're here? A little far from Vancouver, eh?"

"Hey, man, you know how it is. Ran into a little trouble with a bitch and needed a break."

"Me, I never get hung up on one. Wanderer, ya know. But a week back, I met a pretty stu for British Airways, a little kinky, into blow. Had a little party with her in Delhi and hooking up with her again tomorrow in Calcutta."

"She got a friend, Mike?"

"You never know. You heading to Calcutta, too?"

"I came up the narrow-gauge train from Siliguri, eight hours. But yeah, Calcutta's the next stop."

Too good to be true, Halloran thought.

"Well, fuck that train shit. You can catch a ride with me if you want to split tomorrow. I'm pulling out by 7 though. Gotta be back for a little R&R there, if you know what I mean."

"Cool, I'm always up early."

Yeah, thought Halloran, that's because the guards roust your no-good asses out of your bunks at dawn every day in the joint. Peterson continued to help himself to the Glenfiddich. Cavaretta's money couldn't have been spent in a better way, Halloran thought, though the State's Attorney never envisioned this use.

"So, what did the bitch do to you, and what did you do to the bitch?" Halloran broke into some forced laughter to put Peterson further at ease. Third-party admission, he thought, recalling some of Egan's advice. *"If he says anything even alluding to revenge, we could use it, Mike," Egan had counseled.* He knew that already, but it was worth hearing a prosecutor say it.

"Man, you know how it is. Someone fucks with you, you gotta fuck with them. Made that vow in the joint, ya know, man?" Peterson bragged, finishing off his drink but showing no sign of slowing down.

"I know, man. I had a guy in the joint thought I was going to be his Punchin' Judy." Halloran said. "Came up on me from behind in the shower and tried to slip it to me. Said sure, honey. Let me suck you first. Went down and bit half of his cock off. This is pre-Bobbitt, you know, so there was no surgical reconstruction. Flushed two inches down the toilet. Got me a little respect though, ya know."

"No shit? I love it, man. Those fucking queens," Peterson laughed.

Through the years, Halloran had spent enough time talking to cons, ex-cons and wanna-be cons to be able to sling the lingo with authenticity.

"You set things right with the bitch?" Halloran asked.

"That bitch ain't fuckin' with anyone no more. And her old man got a real lesson, too," Peterson grinned.

"Gotta drain the blue vein, man," Halloran said. "Be right back."

Inside, Halloran wrote down the exact words: "That bitch ain't fuckin' with anyone no more. And her old man got a real lesson, too." *Sounds like a confession to me,* Halloran thought. He could hear himself testifying.

When he came back out, Peterson had nodded off. Halloran coughed and Peterson's head jerked up.

"This altitude is getting to me, man. I'm hitting the rack. Besides, it's getting pretty fucking cold up here," Halloran said.

"Yeah, me too." Peterson rose slowly, then nearly fell over as he reached down for the Glenfiddich. He handed it toward Halloran.

"You keep it, but if you want to hit Calcutta with me, I'll roust you at 6:30." Halloran watched Peterson stretch.

"You be right, Jack. See you in the ayem. I'll be up. Don't worry 'bout me."

I'll be worried about you for another 24 hours—until I see you being cuffed and marched off by a couple of Marines, Halloran thought.

CHAPTER 43

In the total darkness of his room, Halloran thought: *Almost there. Easy now. Don't get cocky. Pull him in slowly.* He drifted off to a fitful sleep, images of Syl oozing blood around his right hand and Jennifer Cavaretta with an ice pick in her throat jumping into his dreams.

He was up by 6 to alert Lal they'd be pulling out by 7, and there would be another passenger. By 6:30 he rapped on Peterson's door. He was up and bathed and packed.

"Hey, Mike, another beautiful fucking Himalayan morning, eh," Peterson said. "I'm all set. You?"

"Yeah, man. Just gonna get another cup of coffee, then we're good to go."

Minutes later, he was heading down the hill with Peterson toward Lal and the Land Rover.

"Lal, this is Peters sahib. He's joining us to Calcutta," Halloran said.

Lal saluted Peterson, loaded the bags into the rear and climbed into the driver's seat.

Peterson gave Halloran a mocking salute, then said, "Peters sahib, eh?"

"Yeah, what the fuck. When in Rome, ya know?"

It was a brisk morning, overcast, and the clouds had already moved in to block out Kanchenjunga, so all they could see was the hillside and tea plantations in the valley.

The trip from Darjeeling to Siliguri went quickly, with Lal passing lorries and buses on the cutbacks. Both Halloran and Peterson held their breath a few times as the Land Rover nearly brushed the buses.

Peterson was hungover and slept most of the way to Siliguri, though. Halloran plotted.

By Murshidabad, Peterson had awakened in time for lunch. Lal found a decent-looking place called the Khyber Restaurant and stopped.

"Man, these raghead places make me want to fuckin' puke, and sometimes I do," Peterson said.

"Yeah, well, any port in a storm, ya know. Try the samosas. They're always safe. Deep fried, and Coke. Anything cooked or capped."

Peterson had a beer instead of a Coke, opting for a Kingfisher in a one-liter bottle.

"Little early for me, but you go ahead," Halloran said.

It was 2:15 by the time they finished lunch. While Peterson hit the head, Halloran called Prentiss on the cell. Prentiss answered on the first ring.

"Where are you, Mike, and do you got him?"

"Murshidabad. And he's in the john, so I might make you a broad in a second if he walks up. Driver says we're still about four to five hours away."

"Can you bring him here?"

"That's the plan. Be ready with a couple of Marines. I'll call when I'm 10 minutes away, pretending you're my date."

Just then, Peterson came out of the john, zipping up.

"What a fucking rat hole. Got a cell, huh. Cool. Who you talking to?" Peterson asked.

"Yeah, honey, like I said, he's a Canadian guy. Very cool. Your friend would like him. Yeah, guaranteed." Halloran held his left index finger up to Peterson. "I think 7 sounds do-able. I'll call back if we're running late. But I think we're cool." He disconnected.

"Wazzup, bro?".

"My stu, Ione, has a girlfriend who's a secretary at the American Consulate. Seems there's a dinner party there, and she guarantees it's the best feed with the finest booze in Calcutta. You got a sport coat and tie?" Halloran asked. If Peterson didn't have one, Halloran knew that the Oberoi had a few spares for their best restaurant.

"Got a blue blazer, no tie, but hell, how hard can that be to find?" Peterson laughed.

"Great. Here's the game plan. We go to my hotel—I'm at the Oberoi Grand--change and then hit the party and the broads."

"Very cool. Got an extra tie?"

"We'll get you one," Halloran said, as he jumped into the shotgun seat.

"You can crash tonight with me if things don't work out with the broads, but I got a good feeling. She mentioned she's got a little nose candy. Always nice."

"I'll drink to that," Peterson said, climbing into the back seat of the Rover. He leaned into the back of the SUV and pulled out the Glenfiddich. He tapped the bottle on Halloran's shoulder in the front seat. Halloran held up both hands.

"Too early, but don't mind me."

"Just a hair of the dog to get me started, ya know, man?"

"I know," Halloran said. *I know more than you know, man. I know you're going to be one sorry-ass, murderous ex-con headed back on the long trek back to the joint in a couple of hours.* He winked at Peterson and returned his gaze to the road.

It was rush hour as they approached the outer sprawl of Calcutta, if you could notice the difference in a town as overpopulated as Calcutta. It was a slow go, as Lal weaved in and out of bullock and bicycle and scooter traffic. The sun was setting as they pulled up to the Oberoi Grand.

"Pretty fuckin' nice," Peterson said as he stepped onto the driveway and the doorman saluted.

"I'll check in. You can take a look in the tailor shop and see if you see a tie you like. I only brought one."

After Halloran checked in, the detective and his prey, now with a new red silk Thai tie, went up to the room to shower and change. While Halloran showered, Peterson poured a water-glassful of Glenfiddich. It finished the bottle.

It was 6:45 p.m. when they walked out the front door to find Lal ready to go in the first space of waiting cars in the hotel driveway.

From the car, Halloran took out the cell and phoned Prentiss.

"We're on the way. Should be 10 minutes or so. Hey, what's your girlfriend look like anyway." Halloran winked at Peterson in the back seat.

"Great, great. We'll be there in a bit," Halloran said after a 10-second pause. He rung off and turned back to Peterson.

"Blond, divorced, about 35, and wearing a slinky low-cut red silk dress. Should go well with your tie."

"Should go well with the tie that hangs a little lower but just as long," Peterson said, and let out a guttural laugh.

If only you knew the surprise party I've planned, Halloran thought.

CHAPTER 44

When they arrived at the Consulate, Halloran and Peterson got out of the Rover together. For a second, Peterson hesitated, looking at the American flag fluttering outside, perhaps thinking of what would await him back home.

"This is gonna be a night we won't forget, I'm betting," Halloran said.

"Let's get us some fuckin' pussy," Peterson grinned, joining Halloran step for step up to the Consulate.

Inside, the expansive foyer was deserted but for the Marine seated at the reception desk. As they approached the desk, Halloran asked for an "Amanda Beeler." As soon as he mentioned the name, the Marine corporal rose and walked toward Peterson while another Marine appeared from the rear. Instantly Peterson understood and wheeled away from the Marines, pulling a six-inch switchblade from his back pocket.

"Gentlemen, I got this. He's my prisoner now," Halloran said to the two Marines and turned to face Peterson.

"Mike Halloran, homicide detective. CPD, dickhead, and I'm hauling your sorry ass back for killing Jennifer Cavaretta," Halloran said, approaching Peterson.

"Ya gonna die here, you lying pig," Peterson screamed, crouching and passing the knife from one hand to the other.

"Sure, let's see how tough you are when it's not a woman."

Halloran feinted to his left with a jab step, like an NBA point guard. Peterson took the bait and lunged at Halloran, who sidestepped like a matador, grabbing Peterson's knife-hand and deftly twisting it behind

Peterson's back, jamming it up between his shoulder blades until he screamed in pain and the knife fell to the ground.

With Peterson disarmed, Halloran threw his left arm around Peterson's neck and lifted him off the ground, as his prisoner choked and his feet kicked the air helplessly.

"Is that a free room, guys?" Halloran asked, nodding to a nearby door marked "conference room." Both Marines nodded, wide-eyed.

With that, Halloran dragged his prisoner into the empty room and kicked the door closed behind him.

"Resisting arrest. Thanks for that," Halloran said, tossing Peterson into the corner of the room.

Like a trapped rat, Peterson desperately scanned the room for a weapon and found nothing other than four chairs around a table, and Halloran stood between him and the chairs.

"Make your best move, scumbag," Halloran said.

In a flash, Peterson lowered his shoulders and charged at Halloran. But the former tight end and veteran cop was ready. Stepping quickly to his left, Halloran launched a devastating kick to the groin that landed squarely in an instantly debilitating spot. He then knelt on Peterson's back as he lay gasping on the floor.

"That's for my partner," Halloran whispered into his helpless prisoner's ear. And then he grabbed Peterson's left hand with his right hand and squeezed until he heard bones cracking.

"The handshake? That's from me," Halloran said.

Still grasping his prisoner's hand, Halloran then dragged a groaning Peterson up and back into the foyer where the two Marines stood waiting, one with handcuffs ready.

"He shouldn't have resisted," Halloran said, winking at the stunned Marines, "but I'm kind of glad he did."

They grabbed Peterson by his biceps from either side and shoved him into the wall next to the desk.

"Eric Peterson. You are under arrest under an Interpol and federal warrant for unlawful flight to avoid prosecution," the older Marine said. The other jarhead cuffed Peterson's hands behind his back.

Halloran walked up, reached into his back pocket and pulled out his gold detective star that said Chicago Police Department and thrust it two inches in front of Peterson's nose.

"We got your DNA on the threatening letter you sent to the State's Attorney from the joint, Eric. And we got your DNA match from the cigarette you left in Jenny's car. You're dead meat, asshole. You really think you could get away with this, you shit?"

"Take him away, gentlemen," Halloran said, stepping aside. He turned back to Peterson. "See you in Chicago, asshole."

CHAPTER 45

"How in the hell did you talk him into walking in here on his own?" Prentiss stood in centerfield of the Consulate baseball field with Halloran, watching the chopper carrying Peterson lift and tilt to the right before disappearing into the West Bengal skies.

"One of the linchpins in law enforcement is that it's a good thing the criminals are stupid. This one was stupid and horny," Halloran said.

Back in his office, Prentiss pushed his chair back to reach into a small black GE refrigerator he kept under a file cabinet. He pulled out a six pack of Beck's, withdrew two, then handed one to Halloran.

"Never met an Irish cop who wouldn't hoist one after a righteous collar." They popped the tops nearly simultaneously and clinked cans. The crisp German brew went down smoothly.

Prentiss then walked Halloran through the federal bureaucracy that would ensue before Peterson was turned over to Chicago cops. First, Peterson was being thrown in the brig once he made the ship for a five-day journey to Guam. There, he would be transferred to a military transport plane that would fly him to San Francisco, where he would be taken into custody by U.S. Marshals for a subsequent plane ride to Chicago and ultimately the Metropolitan Correctional Center.

"Figure at least a week and a half before he's in Chicago, given transit and federal bureaucracy."

"You've been a huge help, but there is just one more thing. Without question, dirtbag is going to come up with some bullshit about how he was coerced, beaten or otherwise mistreated, and that's how he wound up getting busted. Can you put together an affidavit by one of the

Marines saying how he was present when Peterson walked in here of his own volition?"

Halloran handed Prentiss his card and asked that he send the affidavit to Area 3.

"Consider it done." Prentiss then stood up, and walked around to Halloran, extending his hand. "Congratulations, detective. It's a long way from Chicago. You must have at least a couple of calls to make. Dial 9-1-888 first and it gets you to an outside stateside line and then dial like you were back home. I got a few things to take care of. Take your time. And help yourself to this beer, right?"

"Speaking of time, what time is it now in Chicago?"

"It's a little after 8 a.m." The diplomat was obviously pleased he was able to help in such a high-profile case. Halloran waited until Prentiss left the room and closed the door behind him.

"Thanks, Bill," Halloran said to the closed door, a little slow on the draw with the thanks.

He dialed the access number first, heard a dial tone, and then punched in Ortiz' cell number. She had made sergeant in his absence, a field promotion, but she was still his partner and on the case. At this time, he figured she would be just dropping the kids off.

She picked up on the second ring.

"Hello." Ortiz was a bit tentative since the caller ID gave her no clue.

"He's no longer in the wind, partner." No hello, straight to the point.

"Jesus Christ, Mike. Where are you? How'd you find him? Are you all right? I can't believe it." Ortiz began pointing to the phone to Joe, who was riding shotgun, after dropping off the last child at school. She mouthed the word "Mike."

"Calcutta. The American Consulate. Back from the Himalayas. And I'm fine. It's a long story, though, and one I want to share with you over a Guinness when I get back. Thought you might want to know, though."

"Unbelievable, Mike. Un-fucking-believable. Did he give it up?"

"No surprise there. He gave up nothing but a batch of shit once he was cuffed. He resisted a bit, but nothing I couldn't handle. But I got a partial admission from him that I think we can use from when I was talking to him before he got busted. It's a long story."

"I can't wait to hear it. Great job, Mike. Did you call Cavaretta?"

"You kidding? You're my first call. But do us both a favor, okay? On your way to work, first stop by Cavaretta's home and deliver the news yourself. We gave him the bad news in person; you should deliver the good news in person."

"Good idea. Jesus, he'll be glad to hear this. You're the best, partner, the best."

"Yeah, yeah, just got lucky. You know that. I may take my time on the way back, see a few things, since it'll take about 10 days to land him in Chicago, I'm told."

"Great. Hey listen, Dr. Moretti called me, said he'd read about my being shot--how Eric had shot me. Told me how Eric was such a bright kid, how he took an intense interest in the anatomy, how he learned to take a pulse by finding the carotid. And he'll testify to that. Said Eric had just gone too far.

"And I interviewed one of his ex-cellmates when he first went into the joint, and he told me all that Peterson could talk about was getting even. Mentioned Cavaretta a couple of times. Called him the 'pretty prosecutor pimpshit.' We can use it."

"Every little bit will help at trial. Oh, and I'm going to give Egan a courtesy call, too."

"Don't *even* want to know how you know she'll be up at 8 a.m., Hal."

"Dirty mind. That's a venial sin and will cost you some purgatory time. Can you take care of notifying the brass? Appreciate it."

"You got it, partner. I can't wait," Ortiz said and hung up. She didn't mention she had made sergeant—no rain on her partner's parade.

Punching the lead-in numbers and hearing the dial tone, Halloran dialed Egan's cell.

"Hello." Halloran could hear traffic in the background.

"Greetings from the mysterious East. One mystery's been solved."

"No shit! You got him? Where?" Egan shouted.

Halloran ran it down for Egan, who listened wordlessly as he recounted the pursuit, the Darjeeling entrapment, the partial admission, and the look on Peterson's face at the Consulate. He made sure to tell her he used no drugs or force to get Peterson to American soil. He mentioned "some slight resistance" and the affidavit that was in the process of being made and sent. He also told her that Ortiz was on her way to Cavaretta's home.

"Sounds as smooth as goose shit, Mike. But I'm guessing you're being modest or taciturn, not wanting to milk the American taxpayers too much on this call. That said, I'm going to ravage you for all the details over some tasty Thai when you get back."

"I'm aghast, offended and chagrined at the sexual overtones, counselor, but I think I'll be ready for a half-pound burger when I get back from Asia."

"It's a deal. Great work, Mike. Really. I can't wait to get all the details."

"Keep the streets safe until I get back, okay counselor?"

"I'm on aggressive patrol, detective. Call me when you get back."

"Will do," Halloran said and hung up.

His final call was to Frank Marone's cell. It was still a little early for Marone, who usually sashayed into the Sun-Times city room shortly before 11 a.m.

"Heh-hello," Marone managed.

"Frank. It's Halloran. This is all background but golden shit. Got a pen?"

"One second." Marone stumbled out of bed with his cell phone, found a pen but no paper handy. He grabbed a book and opened to the white page on the inside cover, pen poised.

"Go," Marone prompted.

"Peterson was just arrested when he walked into the American Consulate in Calcutta. Yes, Calcutta, India. Just listen and take notes. He's on his way back to the U.S. and should be back in about 10 days. The State's Attorney's office will know the details but give them an hour or so.

"No, no one else knows, least way not from me. But the day is yet young. You are my first and only call. At least you got a head start, I guess..." Halloran said. Marone jumped in.

"But how did you—where are you..." Marone spit out.

"Hope it holds until your deadline. Adios," Halloran hung up.

He leaned back in Prentiss's plush leather chair and took a deep swig to finish off the Beck's. He reached over and popped another.

As he sat there, satisfied and slaked, Halloran contemplated his on-again off-again trysts and tribulations with Egan. He smiled as he crumpled the first empty, then tossed it into the circular file 10 feet away in the corner of Prentiss's office.

"Nice shot, big fella."

Going home a winner, he gloated with a smile.

***

On this March morning, Tom Cavaretta was reading the Tribune's editorial spanking the county board for waste when the front doorbell rang. It was too early for his driver, Frank, Cavaretta knew.

"Joyce, you expecting someone?" Cavaretta yelled up the stairs, then leaned to look out the window and saw a Dodge Caravan parked in the driveway.

"Not at this ungodly hour. Who would stop by this early?" But as soon as the words had cleared her mouth, they hung in the air—a reminder of the morning that the Superintendent had rung their bell.

"I'll get it," Cavaretta said. As he approached his front door, he saw through the side window it was Ortiz and opened the door wide.

"Detective, I mean sergeant, is something wrong? Please. Come in."

"No, sir. Nothing's wrong. Something's right. Mike found him. We got him. They're bringing him back." Ortiz spoke fast, anxious. Joyce had come up behind her husband and put her left hand to her mouth.

"Oh, thank God." Joyce Cavaretta took two quick steps before she grabbed Ortiz in an awkward embrace that lasted a full minute, with Joyce sobbing on Oritz' shoulder. When she regained her composure,

Joyce Cavaretta demanded that Ortiz come in and have coffee and tell them everything she knew.

But as Ortiz sat down and before she could begin, Joyce Cavaretta leaned forward and touched Ortiz's right arm.

"How are you? Do you still hurt? How rude of me not to ask earlier."

"I'm fine, just fine. Been back to work for a while now. Thanks for asking." Ortiz then related the little she knew and the timetable for Peterson arriving back in Chicago.

"And how is Mike? This is just outstanding police work, outstanding," Cavaretta said.

Ortiz sat there stiffly sipping her coffee, accepting the congratulations for her partner, and looking for the moment to make a graceful exit.

"Mike is fine. He called from Calcutta maybe 20 minutes ago. I don't know much of the details," she said.

A quick exit was out of the question. The Cavarettas were gracious and grateful. She stayed for an hour, in the end telling the couple about her daughter's soccer game the night before and Joe's struggles to get used to private practice. As Ortiz spoke, Joyce Cavaretta's eyes flitted to her daughter's nearby photo, but quickly fixed back on Ortiz..

As she drove out of the driveway, as she had a half year ago, Ortiz held the same thought she had then: *This is a very strong couple.*

Part III:

The Court

CHAPTER 46

It had been nine days from the time Peterson had been snatched up at the Consulate until he appeared for a bond hearing in Chicago before U.S. Magistrate Judge Jonathon P. Dinkins.

The courtroom was packed with reporters, television sketch artists, agents, cops, prosecutors, and various hangers-on. The room was abuzz when Peterson was led into court in leg irons and shackles attached to a thick leather belt with an O-ring in the middle over his jail jumpsuit.

Pritchard was in the front row left. She weakly raised her right hand to wave as Peterson was brought in, and he winked at her, smirking. It would be his signature look for all the courtroom appearances that were to follow.

In the front row right, behind the prosecution table sat Ortiz, Halloran and Mallory. Peterson ignored Halloran, apparently unwilling to acknowledge he had been snookered by a cop again.

Standing at the defense table was a cross section of the usual suspects: Oliver Hemphill from the People's Justice Office; Shirley Stoddard Thomas, pro bono, from Ellison & Wright, the silk-stocking law firm; and Peter Chance from the University of Chicago.

At the prosecution table were First Assistant Dunne, Egan and Assistant U.S. Attorneys James Hanley and Eleanor Margolis. Hanley spoke first.

"Your Honor, I'm Assistant U.S. Attorney James Hanley, speaking on behalf of the people along with Eleanor Margolis and two Assistant State's Attorneys who have been cross-designated for this hearing, Richard Dunne and Mary Catherine Egan. We are asking that you order the U.S. Marshal's office to tender custody to the Cook County Sheriff's Police for transfer to the Cook County Jail. We are dropping the Unlawful Flight to Avoid Prosecution charge."

"Defense?" Dinkins said, looking down from the enormous walnut bench with the American flag behind it.

"Your Honor, this man was unlawfully arrested in a foreign country and taken back here against his will. This is highly irregular, illegal, outrageous and unprecedented. This man has been harassed by the Chicago Police, the Cook County State's Attorney's office, the U.S. Marines and Navy, and the U.S. Marshal's office. We would ask for a continuance while we do further research into this illicit and spurious misconduct," Hemphill said.

"You've known about this for more than a week. It took me less than an hour to research the law. Request denied. Mr. Hemphill, this is a valid warrant. He is in my court, and I have authority to transfer him and precedent under the law. Look it up. Defendant Peterson is hereby remanded to the custody of the sheriff. Marshal, take him away."

"Your Honor," Hemphill protested. Dinkins cut him off.

"Court adjourned." Dinkins rose and swept out of the court.

As Peterson left, he flipped the bird toward Halloran.

Ortiz poked him and laughed.

"That hurts," Halloran said. "I'm the guy who helped him come home. What an ingrate."

CHAPTER 47

In quick order the case was transferred to 26th and California, where prosecutors had no trouble indicting Peterson within weeks.

When he was arraigned, it was another media circus. The cases at 26th were assigned randomly, but which judge got the case was critical to both prosecution and defense. The computer in the Presiding Judge's chambers spun a theoretical wheel to randomly select the trial judge.

The wheel for Peterson spun out the name of Judge Morris P. Schell. At a perfunctory bond hearing, Schell ordered that Peterson constituted a flight risk and would remain in the Cook County jail without bail.

Schell had been on the bench for four years—one in Juvenile, one in Traffic, and the last two years at 26th Street. Now 40, he was known as hard-working and humorless, but respected by both prosecutors and defense attorneys. Over the last two years, Schell heard countless motions and granted only necessary continuances until all answered ready for trial.

It isn't hard to tell who the prospective jurors are when they wander into the Criminal Court building. They clutch their summons in their hands and look from side to side once they clear the metal detectors and security. Most look bewildered; a few look scared.

And so, it was on a bright spring day nearly three years after the murder, 80 such men and women from all walks of life lined up in rows of two and filed into the courtroom of Judge Schell. Up the black-and-white tiled aisle they strode, scrunching into the dark oak, graffiti-scarred benches of the gallery.

The questioning was mostly the Morris Schell show. Each side had 20 peremptory challenges--opportunities to get rid of a prospective juror without giving a reason. Both sides used most of their challenges during a tedious process that was mostly ignored by the press.

Jury selection took four and a half days and was finished by late Friday afternoon, when the last of four alternate jurors had passed muster with the judge and both prosecution and defense. Gender-wise it was four men, eight women on the jury and two men and two women among the alternates.

Racially the jury broke down to three African Americans, seven whites and two Hispanics on the jury and three whites and one Asian as alternates. All had said they would follow the law as to the death penalty. As usual, neither side was completely satisfied. But the most important person in the court—Schell—was satisfied.

"Ladies and gentlemen, be back here at 9:30 a.m. Monday, when we will hear opening statements from counsel," Schell said.

Stage set. Cast complete.

CHAPTER 48

Like a scene from "War of the Worlds," the TV antennas of the major stations were up and swaying in the brisk southeast breeze as it swept along California Boulevard on the morning of the first day of the historic trial.

Becky Thompson was there for a live stand-up just after dawn with the looming grey mass of the Criminal Court building as her background.

"In just three hours," Thompson began breathlessly, "we will hear the beginning of what many are calling 'The Trial of the Century.'

"Eric Peterson allegedly evened the score with the prosecutor who helped put him on Death Row by plunging an ice pick into the neck of Jenny Cavaretta in the predawn hours on an Old Town street.

"Prosecutors will paint a portrait of a man who stalked the law school student and daughter of State's Attorney Tom Cavaretta and killed her to get even with the prosecutor who helped convict him of the murders of a couple and their son in a drug deal gone bad.

"Defense attorneys are expected to try to portray Peterson as the victim of a criminal justice system run amok, anxious to frame a man who was exonerated in the three earlier murders. They will say Peterson was in fear of his life when he wounded officer Sylvia Ortiz and then fled from police out to frame him for yet another murder he is innocent of."

By 9 a.m., the deputies stood in front of the courtroom doors to control a crowd of about 100 people that snaked down the hallway adjacent to Schell's courtroom.

Inside, the first row was for the courtroom artists and the second and third rows on the right side were reserved for the Cavaretta family. The first row on the left was reserved for Peterson's wife and a few friends. The second and third rows were set aside for the press.

A murmur of anticipation swept through the crowd as Egan, Dunne and Edward Hall Jr., the first chair (senior prosecutor) in Schell's courtroom, marched into the courtroom following the evidence cart being pushed by their law clerk. As a rising star litigator, Hall had joined the team after Schell got the case, and it was Hall who would do the opening statement.

Seconds later, the defense team marched in with three carts and four law clerks, the defense not to be outdone by the state.

"All rise. Court is in session. The Honorable Morris Schell presiding. All cell phones and pagers should be off," barked Schell's bailiff, Sonia Johnson.

"Are we ready, ladies and gentlemen?" Schell asked, looking from side to side to Hemphill and Dunne.

"Your Honor, for the record, I would like to renew my motion for a gag order to prevent this trial from turning into a media circus," Hemphill said.

"Mr. Hemphill, I've already ruled on that, and you know that. My court is not, will not, and has never been, a circus. And any attempted theatrics from either side will not be tolerated and will be punished. Are we straight on that?" Schell looked long and hard at Hemphill before glancing at Dunne.

"Yes, Your Honor," both men said almost in unison.

"Good, bring in the jury," Schell said.

"Ladies and Gentlemen, welcome and thank you for doing your civic duty by responding to the jury summons and taking the oath to fairly weigh the evidence you are about to hear. We will first hear from the prosecutors, who will tell you what they expect the evidence will show. What Mr. Hall will tell you is not evidence; it is his expectation of what the evidence he and his fellow prosecutors will present to you.

"He will be followed by Ms. Thomas, who will also say what she expects the evidence will show. Her expectations, too, are not evidence. When they are finished speaking, we will commence the trial with the first prosecution witness. Mr. Hall, proceed."

Hall stood up to his full 6'4" height and nodded to the judge. Dressed in a dark blue suit, white shirt and striped red and white tie, the former small forward at Purdue strode to the front of the courtroom until the back of his left thigh was pressed against the long oak table where Peterson sat with his defense team.

"This man," Hall said, turning and thrusting his right index finger toward Peterson, "ended the life of a beautiful, kind and intelligent young woman almost before it had really begun. And why? To settle a vendetta he had against the woman's father, Tom Cavaretta.

"He was too much of a coward to try to confront Mr. Cavaretta, the State's Attorney here in Cook County..." Hall continued, only to be cut off by Thomas.

"Objection," Thomas shrieked, standing up and facing the judge. "Objection. This is outrageous."

"No, Miss Thomas, this is opening statements. Mr. Hall, I assume you are leading up to telling the jury that this is what the evidence will show. Objection overruled. Continue."

"The evidence will show that Tom Cavaretta, when he was a young prosecutor, approved murder charges against Eric Peterson and then prosecuted him at trial a few years later. For years after his conviction, Peterson plotted his revenge until he took the life of Cavaretta's daughter on an Old Town street in the predawn hours."

Juror Christina Brigham leaned forward a fraction to get a better look at Peterson, who was partially obscured by Hall's looming frame. Decked out in a dark green blazer with tan pants, a white shirt and blue-knit tie, the clean-shaven Peterson appeared benign, almost dapper, a sartorial cover for his prison tattoos.

As Hall was speaking, Peterson smiled up at the prosecutor. Brigham made a note. Hemphill pulled Peterson's arm and leaned over to whisper in his ear. The smile disappeared.

For nearly an hour, Hall paced back and forth, gesturing to the evidence cart, pointing repeatedly at a now calm and nonplussed Peterson. Hall made eye contact repeatedly with the African American jurists, who appeared enthralled by this articulate and handsome young black attorney.

"And you will hear from his cellmate at Joliet how Eric Peterson had it in for Tom Cavaretta. And you will hear clear and convincing evidence that his DNA matches both samples taken off the threatening letter he sent to Tom Cavaretta and from the cigarette butt found by the body of Jennifer Cavaretta.

"Further, you will hear from Detective Mike Halloran how he tracked Peterson to a remote Himalayan hill station, tricked him with the lure of drugs and sex into following him into the American Consulate, where he was arrested on a warrant by Marine guards. Most important, you will hear how Peterson bragged to Halloran about getting a 'bitch who ain't fucking with anyone anymore.'

"In the end, ladies and gentlemen, there will be no doubt that Eric Peterson killed Jenny Cavaretta, then months later shot Officer Ortiz before he fled the country. The defense will argue reasonable doubt. After you hear the evidence, there will be no doubt--none—that Eric Peterson is a killer who has forfeited his right to be among us. Thank you for your attention."

Just before the judge adjourned for a 15-minute break, Brigham glanced over at Channel 5's sketch artist, who was putting the final touches on a portrait of Hall gesturing at Peterson.

Brigham sighed and joined her fellow jurors as they filed out of the packed courtroom, all spectators standing as the jury left.

***

Standing behind Eric Peterson, Thomas surveyed the jury for 30 seconds before speaking. Then with her left hand she hoisted a copy of the Illinois Criminal Statutes while placing her right hand on the right shoulder of her client.

"This man is innocent. I repeat. *Innocent*. Not because I say so. But because our Constitution says so. He has the presumption of innocence as he sits before you. He is not guilty until you say so. Not because I say so, but because the law says so. He's not guilty because Mr. Hall says he's guilty. Not because the police say so. Not because the press may swallow the state's side. It is not so until you say so."

She walked slowly toward the jury box, then stopped at the witness stand with the American flag on a pole behind it.

"This flag symbolizes our freedom, which was won when our forefathers fought a repressive government. And make no mistake, we have a repressive, oppressive government that has persecuted Eric Peterson, this innocent man, for the better part of the last two decades.

"The persecution would have you believe that Eric..." Thomas continued.

"Objection, Your Honor. Persecution? Please. Ms. Thomas' enunciation is usually flawless, so I believe this is hardly accidental." Hall stood and held his hands up briefly in appeal to Schell.

"There is some leeway in openings, Mr. Hall. Ms. Thomas, perhaps it was a slip of the tongue. Did you mean to say 'prosecution'?"

"Yes, Your Honor. Thank you." Thomas smiled with her eyes as she surveyed the jury for a sympathetic set of eyes. She found such a set when she made contact with Clarice Gordon, a black hospice worker. Thomas continued:

"You will hear evidence that Mr. Peterson was wrongfully convicted nearly two decades ago, and then when Gov. Riley finally acted to free him, the government, the police, hounded him and ginned up this case to bring him down a second time. We ask you to keep an open mind as the evidence is presented.

"There is no confession. There is no eyewitness. There are no prints on the murder weapon. There are none of Mr. Peterson's prints in the car where Ms. Cavaretta was murdered. There is no DNA from Ms. Cavaretta recovered from Mr. Peterson's clothing. What we have is DNA on a cigarette butt. But you will hear no evidence that puts our client with that cigarette in the car. That cigarette could have gotten there in any number of ways.

"What you will hear is a series of circumstantial events, unreliable witnesses, and police and prosecutorial guesswork.

"But ladies and gentlemen, you hold a man's life in your hands. We cannot prevent the prostitution and police from guesswork..." Thomas was saying when Egan leapt up, beating Hall by a fraction of a second.

"Prostitution, Your Honor? This is off the wall. Objection. Objection."

From the third row, Halloran watched in admiration as Egan rose, dressed in a crisp white blouse with a navy-blue Armani suit and three-inch spiked heels, and towered over Thomas' stubby 5'2" frame.

"Miss Thomas," Schell sighed. "Enough. Understand?"

"Freudian slip. It won't happen again, Your Honor. May I continue?"

Schell waved his left hand toward the jury box.

"And in conclusion, you will learn of the unprofessional Gestapo tactics of Detective Mike Halloran, who literally shanghaied Mr. Peterson while he was vacationing in India."

"Objection, Your Honor. Gestapo. Shanghaied. This is unseemly. Is there no end to counsel's histrionics and hyperbole?" Egan asked.

"Histrionics? That seems a bit hyperbolic itself. Is it not, Ms. Egan? But you are mostly right. Ms. Thomas, I assume you are close to the end, and I assume you will not test the court's patience further. Are we clear on this?" Just maybe the Teutonic jurist had taken umbrage to the use of the word "Gestapo."

"Two more sentences and I'm through. The evidence you will hear will not be clear and convincing, nor proof beyond a reasonable doubt. You will have more than reasonable doubt; you will have logical and comprehensive doubt. Thank you."

As she walked back to her seat, she glanced back at juror Gordon, who was rapidly jotting down a few notes, the sole juror so busy.

CHAPTER 49

In every murder trial, there is a "life/death witness," a perfunctory witness that establishes under the law that the victim had once lived, and therefore, could be murdered.

The prosecution loves the life witness, usually the victim's spouse, mother, father or sibling, because they create immediate sympathy for the victim. The defense hates them because the defense attorney cannot cross-examine them without looking like an unsympathetic bully.

For the first day of trial, Joyce Dennehy Cavaretta was wearing a green silk skirt, crisp beige blouse, black stockings and sensible black pumps. Her nearly pure white hair hung to her shoulders but was in stark contrast to her dark brown eyebrows, thick lashes and bright blue eyes. She walked slowly but confidently to the witness stand, with Hall ushering her to her seat. She smiled at Schell and remained standing.

"Do you promise to tell the truth, the whole truth, and nothing but the truth, so help you God?" Schell's clerk asked, her own right hand held high as if to demonstrate. Holding her right hand up just slightly above her shoulder, Joyce said, "I do," and sat down.

Sitting cross-legged in the second row reserved for attorneys and police, Tom Cavaretta smiled slightly at his wife and nodded.

"Will the witness tell the ladies and gentlemen of the jury your first and last name and spell your last name for the court reporter?" Hall asked, standing just 10 feet from his witness and about a half dozen feet from the jury box.

"Joyce Cavaretta. That's C-A-V-A-R-E-T-T-A."

"And did you know the victim in this case, Jennifer Cavaretta?"

"Yes. I did. She was my daughter."

"And how long did you know the victim?"

"Since I gave birth to her at Northwestern Memorial Hospital—for all of her 24 years on this earth."

"And did you see and speak to the victim on the night before she was killed?"

"Yes, I spoke to her and her friend, Anne Doyle, just before they went out for the night."

"Did your daughter carry large sums of money?"

"Not really. Tom, my husband, insisted she carry a $100 bill as emergency money. She would put that behind her driver's license. I don't know that she ever used it. She may have."

"I see," Hall nodded and glanced at the jury. "And when was the last time you saw your daughter alive?"

"When I kissed her just before she walked out the door that night with Annie," Joyce responded, her lip quivering just slightly.

Ordinarily, the defense would object to this redundant testimony, but they did not want to look like they were beating up the victim's mother.

"One last question, Mrs. Cavaretta. Three years ago, did you and your husband bury your daughter at All Saints Cemetery in Des Plaines?"

"Yes, we did, in a plot next to the ones we had bought for ourselves and hoped we would be in before her." Joyce Cavaretta gazed into the jury box, locking eyes with Brigham. Brigham cast her eyes down at her notepad but wrote nothing.

"I have no further questions. Your witness." Hall looked to the defense table, then walked slowly to sit beside Egan.

Hemphill rose and looked at Schell.

"We have no questions at this time."

Next up was Dr. Jane Powers. The defense merely listened as Powers listed her qualifications and then put on a textbook primer on the cause of death. She gave the cause of death as a wound to the right carotid artery and speculated that Jenny Cavaretta had lived no more than two minutes after she was struck.

"The bruising around her mouth. How could that have been caused?" Egan asked.

"That could have been a hand clamped over her mouth."

"To prevent her from screaming?" Egan asked.

"Perhaps," Powers said.

"No more questions of the doctor," Egan said. She nodded to Schell, then joined Hall and Dunne.

"Might the bruising have been an overzealous kiss?" asked Thomas, not budging from her seat.

"I've never seen that."

"But it's possible, isn't it?" Thomas persisted.

"Possible, but highly improbable, based on my quarter century looking at a lot of bodies, counselor."

The doc needed no resuscitation from Egan and was excused.

The last witness in the morning was Betty Kotowski, who testified only that she had heard a woman scream just before 4 a.m. and called police from a pay phone.

With no cross, Dunne rose from his seat.

"If the court pleases, this would be a good time to break for the day since the examination of Detective Mike Halloran is expected to be lengthy," Dunne said.

"The jurors will kindly refrain from reading any newspaper or Internet accounts of the trial, and please walk away if a story comes up on the TV. We resume at 10 a.m. tomorrow."

Right, thought Halloran. *Never happens.*

CHAPTER 50

Looking into his closet, Halloran chose the dark brown woolen tweed jacket he had tailor-made for himself the first time he was in Donegal. White shirt, brown trousers, maroon tie. Brown wingtips. He was ready when Dunne summoned him as court resumed in the morning.

"The people call Detective Michael Halloran." Halloran strode out from behind the brown padded door to the right of the witness stand, glancing into the jury box, not smiling nor avoiding the stares.

After being sworn in and identifying himself for the jury and the court reporter, Halloran related how the case had developed, prompted by a series of questions from Dunne. He took the jury from the day of the murder and the finding of the cigarette in the Jaguar to the match and the chase after Peterson that wound up with his partner being shot. And then to the warrants issued.

He then related how he had tracked Peterson to India, to the Windamere Hotel, and how he lured Peterson back to the Consulate with the prospect of drugs and sex.

"Tell us, detective, what is your understanding of international law or Indian law that you thought it was okay to lie to the defendant and trick him into walking into the American Consulate in Calcutta?" Dunne asked. It was a pre-emptive, fake attack Dunne was launching to catch the jury a bit off guard and take away the sting of the question that the defense surely would let fly if he didn't ask it first.

"Well, counselor, I'm not a lawyer and know little of international law and virtually nothing of Indian law. But I lied to the defendant, yes.

And I tricked him, to use your words, into walking into the Consulate because I doubt he would've walked in there with me if I told him I was a Chicago cop.

"But I did nothing illegal to my knowledge and certainly nothing unethical or even untoward in duping this killer into walking into the Consulate, making him think there was sex and dope waiting for him."

"Objection, Your Honor. Speculative as to whether or what my client would have done if he had been told the truth by this pusillanimous police officer," Hemphill said, rising from his chair, pointing at Halloran. The courtroom artists liked that move and scribbled away on their pads.

"Sustained as to speculative. Nice alliteration, Mr. Hemphill. Pusillanimous? May have to consult my dictionary at the break. Continue, Mr. Dunne." Several jurors laughed quietly.

"Thank you, Your Honor. Moving along now. Detective, did you either threaten the defendant with force or use physical force on him in any way to force him into the American Consulate in India?"

"No, sir,' Halloran testified.

"In your conversation with the defendant, did you discuss getting even with people who crossed him?"

"Yes, sir."

"And do you recall what the defendant said?"

"Yes, sir. I do."

"Please tell the ladies and gentlemen of the jury the gist of that conversation, as best you can recall," Dunne said.

"I asked him about a woman he had referred to as a 'bitch' and he said, 'That bitch ain't fuckin' with anyone no more. And her old man got a real lesson, too.'"

"And what did you take this to mean?"

"Objection, Your Honor, as to what the witness divined from these words. They speak for themselves. The jury does not need an interpreter."

"Nor do I, counsel. Sustained," Schell ruled.

"And how is it that you remember those exact words, detective?"

"Because I knew they were important to our case—I excused myself for a minute and went to my room and wrote the exact words down."

"I have no further questions. Thank you, detective." As Dunne returned to the prosecution table, he tried to read the jury's faces as they continued to look at Halloran. Hemphill stepped forward and walked to the jury box, looking at the jury, not Halloran.

"So, detective, you're asking this jury to believe that this man left the hotel of his own volition and walked into an American post overseas, knowing he had an unjust warrant out on him and risked this for the prospect of a little sex and some dope?"

As Hemphill questioned Halloran, he never took his eyes off juror Jordan.

"I would not want to speculate about what the defendant's motives were, but I can tell you that he walked into the Consulate with me and looked pretty damned surprised when the two Marine guards came to put the grabs on him."

A muted few titters escaped from the jury box. Guffaws came from several rows of young prosecutors there to watch the show. Schell cast a stern look into the gallery.

"We will have decorum in this courtroom. Detective, sometimes a simple yes or no is the most prudent answer."

"May I continue, Your Honor?" Hemphill asked. Schell nodded.

"Would it be fair to say that you were hell-bent on arresting the person who fired a shot at your partner and you, and you would do anything to bring that person here for trial?" Hemphill asked.

"I would not argue with the first part of your question. I was determined to find Peterson and bring back the guy who killed an innocent young woman and tried to kill my partner and me. Yes."

"Even if that meant bending the law, detective, to the breaking point?" Hemphill asked.

Dunne rose. "Objection, Your Honor. The witness has already stated that he broke no law."

"I asked 'bending the law to the breaking point,' not breaking the law," Hemphill said.

"You may answer, detective," Schell said.

"The answer to that would be no, not to the breaking point if that means breaking the law and endangering this prosecution. But what I did was every lawful thing I could think of to bring this man back to face this court and to bring justice to Jenny Cavaretta and Sylvia Ortiz."

This was not Halloran's first cross.

Hemphill could see he was not scoring points. It had allowed Halloran to bring two victims into the testimony, not the best move. So, Hemphill moved to what he deemed more fertile ground.

"When you testified that the defendant spoke about 'that bitch,' did you not take that to mean his girlfriend?"

"Objection. Good for the goose, good for the gander. Now he wants Detective Halloran to speculate on the meaning of words that a moment ago he said speak for themselves. Seems counsel can't make up his mind," Dunne said.

"Sustained. The prosecution has a point, Mr. Hemphill," Schell said. Unperturbed, Hemphill plowed on.

"And finally, detective, did you not attack my client once inside the Consulate?"

"I did not. When the Marine approached him, he pulled a switchblade, and I had to disarm him. Then when I then tried to question him, he tried to tackle me and I defended myself," Halloran continued.

Hemphill soon regretted allowing Halloran to portray his client with a knife.

"Your Honor, I would reserve the right to recall this witness later in the trial."

In retreat, Hemphill was trying to make the jury think that he had not lost, that he had just wanted to let the trial move forward and to spare the jury any more distasteful outbursts from a prejudiced witness. He *hoped* that's what they would think.

As Hemphill walked back to his seat, Peterson shook his head slowly from side to side, either in disgust or in denial. In either case, it would not play well with the jury. Thomas reached over and spoke a few quick words to her client. He leaned over and mouthed something to her. It looked as if he might have said "vacuum" or perhaps it was two words that spoke of carnal intent.

As he rose to leave the witness stand, Halloran caught Egan's eye, and winked with his right eye, so as not to let the jury on his left see. She glanced at the jury and then busied herself with her notations on her yellow legal pad.

Round one: Halloran.

***

Round two: Sylvia Ortiz.

Sylvia Ortiz was waiting in the interview room adjacent to Judge Schell's courtroom waiting for her partner to finish. Egan opened the door and announced: "Show time, Syl."

Dressed in a dark blue pantsuit, a light blue blouse with a red scarf and three-inch black heels, Ortiz looked into the jury box, searching for Edgar Gonzales, a fellow Hispanic. She made eye contact just before she turned right to settle in the witness box.

Egan asked all the perfunctory questions about Ortiz' background, years on the job, and present rank before she brought Syl to the night she nearly died.

"And do you see the man in court today who ran from you that night at the Race Street address?" Egan was standing next to the witness box, between Ortiz and the jury.

"I do," Ortiz said. She leaned slightly forward, craning her neck to the right. "That man is the defendant, sitting at the defense table, dressed in the green sport coat and the blue tie."

Gonzales stared as Peterson stood and nodded to the witness stand. Thomas pulled him down. Gonzales shook his head just once, very slightly. Dunne noticed.

"And Sgt. Ortiz, please tell the jury what happened next, after you saw the defendant run from you and your partner." Egan walked back to the prosecution table to remove herself from the line of sight between the witness and the jury. Ortiz leaned slightly forward and looked into the jury box.

"Mike--Detective Halloran--was driving. We were weaving in and out of traffic—the traffic was heavy, and he didn't want to kill anyone. When we got to Grand and Paulina, we could see Peterson's car slide to a stop at Ashland. Mike dodged some traffic and skidded to a stop a few car lengths away from Peterson. I saw the driver's side window go down. I looked to the left and yelled to Mike. Then the window exploded, and I knew I was hit.

"Mike got out and got off a few rounds. I remember seeing and hearing that, but I was losing it. I remember Mike pulling me over to him. I was on my left side, my head on his shoulder. I could feel him force his finger into the wound. It hurt like hell, and I wondered what he was doing just before the lights went out. That's all I remember until I came to in the recovery room."

Several of the women jurors were dabbing their eyes. Halloran watched from the third row and winked at his old partner. She had done well.

"Nothing further," Egan said.

Thomas rose slowly from her chair.

"You are back on the job now, officer, fully recovered, I hope," Thomas asked.

"I am back on the job. The doctors say there was some muscle damage, and they doubt my tennis career will ever be the same. But mostly recovered, thank you." Ortiz let a slight smile cross her face.

"Let's go back to the instant you say you saw the defendant, Mr. Peterson, fleeing his apartment. Did you tell him you had a warrant for his arrest?" Thomas asked.

"We never had the chance. He took off." Thomas walked closer to the witness stand. "Were you in uniform that night, detective Ortiz?"

"Sergeant Ortiz," she corrected. "I was in plainclothes, the way I always dressed as a detective."

"Did you have your weapon out?"

"At what point?" Ortiz asked.

"At the point where you and your armed partner showed up at the home of a man who had just gotten out of prison after spending 20 years for a crime he did not commit."

"Objection, Your Honor," Egan said. "Is there a question in the middle of that diatribe, please?"

"Sustained, Ms. Egan, and you injected a little speech into your objection too, didn't you? No more speeches, please, counselors. Proceed."

Ortiz spoke up.

"We did not have our weapons out. There was no need at that point. It wasn't until we arrived at the intersection that there was a need. I never had a chance to get my weapon out before I was shot."

"Did you ever show your badge or announce your office to the person who shot you, Officer Ortiz?"

"It was a chase. I never got my window down, the door open, my weapon out or any words out of my mouth before I was shot," Ortiz said, brown eyes flashing.

"And you were in an unmarked squad car, is that right?"

"Peterson knows what an unmarked squad car looks like."

"Is that a yes?"

"Yes," Ortiz said through clenched teeth.

"Thank you, officer. That will be all."

Egan was on her feet before Thomas had a chance to turn back toward the defense table.

"During this chase, did Detective Halloran have his flashing emergency lights on and the siren blaring?" Egan asked.

"He did."

"And Sergeant, were other cars pulling off to the side to get out of the way because they could see you were in a squad car, albeit unmarked, but in pursuit of a fleeing felon?"

"Objection as to what the other motorists could see or knew about a fleeing felon," Thomas said.

"Sustained."

"Were other cars getting out of the way?" Egan rephrased.

"Yes."

"No further questions."

"Re-cross?" Schell asked, turning to Thomas.

"No, thank you, Your Honor." Thomas was getting out after noticing that a few jurors seemed a bit annoyed with her questions.

The last witness for the day was Maisy Morowski.

Looking every bit the efficient legal secretary that she is, Maisy sat in the witness block with her eyes locked on Hall as he asked a few set-up questions on how long she had been with Cavaretta and how she filed letters. Then she detailed how she kept and filed the threatening letter from Eric Peterson that he wrote after his incarceration for a triple murder.

Hemphill declined to cross.

CHAPTER 51

The ride from Dixon Correctional Center penitentiary to the Cook County Courthouse took about two hours in the predawn traffic. Two investigators from the State's Attorney's office, Joe Hannon and Jesse Washington, both retired Chicago cops, had picked Edward Konsler up and slapped the cuffs on him in the waiting room before taking him out to the waiting car.

"Can we do the cuffs in front so I can smoke, guys, please?" Konsler asked. Konsler was a repeat rapist and petty burglar. He had never used a weapon in his most recent assaults, both of which targeted women in their early 70s. He burglarized their homes in a rural area just miles south of Belvidere, and thought he would top it off with a little sex. In previous burglaries, he had either urinated or defecated on the dining room tables of his victims. He was a sick cat, but not much danger to these two veteran cops.

"Sure, what you think, Jesse?"

"You're going to be puffing on that foul cigar, and I ain't gonna go without a butt for two hours, so what the fuck? You try anything, asshole, and we will break both your arms, and no one will ever believe you didn't deserve it. Got it?" Washington said.

"I'm cool, cool. Take it easy. I just want to smoke, not stage the Great Escape. Notch it down, detectives." Konsler revealed his graying teeth in an unctuous smile as Washington recuffed him in front, then shoved him into the rear seat, separated from the front seats by a metal screen.

Twenty years earlier, after his first rape conviction—for assaulting the 13-year-old niece of his boss—Konsler wound up in a cell at

Stateville with Eric Peterson, just a few days after he was sentenced in the triple murder and rape, then dispatched to the Illinois Department of Corrections.

"I'm gonna get that fucking prosecutor. The cops are all crooks, but the prosecutor is supposed to be better, the buffer between us and those jagoff cops," Peterson had said. "He knew I hadn't confessed, but he approved charges anyway. I shouldn't be here. Motherfucking Cavaretta. And then I caught the dirty dago again at trial."

Konsler remembered the conversation because the name of the prosecutor was the same as his dad's hero on the Cubs, Phil Cavarretta— different spelling, same pronunciation. And that's what he told Ortiz when she came to talk to him in Pontiac while Halloran had been hunting in India.

After they arrived at the rear of the 26th Street courthouse, Washington and Hannon handed off their prisoner to two burly deputies assigned to the sheriff's SORT (Special Operations Response Team) unit.

"How come he's cuffed in front?" asked one of the deputies as Washington took his cuffs off.

"He's a fucking Houdini, slipped them around the front on us." Hannon winked at Washington.

"Right, pal." The deputy slapped his own cuffs on Konsler—in the back-- for the trip to the courtroom.

A short time later, still dressed in his IDOC jumper, Konsler walked into Schell's courtroom and smiled at the jury. Not one juror smiled back. Several just looked to the back of the courtroom to avoid making eye contact.

After being sworn in, Konsler sat and nodded up to the judge as if they were somehow peers, the two parties in the courtroom without agendas. Schell frowned at the witness and instructed Egan to proceed.

Egan first led Konsler quickly through his extensive criminal record to take that arrow out of the defense quiver. Then she took him through the events that led to his being in the same cell with Peterson. Peterson glared at him with a laser focus.

"And do you see that man in the courtroom today?" Egan asked.

"Yes, ma'am. Hey, Eric, how ya doin?" Konsler waved over to the defense table. Peterson kept glaring.

"Can you describe what the man you were cellmates with back then is wearing and point him out?"

"Oh, yeah. He's at the defense table there,' Konsler said pointing and grinning, "dressed up like a legit guy in that green blazer. Lookin' good, man." Peterson sat mute and seethed.

Thomas spoke up. "We stipulate to the identification, Your Honor."

Egan then brought Konsler to the day and time he heard Peterson talk about the prosecutor whom he wanted to get even with. He repeated for the judge and jury exactly what he had told Ortiz in prison.

"Was there any other reason you had to recall your brief time with the defendant?" Egan asked.

"Yeah, he was a cheap fuck."

"The witness will watch his language," Schell interrupted.

"Sorry, judge," Konsler said.

"And why do you say that?" Egan asked.

"Because when I was out of smokes, he would never loan me one. My brand too, he smoked. Camels unfiltered."

"Thank you. I have no further questions of this witness."

Defense counsel Peter Chance nodded to Egan, and then stepped before Schell.

"If the court pleases," Chance said, resplendent in his charcoal brown tailor-made suit, pale blue shirt and red and white polka dot bow tie. A graduate of Berkeley undergraduate and Harvard Law, Chance was every bit the aristocratic patrician. He raised his nose just slightly to address Konsler.

"You speak of your criminal past as if you are proud of it. Are you?"

Egan stirred to protest, but Dunne knocked her knee with his at the prosecution table. She remained seated and silent

"Hey, it is what it is, man. I ain't going to lie or sugarcoat it."

"Well, that's good of you. So, let's pursue that a bit. Let's talk about the truth, unvarnished and naked. Did the prosecution offer you anything for your testimony?"

"Not a thing," he said, smiling at Egan.

"But is it not so that you have been moved from maximum security Pontiac to medium security Dixon in the past few months?" Chance asked.

"Yes sir, but I'm thinking that was for good behavior."

"And our prosecutors from Cook County, who send more prisoners to the state system than any other office of State's Attorney in the state, would have had no hand in that, is that what you are telling me and this jury of 12 intelligent people?" Chance arched his eyebrows, looking to the jury.

Egan shot out of her seat.

"Your Honor, counsel can't possibly be hinting that Mr. Konsler knows about what the Illinois Department of Corrections is basing its decisions on."

"I think that is exactly what he is hinting. You may answer," Schell said to Konsler.

"Beats the shit out of me. I've been good in the joint. But I didn't ask and they didn't say. Kind of like the Army these days, you know?" Konsler said, turning to grin into the jury box.

"Watch your language--again," Schell admonished. "This is not the prison yard, sir, but a court of law. Continue, Mr. Chance."

"Moving on. Would you say that your memory of the events of 20 years ago is better today than it would have been, say, the week after you had this alleged conversation with the defendant?"

"Well, I sure would hope it would've been better back then, wouldn't you?" Konsler said.

"My opinion is neither sworn nor relevant. But yours is both. Would you say your memory is not as good as it once was of these alleged events and conversations?"

"If you think this is scoring points, counselor, I'd say you're nuts. But yeah, I would say that the memory was better a week later. And the cheeseburger I'm going to have for lunch will taste better today than my memory of it will be tomorrow," he turned to see if that got a reaction from the jury. They just stared, but he had made a point with some of them.

Chance was not where he wished to be but had scored a minor point he could use in his closing argument.

"I have nothing further to pursue with this witness."

"Redirect?" Schell asked.

Egan rose quickly but stayed in place at the prosecution table.

"Did the prosecution make you any promises in return for your testimony?" Egan asked.

"Not a thing." Konsler continued, grinning.

"Was your sentence reduced after you testified before the grand jury?" she asked.

"Not a minute."

"Has anyone at this table given you anything or promised you anything for your testimony?"

"Nope."

"Did anyone at this table or in the State's Attorney's office promise you that we would intercede with the Illinois Department of Corrections on your behalf?"

"No, ma'am."

"Is there some particular reason that you remember the cigarette brand?" Egan asked.

"Yeah, we talked about how it was just one more nail in the coffin with them unfiltered Camels. But he said he was looking at death anyway, so he laughed about getting lung cancer and cheating the needle."

"Thank you. That is all." Egan sat back down after linking Peterson to the same brand of cigarette found next to Jenny Cavaretta's body.

Chance looked to his co-counsels as Schell asked if he had anything to ask on re-cross.

"I think we are finished with this witness, Your Honor," Chance said.

"You may step down," Schell said.

"Mr. Pomposity looked just great with the con, eh," Hall whispered to Dunne. Dunne nodded and leaned over to Egan.

"Smarter than he looks. And without the benefit of an Ivy League education."

Egan smiled and tried to read the jury. Always tough with a con on the stand.

***

Karen Svenson seldom took a hit from a defense attorney. It was never a fair game. She knew the book on DNA better than any defense attorney alive.

Dunne was the prosecution's best-versed attorney on DNA, so he did the direct examination on Svenson.

After reciting all her degrees, articles she has written, and courses she has taught and taken, Svenson got to the key testimony. The unfiltered Camel and the letter.

When she gave the odds of the DNA coming from someone other than Peterson, every juror scribbled down her words, "14 quadrillion to one."

"And that would, would it not, be more people than have ever walked on this earth?"

Dunne knew the answer well, having asked it before of the same witness.

"That is true."

"And the DNA you gleaned from the letter the defendant sent Mr. Cavaretta matched the DNA lifted from the cigarette recovered in the victim's car? Dunne asked.

"It did," Svenson answered crisply.

Dunne walked over to the prosecution table and sat down. "Nothing further, Your Honor."

Hemphill rose slowly, glancing at Svenson, but then looking to the jury.

"Miss Svenson, you would have no idea how that cigarette allegedly got in that car, would you?" Hemphill was planting seeds for closing argument.

"No, sir, that is not my field. I analyze evidence for DNA, not collect it." Svenson had played this game before, and knew to keep it short, tight, on point.

"So, if that cigarette had been taken from the defendant's home and planted there, you would have no way of knowing that, would you?"

"Objection," Egan said, rising. "There is no evidence whatsoever that the cigarette was planted, nor will there be."

"Sustained. Anything further, counselor?" Schell asked.

"I think that is sufficient," Hemphill said.

"Redirect?" Schell asked.

"Nothing more. Thank you, Miss Svenson," Egan said.

Juror Samuel Jackson smiled at Svenson as she stepped down and filed past the jury box. Dunne caught it and nodded to Hall.

Next up was Sgt. Tom Sheehan, who testified that he found the purse empty and the credit cards missing and no cash. Near the car, he said, police found a plastic bag containing marijuana, which the defense would stipulate was indeed cannabis as tested by the crime lab.

"Who did the marijuana belong to, Sergeant?" Hemphill asked in cross-examination.

"I would have no idea, counselor." Sheehan was then excused.

Schell cleared his throat and looked to the jurors.

"Ladies and gentlemen, Mr. Hall is now going to read into the record a stipulation. A stipulation is a statement of facts that both the prosecution and the defense agree would be the testimony if the witness were to take the stand. Mr. Hall, proceed."

Hall rose and began to read off a legal pad that held the words that he had worked out with Peter Chance.

"If called upon to testify, Marine Lance Corporal James S. Hayes would testify that on March 16, 2003, he was on duty at the front desk of the American Consulate in Calcutta, India. At about 7 p.m., or 1900 hours military time, an American named Michael Halloran walked into the consulate and asked for an Amanda Beeler. Behind him was another civilian whose name I came to know was Eric Peterson. He was carrying a Canadian passport identifying himself as Harry Peters. He appeared to be there of his own volition since he had been smiling and laughing with Mr. Halloran as they entered. I witnessed the suspect pull a knife and threaten us. Officer Halloran disarmed him, and we subsequently handcuffed him and took him into custody. On orders from Deputy Consul Bill Prentiss, I and Corporal Edward Price placed Eric Peterson under arrest under a UFAP warrant issued by the U.S. District Court in Chicago, Illinois."

"So stipulated counsel?" Schell asked.

"So stipulated," said Chance.

"So stipulated," agreed Egan.

So much for entrapment, coercion, and force, thought Egan.

After that, Patrol Officer Eduardo Martinez testified how on the evening of July 29, 2002, he had observed a Buick LeSabre glide through a stop sign at Grand Avenue, while northbound on Hermitage. When he pulled over the defendant, Eric Peterson, he smelled cannabis emanating from the car. He then ordered Peterson out of the car, searched the car, and found some plastic bags and a one-pound brick of what appeared to be marijuana on the back seat.

"Dealer size," he said.

The defense stipulated to the lab reports that the brick of marijuana tested positive for cannabis at the crime lab. There was a further stipulation that Peterson was under indictment for possession of that marijuana at the time of the murder.

There was no cross.

The circumstantial noose was tightening.

CHAPTER 52

Two witnesses put Peterson at the bar that night with Jennifer Cavaretta. Sort of.

Tom Reynolds testified he recognized the tattoo when Peterson stood up as instructed, took off his suit coat and rolled up his blue dress shirt. Anne Doyle said Peterson looked like the man she had seen in the bar talking to Jenny the night she was murdered, because she also had noticed the strange tattoo on his wrist. She also testified that Jenny said she had seen him around school.

Neither did well on cross examination, admitting they could not be sure it was Peterson they had seen that night in the bar.

A subdued Dr. Moretti took the stand and testified how Peterson had been a quick study and learned to take a pulse by finding the carotid. He shook his head as he passed Peterson, who kept his head down for the entire testimony.

By the end of the fourth day of testimony, the prosecution rested with a strong circumstantial case based on DNA, corroborative third-party statements and a confession of sorts to Halloran. Plus, motive and opportunity.

The defense called as its first witness Joan Pritchard-Peterson.

Dressed in a flowered peasant blouse, a pink skirt and black Birkenstocks, Pritchard-Peterson walked to the witness stand and raised her right hand without being prompted, like a professional witness. Her stringy dishwater blond hair was pulled back into a tight bun held together by a leather hair clasp with a pencil stuck through it.

She swore that on the night of the murder Peterson was with her all night, and she remembered because they had eaten Thai food that night--her favorite, Pad Thai. She remembered waking up at 4 a.m. with heartburn, her acid reflux acting up and awakening her. She said her husband was sleeping soundly by her side when she went back to bed after taking some Tums.

Thomas did the direct examination, woman to woman, often staring into the jury box, making eye contact with Gordon, the Quaker hospice nurse who by now the defense had fixed upon as their most sympathetic juror.

At the end of direct, Egan stood and walked up to Pritchard-Peterson. "It would be safe to say that you love your husband very much. Would it not?"

"That would be true," Pritchard-Peterson said warily.

"That you would do anything for him?"

"Most anything," she said.

"And that is, of course, understandable. On the night of Sept. 1, 2002, did you call the police to report that your husband was beating you?"

"That was a little disagreement, the kind that most couples have."

"So that would be a 'yes,' would it not?"

"Yes, I suppose." A frown creased Pritchard-Peterson's pinched features.

"And according to the police report, your right eye was swollen and some blood was observed under your nose. Why is it that you decided not to testify against your husband in that case?"

"It was simply a lover's quarrel. He is not a violent man."

"Not violent is it? Where did you meet your husband?"

"I met him through the mail, through correspondence."

"But where is it that you first set eyes on him?"

"In Joliet, Illinois."

"In Stateville Penitentiary?" Egan asked.

"Yes."

"And why was he there?"

"Objection," Thomas said. "This is beyond the scope of the direct examination, Your Honor."

"I'll allow it. That door has long been opened," Schell said, turning slightly to the witness stand making a small gesture with his left hand to continue.

"He was wrongfully convicted and later exonerated." Pritchard-Peterson's eyes flashed toward the jury box.

"Convicted of what?"

"Does it matter? He was innocent," Pritchard-Peterson said. "They said he killed three people. Never happened."

"I see. And who said so? Was it the jury or trial judge, the Illinois Appellate Court, the Illinois Supreme Court, the 7th Circuit U.S. Court of Appeals, the U.S. Supreme Court? Who said Eric Peterson was innocent?"

"Gov. Riley said so. He was the only one who listened to the facts of the case." Pritchard-Peterson's voice rising in anger, she looked to the defense table for help.

"But you were aware he was convicted of that triple homicide, including the murder of a child?" Egan asked.

"Yes, but I am also aware that Gov. Riley dismissed that bullshit case," Pritchard-Person spat out.

"And that would've been just two days before the governor left office in disgrace, would it not?"

"Objection, Your Honor. This whole line of questioning is way beyond the scope of my direct. And the prosecutor is making a speech, not conducting a cross-examination."

"These are indeed speeches. Sustained. The jury will disregard the last question from Ms. Egan."

Thomas sat down fuming, glaring at Egan for making the same kind of cheap points she had made. Egan was a streetfighter in court and knew the limits the judge would allow and would restrain herself just short of overstepping the law. Neither Egan, nor Dunne, nor Hall, nor Cavaretta wanted this trial declared a mistrial or later sent back by a higher court for a new trial. She moved on.

"Let's go back to the night you answered the intercom when detective Ortiz stopped by to question your husband about the Cavaretta murder. You remember that night, right?"

"Yes," Pritchard-Peterson said. "But he didn't know what the cops were there for. He probably thought it had something to do with that bullshit pot bust a few months before." Thomas winced. The defense team had warned her to stick to yes and no answers on cross.

"And your husband ran from the police that night, is that correct?"

"The cops had hassled him for more than 20 years. They were never fair or honest. He ran because he knew he would never get a fair shake. Look at him now. He shouldn't be here."

"So, the answer is 'yes.' Is that correct?"

"You bet he ran. Correct."

"Two final questions. Miss Pritchard-Peterson, would you give your life for your husband?"

"I would," she said proudly, jutting her lower lip slightly forward.

"Would you lie?" Egan said.

"Objection," Thomas shouted.

"Overruled. You may answer," Schell said.

"I would not," Pritchard-Peterson said, looking into the jury at Gordon. The juror scribbled a note.

"I see. Thank you," Egan said.

"Redirect," Schell said.

"Are you a good Christian?" Thomas asked.

"I was raised Episcopalian," Pritchard-Peterson said, avoiding her diversion into Hinduism.

"Did you just lie on the witness stand after taking an oath to God not to?"

"I did not. I would not."

"Thank you, no further questions."

"Ms. Egan?" Schell asked, the questions having hit the bottom of the inverted pyramid of cross-examination.

Egan was taking notes, and merely looked up briefly and told the judge, "No thanks, Your Honor."

"Next witness," Schell said.

Hemphill rose slowly and looked into the jury box, looking into the eyes of Jackson.

"The defense rests," he said.

"Rebuttal witnesses?" Schell asked. Dunne glanced to Egan and Hall. They shook their heads slightly.

"No thank you, Your Honor." It was 4:45 p.m.

Schell looked to first the prosecution and then the defense table.

"The jury is dismissed. We will see you again at 9:45 a.m. Good night," Schell said.

***

"That's the best they got? The wife alibi? Jesus, this is a slam dunk," Hall was fairly exploding as the three prosecutors gathered in Dunne's office.

"Let's not get cocky. We still have a way to go with this. But maybe they're going for an 'ineffectiveness of counsel' reversal from the Appellate Court," Dunne said.

"Unlikely. Half the Appellate Court goes to the same charity galas as Chance. How would that play at the next cocktail party at the Union League Club?" Egan asked. They all laughed.

Egan resumed. "I'm going home to do this close for the 200th time. I will be back at—what Dick?—7:30--to run it by you guys?" Egan asked.

"We'll be here. I'm gonna stay here and do my best to counter their close. Ed, I may need a little help, okay?" Dunne said.

"Absolutely," Hall replied.

CHAPTER 53

Just after dawn, the TV trucks were already lining up along California Boulevard--10 of them, all of the local stations plus CNN, CNBC, and C-Span. CNBC was feeding into the BBC.

Truly, the world was watching.

The line outside the courthouse on California had snaked around to 26th Street long before the deputies opened the front door at 8 a.m. The second and third rows in Schell's court had been reserved for the Cavaretta family, right behind the sketch artists. The next three rows for the press. The lines for the general public were backed up down the hall towards Schell's chambers' door.

Inside, the hard and scarred oak benches were jammed, divided almost equally between prosecution supporters on the right side and defense supporters on the left.

The mood in Schell's courtroom was electric. Tom Cavaretta entered with Joyce on his arm at 9:25 a.m. He nodded to Egan, Dunne, and Hall, mouthing a "good luck" before sitting down. Anne Doyle and Tom Reynolds were already there. Anne hugged Joyce. Reynolds shook hands gravely with the State's Attorney.

Pritchard-Peterson sat alone with her thoughts in the second row on the left, just 10 feet from her husband's seat. After Peterson was escorted in by two deputies, he blew her a kiss and gazed into the defense side of the gallery for another friendly face. It was just strangers who were there to support him.

At 9:29 a.m., Schell walked purposefully into his courtroom and up to the bench. He looked from side to side.

"All here? Good. Bring in the jury." Schell nodded to the deputy standing by the jurors' door.

The courtroom was overflowing. Given the crowd outside, Schell had allowed the deputies to line the back and side walls with spectators.

Before the jury entered, Schell looked up to admonish the throng.

"I have allowed you folks to stand in my courtroom today as a courtesy. You will all conduct yourselves with decorum in this court or suffer the consequences. Thank you for your cooperation."

After the jury filed in and seated themselves, Schell turned to Egan. She walked slowly toward the lectern and placed her yellow legal pad on top before she positioned the wooden stand at a 45-degree angle aimed at the jury.

"It would be easy if we had all witnessed the murder of Jennifer Cavaretta, or if we had a videotape of the crime, if Eric Peterson had been as upfront and obvious as Jack Ruby. But that is not what we have here.

"What we have is a circumstantial case, but a tight circumstantial case backed by DNA science that has parts that fit together as snugly and completely as my two hands and fingers fold together." Egan interlocked her fingers together and held them up for a moment just beneath her nose.

"What you will hear from the defense when I sit down is that there is reasonable doubt in this case. There is not. There is not only no reasonable doubt; there is no doubt. How could there be doubt?

"We know that Eric Peterson harbored a grudge against Tom Cavaretta for more than 20 years. We heard that from Ed Konsler. The defense will tell you that Konsler is a career criminal, a scumbag. And it's true. He is. But we didn't choose him. This man chose him."

Theatrically, Egan walked over to the defense table and pointed to Peterson, her right index finger a foot from the back of his head. Peterson jotted notes on a legal pad as if whatever Egan had to say bored him.

"We know that he's violent. His wife acknowledged that. You heard from her how he was convicted in a triple murder years ago. We know that Peterson matches the description of a man who was seen the night of the murder, just a block from the murder scene. Tom Reynolds did not get a good look at Peterson that night, but he did remember this unique tattoo, the scorpion one that he has kept under wraps for most of this trial. Anne Doyle said Peterson looked like the guy she had seen talking to Jenny at the bar and that Jenny had said she had seen him around school.

"We know that his DNA was on that cigarette butt in Jenny Cavaretta's car. And you heard Tom Reynolds say Jenny never smoked. Konsler told you that Peterson smoked Camels unfiltered, the same kind of cigarette found in the Cavaretta car.

"You heard from Officer Jackson that he found a lid of marijuana a short distance from the Jaguar Jenny was found in. We know that Peterson was peddling because he had a pending case against him for possessing a dealer's amount of marijuana. We heard from Maisy Morowski that she kept a threatening letter from prison from Eric Peterson that he wrote after his incarceration for that triple murder. And you heard from Karen Svenson that the DNA on the cigarette in Jenny's car matched the DNA left on the dried saliva Peterson used to send that letter to scare a young Tom Cavaretta. It was the coward's way, to send a threatening letter. He dared not threaten the prosecutor to his face. He didn't go after the State's Attorney when he got out of prison. No. No, ladies and gentlemen. He saw that Tom Cavaretta--whose office puts thousands of violent people in prison every year-- had bodyguards. Armed policemen. So, this coward started stalking Cavaretta's daughter, plotting his move.

"He found it that night on a darkened street when he took just one swing to land that lethal wound. Dr. Moretti told us Peterson knew at an early age how to find the carotid. Coincidence, ladies and gentlemen? I think not. There are no coincidences in law enforcement. There are connections. And the connections that link Eric Peterson are many, and interwoven, like a spider's web. And in the center of the spider's web was Eric Peterson.

"Unfortunately, Jenny Cavaretta became ensnared in the web Peterson spun around her. In the last moments of her young life, Jenny was stung by Peterson and infected with the venom Peterson had been harboring and storing for two decades. And in the end, the cowardly predator, Eric Peterson, plunged his deadly ice pick into Jenny's throat like the venomous killer he is and has proven himself to be. In his haste to flee, he left behind his cigarette butt. We will never know exactly how he conned his way into that Jaguar, but we assume he did.

"In a short time, you will hear a lot of talk about reasonable doubt. Think of this term and how you've used the word 'reasonable' in your everyday lives. If you were told the facts of this case by a neighbor and were asked if you thought Peterson committed this horrific, deadly, planned attack, you would probably say that it was reasonable that he did it.

"What you've seen and heard in this case is a cascading avalanche of evidence that flows right to Eric Peterson. We know that Peterson had dealer-level amounts of marijuana because he was arrested with a pound of it. We know that a baggie, or lid, of cannabis was found a short distance from the Cavaretta car. We can make a leap in logic to picture Peterson in his haste to get away from the murder scene dropping one of his lids on the street.

"You heard Detective Halloran testify how Peterson talked about evening the score with the 'bitch and her old man'. It's an avalanche of facts and logical inferences that lead to the inescapable conclusion that Eric Peterson, this defendant," Egan said, walking from the place she had established at the lectern in front of the jury to walk over to point emphatically again at Peterson, "this man, this violent career criminal, plunged the ice pick into the carotid artery of Jenny Cavaretta, ending a life filled with a rich future, ripe with promise and love, to settle his fantasy of vengeance. This is really a very simple case, ladies and gentlemen. We have before us a habitually violent criminal who uses violence to settle scores and eliminate those who cross him.

"Ladies and gentlemen, there is no doubt. I ask you to do your sworn duty and find Eric Peterson guilty of the first-degree murder of Jennifer Cavaretta.

"Thank you."

The only sound in the courtroom was the quiet sobbing of Joyce Dennehy Cavaretta.

"We will take a break before proceeding with the defense," Schell said.

CHAPTER 54

In long hours of preparing for this high-profile case, the defense team had decided it would be Hemphill who would be the clean-up hitter, the one who would have the last word with the jury, the last person to rip into the case the prosecution would deliver.

When the jury returned from lunch, Schell turned to the defense table, and said, "Mr. Hemphill, if you please."

"Thank you, Your Honor. Your Honor, counsel, ladies and gentlemen of the jury." He paused as he stood in front of the judge and to the right of Peterson. "This man remains innocent to this point. Innocent until you say otherwise. There is no more serious matter that any jury has to decide than this.

"Eric Peterson has lived a hard life, perhaps a life that many of you might not approve of. He may not be your kind of guy. He has a prison tattoo. He's done time, but we also learned that that conviction was thrown out. So, you must put that aside. But Eric Peterson cannot put aside those years he spent in prison for a crime he did not commit. We did not learn all the details of that crime and we need not. Those details were dealt with by Gov. Riley when he freed Eric. There are things we know and don't know, as it is in life.

"We know, for instance, that the victim, Jennifer Cavaretta, was bright, lovely and had a wonderful future. No one in this courtroom has anything but sympathy for the Cavarettas for their loss. But will it make their loss any less painful if you convict an innocent man of a crime he did not commit? Ms. Egan struck an analogy of a spider's web. Let's run with that a bit further. The spider's web is translucent and delicate in its appearance. It captures leaves, dust, insects--without discrimination. The prosecution and the police have spun a web that has ensnared an innocent man who happened to be in the wrong place at the wrong time.

"We did not waste your time or the court's in a lengthy cross-examination of Mr. Reynolds about what or whom he might have seen that night at the bar. Let's say he did see Mr. Peterson. What does that prove? But he did not say he saw Mr. Peterson. He said he saw a man with a tattoo. We would need a jail the size of Rhode Island if we were to go after every man with a tattoo who may have been near Jenny Cavaretta in her last few days, weeks or months on this earth."

Hemphill was pacing now, back and forth in front of the jury, making sure that he made good eye contact with the African Americans and particularly with juror Gordon, the defense hope.

"The prosecutor would have you believe that Eric Peterson plotted to kill Tom Cavaretta, the victim's father, for taking an alleged confession, *unsigned,* that turned out to be worthless and for prosecuting a case that was eventually tossed. And how would they like you to come to that conclusion? Based on the worthless testimony of a con named Ed Konsler. He tried to be cute on the stand. Did you find him cute? I don't think that one of you good people found him cute. Don't find him credible either. He got moved to a better prison right after he agreed to testify. Ms. Egan says she doesn't believe in coincidences, but she would have you believe that Konsler took the stand out of the goodness of his heart. He has no heart; he has no goodness. Toss his testimony in the trash, where it and he belong.

"The prosecution will make much in the rebuttal in a few minutes dealing with the DNA evidence in this case. We do not dispute that Eric Peterson, in a moment of desperation and frustration, wrote Mr. Cavaretta a letter that was vaguely threatening. Why would he not be frustrated? He was in prison for a crime he did not commit. And we do not dispute that it was his DNA on that cigarette butt. But the question that you must ask is: How did that cigarette get there? There is no evidence that Mr. Peterson ever was in that car. You heard not a whisper about his fingerprints being found in or on the car. No one said they saw him in the car, near it or leaving it.

"What we are left with is that a cigarette was found there, and it had his DNA on it. We know that the police had once wrongfully convicted Mr. Peterson and we know that he had been arrested by them just a few months before the murder on an alleged dope possession—which by the way has never been proven—and that the police wanted to press felony charges against Peterson for a domestic dispute that his wife was not interested in pursuing. How did that cigarette get there? We simply do not know, so we are left to guess. A man's freedom is at stake here-- should we be guessing?

"None of us who listened to Officer Ortiz could be unaffected by the trauma she suffered. We do not deny that Eric Peterson fired the shot that wounded her. But you must consider the thoughts that must have been running through Eric Peterson's mind as he ran for his life that night. There is no evidence that he knew these officers in civilian clothes in an unmarked car were police. But okay, let's say he knew they were the police. This is the same police department that 20 years earlier brought the charges that he was innocent of. It is the same police department that brought up the trumped-up charges of dope possession..."

Egan jumped to her feet.

"Objection, Your Honor. There is absolutely no evidence, not a scintilla of evidence that the arrest for possession of more than a pound of high-grade, dealer-level, cannabis was trumped up. That case—by the way--is still pending. Move to strike."

"Sustained. The jury will disregard Mr. Hemphill's characterization of the marijuana case as 'trumped-up,'" Schell said. "Proceed."

"No evidence that it was a valid arrest," Hemphill continued.

"Objection," Egan said.

"Sustained. Let's move along, shall we, Mr. Hemphill?" Schell said.

Unfazed by two sustained objections, Hemphill plowed on.

"So, you have this man who has had questionable, at best, contact with the police being pursued by two officers with no clue as to what this is about. And yes, he takes a pistol out and fires in self-defense.

And then he is so frightened, he flees the country. Then, while lawfully visiting the beautiful Himalayan hill station of Darjeeling, he is hijacked by rogue detective Mike Halloran and delivered to the American Consulate in Calcutta. We have only the stipulated testimony of a Marine that Mr. Peterson was not coerced, lied to, bamboozled, or shanghaied by this vengeful, out-of-control detective.

"Under international law, Mr. Peterson should still be traveling peacefully on the subcontinent so identified with the peaceful philosophy of Mahatma Gandhi.'

"Objection, Your Honor. Learned counsel may know Illinois law and the judge will instruct on its applicability in this case, but there has been no evidence of violation of international law or of Mr. Hemphill's expertise in this area."

"Sustained, let's stick to Illinois law," Schell said.

"You've heard from Mrs. Pritchard-Peterson that her husband was with her the night and morning of the murder. She took an oath and swore to tell the truth. She said she loves her husband but would not lie to protect him. Let's say that he did strike her during a domestic dispute, just supposing, not admitting, since there is scant evidence of that. Would it not be more likely that she would turn on him, would not lie for him, but rather would take this opportunity to get even with him?

"What you have here is reasonable doubt. Doubt that she would lie for him. Doubt that it was Eric Peterson who left behind a DNA calling card in the victim's car. Doubt about how that cigarette butt got there. Doubt that he was anywhere near Lincoln Avenue that night. Doubt that if he did commit this crime, what did he do? Wear latex gloves to prevent leaving prints or wipe the ice pick and car clean of his prints inside and out in the seconds it took for the police to arrive? Highly unlikely.

"There is no smoking gun here, ladies and gentlemen. There is reasonable doubt. Doubt by the boatload that this man, this formerly wrongfully incarcerated man who lost 20 years of his life, would risk his freedom to commit such a vile murder.

"We ask you to find this persecuted man innocent of the murder of Jennifer Cavaretta. We ask you to search your minds, your souls and your common sense and return a just verdict in this case. Not guilty.

"Thank you."

Peterson nodded to the jury. Not one juror nodded back. Gordon cast her eyes into her lap.

"We resume at 9:30 for rebuttal," Schell said. Hemphill patted Peterson on the back.

"Great job," Thomas said.

"Well done," Chance said. Hemphill picked up his yellow pad and stuffed it into his valise. Hemphill nodded.

"We'll see."

CHAPTER 55

The voice of WBBM morning anchor Pat Cassidy jolted Dick Dunne awake the next morning. He was one of those rare men so comfortable with his skills and preparation that he can sleep like a baby before a command performance like he was set to deliver on this day.

"Good morning, breakfast lovers. This is Pat Cassidy with Felicia Middlebrooks. It is 6:05 on a bright but windy morning. The lead story is closing arguments in the explosive murder trial of Eric Peterson..."

This day could be a career-maker. The eyes of the county, of the country, would be on the courtroom of Morris Schell. On Dick Dunne, on the son of a fireman and grandson of Irish immigrants.

His whole career had been pointing to this hour that he would have to wrap up the case against Peterson. The other 109 jury trials, 107 of which he had won, had been warm-ups for this. He knew that, and he relished it.

As he showered, he rehearsed his close. He parsed the words carefully. There would be no wasted rhetoric. He would be Hemingway in the courthouse delivering the final graph of Farewell to Arms—written, rewritten, edited, tailored, cut, polished and finalized.

He chose his dark grey, pinstriped suit, white shirt, navy blue striped tie, black wingtips. Professional but not flashy, not overdressed like Chance, the dilettante from the grey towers of academia taking a sabbatical for a few weeks.

Not Dunne. This was his life--26th and California was not a vacation; it was a vocation. It was who he was. Had it been 27 blocks north, on the North Side, it would not have been who he was. Dunne was a South Sider, through and through. His father only started cheering for the Bears when they stopped playing at Wrigley Field and moved to Soldier Field, on the South Side--just barely.

Dunne drove slowly to the courthouse that morning, with the traffic, not looking to make time. He was going over the rebuttal for the last time in his head. It would be good, tight, terse, tying up any loose ends Hemphill had sought to untie.

Egan had been terrific, a hard act to follow, anticipating well what the defense planned to say. But Hemphill had gotten the attention of the jury, and of the press, always a good indicator of how effective a closing argument was. If the press left before you finished, you were dead. You were boring. No one left during Hemphill's close. It was very good. Dunne had to be great. He would be, he told himself as he parked the gleaming black Crown Vic in his spot behind the courthouse in front of the old Division I cellblock.

"You're going back there, fuckhead," Dunne said to the grey walls that held Peterson.

In his office looking west across the jail complex, Dunne thumbed through the police report of Peterson's arrest on the marijuana beef. He really did not need to look it over for the 10th time; it was just something to do while he waited. Cavaretta walked in.

"Morning, Dick. Ready?" Cavaretta's face revealed no sign of stress. He looked calm. Dunne hoped he portrayed the same placid façade.

"He's dead meat, boss."

"Good. Good luck. I'll leave you alone. I know you're ready, but I know you need a few minutes." Cavaretta ducked out to retreat to his adjacent office.

Egan walked into the State's Attorney's office seconds later. Dunne could hear her muted conversation with the boss; he knew Cavaretta was congratulating Egan. She deserved it; hers was a great close.

"Break a leg, boss," Egan said, poking her head around the partially closed door that Cavaretta had left slightly ajar.

"Thanks, partner. You set the table. I just have to be careful not to drop the hors d'oeuvres tray on the jury. Tie it up without fucking it up. Right?"

"Hemphill's bullshit about reasonable doubt did not play well with this jury. I could feel it. You, too?"

"Yep. Give me 10 minutes, will you?" Dunne was about three supervisory levels over Egan, and she knew it, but she was his trial partner and partners did not pull rank. But he wanted just a few more minutes to himself.

"You got it." Egan closed the door behind her.

Dunne paced back and forth in his empty office, rehearsing even his hand gestures. By 9:15 he was ready.

In court, the gallery was packed again. Standing room only. By the time Dunne arrived with Egan and Hall and the evidence carts, the Cavarettas were in their spot in the second row right, behind the courtroom artists. Halloran right behind them.

The defense table was full, but for the defendant. By 9:25, the deputies led Peterson into court.

At 9:30 a.m. sharp, Judge Schell exited his chambers and scaled the three steps up to his leather swivel seat, situated at the highest point in the courtroom.

"Are we ready for the jury?" Schell asked. Dunne spoke for the prosecution.

"Yes, Your Honor."

"Ready," said Chance.

"Bring out the jury, please," Schell ordered.

Brigham led the group out as usual. And as usual, she gazed into the throng gathered for this final show. The murmurs quieted as the jury shuffled in.

When they were seated, Schell nodded to Dunne. "Proceed, Mr. Dunne."

Dunne moved the lectern until it faced the jurors directly. He straightened his notes on his legal pad and put West's Illinois Criminal

Law and Procedure on top. He walked around the lectern to face the jurors, five feet from the dark oak box that held them.

"First of all, on behalf of Ms. Egan and Mr. Hall, I would like to thank you for your attention during the last two weeks. I have watched as you have taken notes and paid close attention to the evidence in this difficult case. I've watched as a few of you have wiped away a tear, some embarrassed by your involuntary show of emotions. That reaction is understandable. This is an emotional case. But I want you to cast aside your emotions, hold them in abeyance and think clearly and logically as you sift through the evidence in this case.

"Mr. Hemphill spoke of reasonable doubt. Well, folks, you know from your grammar school days that doubt is a noun and that reasonable is an adjective that modifies it. There are all sorts of adjectives we could apply. Little is an adjective. Is there little doubt Eric Peterson killed Jenny Cavaretta? I would submit there is little and little is stronger than reasonable here.

"Grave is another adjective. Do we have grave doubt that Eric Peterson plotted from his prison cell to get even with Tom Cavarretta? No doubt. Ed Konsler is no angel, but he had no motive to lie. Mr. Hemphill would have you believe there is a grand conspiracy to get Eric Peterson, that the powerful tentacles of the Cook County State's Attorney's office reached into the bowels of the Illinois Department of Corrections and got Ed Konsler assigned to a better prison. There is no evidence of that. And the reason there is no evidence is that it simply did not happen. Why did Konsler testify? We could guess about his motive, but we are not in the guessing business. We are in the evidence business. And there is no evidence that Konsler got anything for his testimony. Have no doubt about that—little, reasonable, or grave.

"Mr. Hemphill would have you sign on to another vague conspiracy theory-as gossamer thin and translucent as the web of words he spun for you. He cannot explain away how Eric Peterson's DNA got in Jennifer Cavaretta's car. He cannot deny and did not deny that Peterson sent the threatening letter to Tom Cavaretta. So, he uses a little misdirection.

He wants you to believe through subtle suggestions that the DNA was planted…"

"Objection, Your Honor. I said no such thing. Objection and move for a mistrial," Hemphill said.

"Overruled and denied. This is argument, rebuttal. I let you speak and now it is the prosecution's turn. Continue, Mr. Dunne," Schell said. Dunne did not so much as glance at Hemphill as he continued.

"Use your common sense. Don't be misled by idle speculation based on no evidence. Did the police trail Eric Peterson and wait for him to drop a cigarette, grab it and then kill Jennifer Cavaretta to frame him? Talk about reasonable doubt that this ever happened. How logical is that? Or else perhaps Mr. Hemphill would have you believe that someone else killed Jennifer Cavaretta, then the police planted the evidence in the car. How preposterous. The other possibility is that either Tom Cavaretta or his Jenny were pals with Eric Peterson and that one day he dropped the cigarette while getting a ride home from one of the Cavarettas. Again, preposterous and no evidence.

"What we believe you can glean from the evidence proved in court is that Eric Peterson had met Jennifer Cavaretta at Northwestern by some seemingly random event. Perhaps he asked her a question about a book she was carrying, or perhaps he bumped into her and then spilled his books all over the library floor and she helped him pick them up. Whatever the contact was, he renewed it again briefly in the bar that night. He had undoubtedly trailed her, stalked her, staked her out, and had followed her to the bar. He then waited outside and watched her go to Tom Reynolds' apartment. And then waited some more. He was patient. He had waited for years, decades, to even the score with Tom Cavaretta, this good man who has sat through this trial with his wife, Joyce, who you heard from early in the trial.

"Then in the early morning hours of Oct. 9, 2002, Eric Peterson staged another 'accidental' meeting with Jenny Cavaretta as she walked to her car. He asked perhaps where she was going and maybe asked for a ride. He knew she was heading to the Eisenhower because he knew where the Cavarettas lived, so he may have made up an address somewhere between Lincoln Park West and the Ike. We'll never know.

"You now have a sense of the kind of young woman Jenny was, so you would not be stretching your imaginations to assume she may have agreed to give him a ride. They got into the car, and he still had his cigarette going. But he would need both hands for his murderous act. So, he stubbed out the cigarette, and then turned on Jenny Cavaretta. Perhaps the butt fell to the floor as he made his lethal move on Jenny. We can imagine that the scream that Betty Kotowski heard came from Jenny in her last few seconds of life after she saw the ice pick—this ice pick," Dunne said, theatrically holding the weapon encased in plastic and marked as Prosecution 1.

The veteran prosecutor walked slowly by the jury box, holding the weapon at arm's length and shoulder high.

"And perhaps Jenny heard from Eric Peterson who he was and why he was going to take her life. We have no evidence of that, no proof, so we can only guess what Jenny's last moments were like. And then he plunged the ice pick into her throat into the carotid, just below the mandible line where it curves up toward the ear." Dunne stopped to point for a full five seconds to his throat just beneath the jawbone.

"At this point, he probably put his hand over her mouth to stifle further screams. You heard from Dr. Powers that there was some mild bruising over her mouth. Then in the minute it took for her life to ebb away, he held her. After she went limp, he looted her purse for her credit cards and cash. We have no evidence that he ever used her credit cards, but we do not need to present proof of that. The $100 bill her father insisted she always had hidden in back of her driver's license was missing. Perhaps he saw it and took it. Maybe she had already spent it. We will never know. Perhaps he saw this as his tip for a job well done. More probably he thought if he took the money and credit cards, police would think that it had been a robbery. We heard from Sgt. Sheehan that there was no money nor credit cards in the purse that he found under her body.

"We can use our common sense that if it had been a carjacker or robber, he would have simply taken the purse with him, rifled it and then dumped it. But not Eric Peterson. We surmise that he took the money and the cards out as he held her dying body, then for reasons we can only guess, he let her limp body fall back on it.

"But that is the only guesswork you have in this case. The rest of this case is based on the evidence. And about the guilt of Eric Peterson, you can have no doubt. There is no doubt he had a motive. He stated it in his letter to Tom Cavaretta. That was corroborated by Konsler. There is no doubt he had the knowledge of where the carotid is located. You heard from Dr. Moretti that he knew how to take a pulse there. We have no doubt Detective Halloran testified that Peterson said he had settled a score with a 'bitch.' We have no doubt that he ran from the police, tried to kill Officer Ortiz, and then fled the country.

"We watched Joan Pritchard-Peterson testify so we also have no doubt that his wife loves him. Why, you may ask, but she does. But you can have reasonable doubt that she is telling the truth. She sought this man out in prison and then married him there. She would do anything for him. She suffered at his violent hands but refused to press charges against him. Her alibi is simply not credible and not backed by any other person or event or shred of evidence. You should give her testimony no credibility whatsoever.

"What you are left with in this case is a pyramid of evidence that is strong at its base with the DNA evidence, which is unchallenged and rock solid. We build upwards with the sturdy blocks of motive and opportunity. He clearly hated Tom Cavaretta and plotted to get even. He had the opportunity because we can put him in the neighborhood the night of the murder. And at the top of the pyramid, we have Eric Peterson alone, the only suspect in this vicious and premeditated assassination of a public official's daughter."

As he warmed to the end, Dunne began gathering up his notes, stacking them up anew, and piling them neatly atop the law book. He walked away from the lectern and stared straight into the jury box, making eye contact with each juror slowly.

"What you have, ladies and gentlemen, is a tsunami of circumstantial and physical evidence that links Eric Peterson to the murder of Jennifer Cavaretta. There is no doubt in this case. No grave doubt, no reasonable doubt, not even a little doubt. Please do your sworn duty when you return to the jury room for deliberations and return a verdict of guilty in the first-degree murder of Jennifer Cavaretta and the first-degree attempt murder of Officer Sylvia Ortiz. Thank you."

There was no sound in the packed courtroom save for the fevered scratching of the sketch artists.

As Dunne walked slowly back to his seat, he looked up to see Joyce Cavaretta mouth: "Thank you."

***

Hours later, the Cavarettas sat mostly silent as they dined in a rear table in Tufano's in Little Italy, just 10 minutes from the courthouse.

Joyce Cavaretta broke the silence after turning down the waiter's suggestion of tiramisu for dessert.

"Will we ever feel we've gotten justice for our baby, even if this jury convicts?"

Cavaretta hesitated a moment, then whispered to his wife.

"We will get a conviction; I have no doubt. But justice? Never as long as that man lives."

CHAPTER 56

It had been after 4 p.m. by the time Schell finished instructing the jury that they would first have to decide if Peterson was guilty of first-degree murder and then if he deserved the death penalty. The somber jury filed out slowly to begin deliberations.

In the jury room, the vote on guilty took just two hours, with Gordon reluctant but finally willing to convict.

But when it came to sentencing Peterson to death, Gordon was intractable.

"It is never right for any person or any institution to take a life," she argued. Again and again. For three days. Jaw tight, arms crossed.

Finally, late on the third day, jury foreman Gonzales told the deputy sheriff they had reached their verdicts.

The deputy sheriff reading the Trib outside the deliberations room looked startled.

"Yes?" she said.

"Please tell the judge we're ready," Gonzales said.

CHAPTER 57

Word of the verdict ricocheted through the courthouse like a fired bullet.

Egan was in the middle of reading through the police reports of a complicated triple rape case, an unsavory assault on a drunken 15-year-old girl by three fine Catholic thugs who took advantage of her at a party that was launched just hours after the parents of one thug had taken off for a week in Bermuda.

"We have a verdict," Hall said, rushing into Egan's office.

"About time," Egan said. "Dick know?"

"I'm not sure. The deputy in Schell's court just called me. Want me to call Dick?" Hall asked.

"I'll do it," Egan said. She grabbed the phone and punched in the four digits to get Dunne's extension.

"Yeah, I just heard," Dunne said, having seen it was Egan from his caller ID. "Meet you there. I'll tell Tom."

Tom Cavaretta had just finished a call to the U.S. Attorney on a joint drug investigation when Dunne burst in.

"They have a verdict," Dunne said, a bit breathless. Cavaretta was sitting in his huge black leather chair, his tie pulled down, his navy-blue suit coat hanging on the coat tree nearby, his face haggard. It had been a brutal few weeks for the State's Attorney and his wife.

"Thanks, Dick, you go ahead. I'm going to call Joyce and wait for her. Stall for a few minutes down there for us?"

Dunne closed the door and nodded as he hustled past Maisy. They could hear muffled movement behind the closed door.

"I think he's getting ready, maybe changing his shirt. He's waiting for Joyce and said he would see us in court," Dunne said quietly.

A minute later, the State's Attorney dialed Joyce's cell phone.

"There's a verdict," he said. "No, we just know there's a verdict, not what it is. I'll wait for you, and we'll go into court together."

Joyce Cavaretta excused herself without explanation from the River Forest Library Board meeting, which she chaired. No one asked. There was no need. She jumped into her Lexus and sped east to the court-house. Tom Cavaretta was in less of a hurry as he slipped on his suit coat. Joyce joined him in less than 20 minutes.

***

Minutes after the deputy informed the judge, the courtroom was packed with reporters, prosecutors, public defenders, clerks, bailiffs and the merely curious. All parties were present, and the jury was waiting.

At 6:15 p.m., the judge summoned the jury into court. They filed into the courtroom. Superstition had it that if the jurors could not look at the defendant or the defense table, it was a guilty verdict. It was just that. Only Gordon looked furtively at Peterson, then looked away into the rear of the courtroom as soon as he looked back. Tom and Joyce sat in the second row. Halloran right behind.

"Has the jury reached a verdict?" Schell asked the foreman.

"We have two, Your Honor," Gonzales said.

"Please give the verdicts to the bailiff," Schell said.

Bailiff Johnson took the ballot and walked swiftly over to the bench to hand it up to Schell. He put on his reading glasses and studied the ballot for a moment before handing it to his clerk.

"Please read the verdict," Schell said. The bailiff cleared her throat. As instructed by his attorneys, Peterson stood and faced the jury.

"We the jury in the matter of the State of Illinois vs. Eric Peterson find the defendant guilty of first-degree murder in the death and armed robbery of Jennifer Cavaretta. We the jury find the defendant, Eric Peterson, guilty in the first-degree attempted murder of Officer Sylvia

Ortiz. As to the death penalty, we do not believe that the defendant should be executed."

Joyce Cavaretta threw her arms around her husband and began sobbing. Tom Cavaretta held his wife for a second and then freed himself.

Ten feet away, Peterson shouted at the jury.

"Fuck this. I'll do life like a walk in the park," turning to smile at the Cavarettas.

Tom Cavaretta stood quickly, staring straight at Peterson, and pulled his .45 from his suit coat pocket.

"No you won't," he said, pointing the gun at a wide-eyed Peterson. He fired once, hitting Peterson in the middle of the forehead; Peterson flew backward onto Thomas. Then the father and head prosecutor lowered his semi-automatic to his side and sighed.

Halloran reached over the bench and took the weapon in the still and stunned courtroom.

"Nice shot,' Halloran said.

Then, turning to look at the killer's still body, he added:

"No, scumbag, Death before life."

Note: The last person to be executed in Illinois was in 1999.

*The death penalty was outlawed in Illinois
by the state legislature in 2011.*

Epilogue

The *State of Illinois vs. Thomas Cavaretta* was handled by the Illinois Attorney General because of the obvious conflict of interest.

In short order, Cavaretta pleaded guilty to second degree murder by reason of insanity and was sentenced to six months at the Read Mental Health Center by Judge Sheila Ryan O'Brien. Doctors there evaluated Cavaretta, and at the end of six months deemed him no threat to society. O'Brien agreed and ordered Cavaretta to be confined at home with electronic monitoring for six more months. At the end of that, O'Brien allowed Cavaretta to serve another two years of probation at his summer home in Union Pier, Michigan. There, Joyce and Tom kept to themselves, sold their River Forest home, and occasionally saw a few close friends and relatives.

***

Only Pritchard-Peterson and Hemphill showed up at the graveside ceremony for Eric Peterson at Graceland Cemetery.

A Hindu sadhu in saffron robes spoke a few words of comfort to the widow, who placed the urn containing Peterson's ashes in a mausoleum slot provided by an anonymous donor from the University of Chicago who had contacted Chance. Chance had a law school class to teach that morning. Thomas was on trial.

Two weeks after the burial, Pritchard-Peterson, took off for Canada to protest the annual slaughter of baby seals.

***

With Cavaretta no longer able to serve, Dunne was appointed interim State's Attorney by the County Board. Dunne's first move was to appoint Egan as his First Assistant and make Hall his Chief Deputy.

"Why break up a winning team?" he said to the two astonished assistants when he broke the news to them in Cavaretta's old office.

***

Syl Ortiz was transferred to police headquarters to serve as the deputy chief of Gang Crimes, a promotion that leapfrogged her career over a host of other higher-ranking cops. It was mostly a nine-to-five job with a male secretary and a plush office just down the hall from the superintendent. It gave her more time for her family and her salary nearly doubled. She took the lieutenants' test the day after Tom Cavaretta's sentencing and placed second in a field of 97.

***

Supt. Johnson summoned Halloran to his office a week after the courthouse shooting.

Halloran arrived 10 minutes early and waited for 15 minutes to be admitted while the superintendent spoke by phone to the mayor.

"Mike, come in. Sorry. A little politics with the mayor. An alderman's son caught in a massage parlor. No attempt at a fix--just wanted information," Johnson said, guiding Halloran by the elbow to his couch. "Sit down, detective."

Halloran's antennae were twitching. They did every time a boss was being nice to him. And this was the boss of bosses.

"We've not had a chance to speak since the outstanding work you did in the Peterson case. This department, this city, this county are in your debt, Mike. I mean that sincerely. What is it you want to do in this department? Just ask."

Halloran was floored but not mute. Never before had he been asked such a question; and he doubted it would ever come again. He paused for a minute, looking into the superintendent's eyes the way he studied a suspect for signs of bullshit, subterfuge, disingenuousness. He saw none.

"Superintendent, I love being a homicide dick. I think I'm good at it and want to continue. It was great shit finding Peterson and pinning his ass to the wall. It's who I am. That said, there is that joint task force with the feds looking into cold cases. I've often thought that would be fun--solving an old one," Halloran said.

"Done," Johnson said. "And if you change your mind in a month or a year, my door will always be open. You're my kind of cop."

"Thank you," said Halloran and shook the strong right hand of his boss.

***

Every five or six months, Halloran would get a call from Egan, and they would get together for lunch, dinner, or a discreet escape to Door County to Egan's parents' cottage just north of Algoma. If she didn't call in a few months, he'd call her.

Theirs was a relationship of convenience, both too content with their single lives and careers to make the sacrifices and compromises necessary to wed.

***

While investigating a 25-year-old murder, Halloran drove four hours to interview a witness just west of the Illinois-Iowa border, in a suburb of Davenport. As he crossed the bridge into Iowa, he spotted a majestic American bald eagle circling above the Mississippi, peering down for any sign of a catfish surfacing.

"Good hunting, buddy."

Acknowledgements

Any ink-stained wretch of a newspaper reporter has thought there was a book in him, or her. This scrivener is no different. This book sprang from my years as the press guy for the Cook County State's Attorney's office, but much of it traces to my 28 years a reporter, chasing cops, fires, thugs and any witness who would stand still for a few questions in person or on the phone.

So many thanks to the hardworking prosecutors I dealt with and who trusted me to interpret their work to a skeptical press and for stories I ripped off for this book. They will hopefully understand certain liberties with the law I took to facilitate the narrative.

Specifically, I would like to thank Dr. Nancy Jones, former Cook County Medical Examiner, for her help with how wounds work; and for the insights of retired CPD District Commander William Guswiler; and retired CPD Chief of Detectives Eugene Roy. Also thanks to two clever colleagues, Jim Elsener and Ross Werland, for their editing skills.

Lastly but most importantly, I want to thank my family for their patience and encouragement through the years of stopping and starting this novel. Not surprisingly, as they and this novel grew old together, my children, Katie and Mike, found time to graduate from college and law school, pass the bar, and forge admirable careers as attorneys. And, of course, my wife, Janice, who held my hand through all of this.

About the Author

John Gorman started his journalism career at the storied City News Bureau of Chicago before joining the Chicago Tribune. He spent half of his 26 years at the Tribune as a reporter covering courts, cops and catastrophes and was twice a runner-up for the Pulitzer Prize. As an Assistant City Editor for 13 years, he oversaw the city desk, herding, helping and harassing reporters. Later, he spent nearly a decade as the Communications Director for the Cook County State's Attorney's office. He lives in Chicago with his wife, Janice, and not far from his children, Katie and Mike, and two grandchildren, Grace and Michael.